NEVER FORSAKEN

NEVER FORSAKEN
THE KURTHERIAN GAMBIT™ BOOK 5

MICHAEL ANDERLE

This book is a work of fiction. All of the characters, organizations, and events portrayed in this novel are either products of the author's imagination or are used fictitiously. Sometimes both.

Copyright © 2016 Michael T. Anderle
Cover by Gene Mollica and Sasha Almazan
https://www.gsstockphoto.com/
Cover copyright © LMBPN Publishing

LMBPN Publishing supports the right to free expression and the value of copyright. The purpose of copyright is to encourage writers and artists to produce the creative works that enrich our culture.

The distribution of this book without permission is a theft of the author's intellectual property. If you would like permission to use material from the book (other than for review purposes), please contact support@lmbpn.com. Thank you for your support of the author's rights.

LMBPN Publishing
PMB 196, 2540 South Maryland Pkwy
Las Vegas, NV 89109

Version 2.56 February 2023
ebook ISBN: 978-1-68500-021-9
Print ISBN: 978-1-54678-543-9

The Kurtherian Gambit (and what happens within / characters / situations / worlds) are copyright © 2015-2023 by Michael T. Anderle.

NEVER FORSAKEN TEAM

Thanks to our JIT Readers for this Version

Timothy Cox (the myth)
Deb Mader
Rachel Beckford
Diane L. Smith
Peter Manis
Daniel Weigert
Jackey Hankard-Brodie
Kerry Mortimer
Veronica Stephan-Miller
Billie Leigh Kellar

If I've missed anyone, please let me know!

Editor
Lynne Stiegler

DEDICATION

To Family, Friends and
Those Who Love
To Read.
May We All Enjoy Grace
To Live The Life We Are
Called.

CHAPTER ONE

<u>Germany</u>

Beneath the snow and ice, the stone building was centuries old. Materials had been carried into the small valley on the backs of slaves whose bones had long since turned to dust in the countless graves surrounding the massive castle. For hundreds of years, the trees had stood as silent living headstones, and the undergrowth covered the only physical remains of lives used up as self-serving expedients without a thought to the people who had died to build this fortress.

David hadn't cared about humans then, and he cared even less now. He walked into the massive room beneath his castle. Over twenty feet wide and thirty feet long, rising over twenty-five feet in the air, it had taken an immense effort in time and lives—time and lives he couldn't be bothered to remember. He finally stopped, staring at the hermetically sealed container in front of him. Rage infused his countenance, his eyes red, his voice full of anguish and hurt, and his voice barely above a whisper, albeit one that could be heard in the four corners of the room.

"Father, Father. Why did you bring me to this? Instead of being locked up in this holding cell, you could be taking your rightful place at the head of our new order. You should have been the prince these cattle would have recognized and followed. Now, I am stuck with Anton, that degenerate mind-fuck, and the Nazi scientists whose lives he has extended. Their pitiful existence is needed to continue their research toward recreating the serum." David stepped closer to the glass. "Why you sacrificed others to destroy the effort in Japan is beyond me. We were finished. We were complete. We had the answer in our hands, and your American lackeys destroyed it all in the inferno of their atomic bomb—all our priceless research gone. All they left me were a few samples to try to reverse-engineer."

David, a tall aristocratic-looking man with dark peaks on either side of his forehead, paced in front of the rectangular copper-colored metal and glass container. Iron anchor bolts held it steadfastly and solidly to the bedrock beneath it.

"Now I am forced to kill another sibling. Stephen has annoyingly decided living is a better solution than simply fading into the sun, so I will have the blood of another brother on my hands. I've despised myself since I sent Hugo to the eternal sleep, and now Stephen is forcing me to end his life." His voice became harder. "This time, however, *you* are to blame. You brought this new woman into existence, and she pulled him back from his final rest. His blood will be poured at *your* feet, his death on *your* head. Your Bethany Anne is causing all sorts of trouble for Anton, and Stephen is now beyond being a simple annoyance." He stopped and considered his next steps. "I cannot allow his continued interruptions of my European plans. Eventually, he might impede the progress of projects which are critical. So, I tell you this and you may grieve in advance, knowing your choices have already led to so many of our race dying…*dying!*" David slammed his palm against the copper exterior, and a deep ringing echoed off the wall.

He drew himself to his full height. "Do you know how many have died since she was brought forth? *Do you?* You preach honor, but she is the most dishonorable of all. She treats humans as having value and werewolves as deserving of respect. This filth she teaches cannot be allowed to spread. It cannot be allowed to take root in any more minds than it already has. She has affected far too many of my plans." He stopped, his voice dropping to little more than a thread. "As powerful as she could become, it was with little happiness that Anton decided to kill her. She would be a supreme choice to become the new leader of our race." David paused, envisioning a future that could not be. "Of our existence. Compared to her, even you pale. The cattle would form a line, and the sheep would bleat out their willingness to sacrifice everything merely to feel her touch."

He turned around, looking up and into the distance from beneath so much soil. Up to where he imagined the sun must be shining, those rays which were too painful to see or to enjoy, and spoke into the air. "She could take us into such a glorious future, but she must be sacrificed to the greater righteousness and make amends for the millions killed while seeking our rightful place." He paused, imagining what would not be. "Pity, that."

David walked toward the steps which would take him up to the castle proper, wrapped in his own thoughts, his anger from a minute before completely forgotten. He called over his shoulder before disappearing up the stone stairs, "Do say your goodbyes to Stephen. He won't be long in this world."

In the copper container, Myst swirled from top to bottom and back again, agitated. The pressure inside was too great for it to become a flesh and blood being; a human form would immediately disintegrate. The Myst had been in this container for a time that seemed an ongoing, never-ending pain as its energy continued to fade. It had too much time to think, to listen to its child rail in rage and dishonor. Time for even a thousand-year-old being to consider the mistakes an unbreakable belief in absolutes might bring about. To realize his whole existence and knowledge had been laid low, his superior standards broken on the anvil of reality. If the Myst could have wept, it would have shed ten thousand tears.

The Queen Bitch's Ship *Ad Aeternitatem*

So, what are you saying will happen?

Would a qualified "I don't know" satisfy you?

Bethany Anne snorted; why TOM thought anything of the sort was beyond her. She stood in front of the Pod-doc in TOM's ship. They had been going through the results of the German Shepherd's medical review for the last fifteen minutes. Well, as much as, "Push this button. Hmmm... Push that button and slide that digital representation up. Hmmm... Not sure about this. Push this..." was a review. She was now a little irritated at the alien symbiont inside her.

Okay, give me your unqualified best guess, TOM. I'm a little impatient.

Really? When did we start with patience so you could reduce it? I thought that if something was lacking in the first place, you couldn't lose what you didn't have?

TOM, if it didn't hurt so much, I would slap you smart.

Good for me that you can't at the moment, hmmm? Wait, what was that?

Bethany Anne grinned. TOM had become his own complete personality with idiosyncrasies she both enjoyed and deplored. She'd finally figured out the other night that he could hear another trashy reality tv show which vibrated down from the deck above, and quickly went up and walked in on a group of Navy folks working in the kitchen.

She looked at the tv, walked over, and yanked the plug out of the wall, which got everyone's attention. "See this tv?" Lots of heads nodded. She reached down while holding it with her left hand and yanked the cord out with her right. "This was giving TOM all sorts of bad human ideas I have to listen to all the time. Now, any program that plays in here better be family-friendly, or the tv goes overboard with the person who was using it, *capiche?*" Lots more nodding. One or two tried not to smile. Some of TOM's comments had run through the grapevine, and there was a small but growing cadre of TOM fans.

It was driving her nuts.

She quit woolgathering and got back to the task at hand.

Never mind what I said. What's the diagnosis?

We have our own version of the Six-Million-Dollar Mutt?

Gott Verdammt! She was going to find John and slap the ever-loving shit out of him. TOM had asked about that deplorable old tv show after he'd heard a conversation between John and Frank, and now fancied himself a creator of new and better versions of reality. Maybe she should slap Frank as well for good measure.

Bethany Anne pulled aside the cover which allowed her a view inside and looked into the Pod-doc. "Oh, holy shit. I don't remember him looking like that when I put him in there, TOM. What happened?"

You're talking to the air again.

"Shut up and just get on with it. Anyone inside this ship right now knows you're in me."

There is no one else in this ship.

There was a pregnant pause, during which Bethany Anne didn't reply.

Okay, got it. It seems the Pod-doc decided to move forward after we put the canine in.

Why would it decide to do that? I was under the impression we were only checking it out.

Human error?

How could it be human error, ass? I was the one to set it up, and we both know I don't know shit about how to operate your machinery, including Bones here.

Bones? Oh, Dr. Bones. Nice one.

Bethany Anne had pulled the *Star Trek* series to watch with TOM, and they had made it through Season One so far.

Well, Jim, it's like this—I fucked up.

Bethany Anne was poleaxed for a moment as his words washed over her. She could feel his slight embarrassment through their connection. A little surprised, she straightened for a second, then leaned over and looked through the small window before standing upright again.

"TOM, buddy, that might be a small understatement. We put a normal if pretty aggressive German Shepherd into the Pod-doc. What I have in there is an all-white monster-sized German Shepherd with what I imagine are small knives for teeth and feet the size of a draft horse's. I don't know if he can eat a side of beef, but I'm pretty sure I don't have enough cow on board for that dog. If the aggressiveness has been increased, I might have to kill it, and that is a hell of a thank you for helping me in the fight."

True, and I would feel bad about that. But on the positive side, he isn't ready to come out yet, so we have a little time to discuss this situation.

"'Situation.' Yeah, that about sums up this SNAFU. Well, take your readings, and set them to give it what we can. If we're going to change him—and that train has left the station—we might as well up the settings to eleven."

Bethany Anne, the settings don't have an eleven.

Turn of phrase, TOM. It means we turn them up past what others can turn their... You know, I'll just have to let you watch an old movie called **Spinal Tap.**

Okay, up to eleven it is.

Five minutes later, she turned to her right and took a step to translocate through the Etheric. She disappeared before putting her foot down.

The Queen Bitch's Ship *Polarus*

Bethany Anne completed her step by appearing inside her protected wardrobe, then unlocked the door and walked into her personal suite. Ecaterina was working at her desk, giving off a dissatisfied energy the vampire was almost able to feel, even if it didn't show on her face.

Jumping up on her bed, she crossed her legs and put her chin on her palm, her elbow resting on her leg. "What you got for me, Kat?"

Ecaterina was accustomed to Bethany Anne appearing from any direction. Since her human senses wouldn't register much of what the vampire could do, she tried to dampen her reactions, which had been honed by years in the wilderness. A wilderness, she could admit to herself, she was missing.

Ecaterina worked down the list of tasks.

"The Weres are on their way down to Miami. They will stop and talk to Nathan and Pete, and then Pete will bring them down to us. Bobcat will pick them up at the closest airport—not sure which one that is yet. Nathan is working on a project with Frank and Lance in Miami at the moment, so he's staying there. Dan and the team are getting ready to have the meeting with the Weres. We've been able to track a little of what is going on in San José because of the newspaper and the reporter you guys helped. She has some sort of love-fest going on for you guys. Except, she says her butt was pinched."

Bethany Anne retorted, "She wishes. It was a dart from my gun when I shot her to put her to sleep. We needed her quiet at the time, and it seemed like the easiest solution. She was freaking out like a little girl."

Ecaterina looked over her laptop at Bethany Anne on the bed and raised a questioning eyebrow. "She *is* young. Maybe not a little girl, but she certainly had enough guts to try to get the story, no?"

"Yeah, okay. You might consider that rash, stupid, or any

number of other things. I suppose you could attach bravery as an alternate possibility."

"In my country, freedom of the press is permitted, but we still remember when it was not so easy to get the truth out. I appreciate her effort to tell the truth, even if we don't personally want it known."

"Consider me duly chastised. Her stories have helped us, or at least the politicians aren't trying to track us down. I don't think we've gotten a single call in a week, right?"

"That is true, so I consider her an asset. Asset—this is the right term, yes?"

Bethany Anne thought about that. "Yes, she's definitely an asset. Nothing she has done has hurt us. You're right, she is a benefit." There was more going on with Ecaterina than she thought. "Are you missing Nathan? He's only been gone a couple of days."

The Romanian woman looked up from her laptop and pursed her lips, then closed the lid and frowned. "Nathan is not happy I want to do more, and we have had a disagreement. I don't like being stuck on the ship all the time when everyone leaves to go on operations. He thought I would be happy for a while with the new sniper rifle, but it was a ruse. A ruse? Maybe that is the wrong word. I am not unhappy to be with you, and I will wait however long I need to be a part of your ops team. But I am ready to be more than just…this." She waved her hand over the laptop. "More than one who manages people and things."

"You're going stir-crazy."

"What is this? You mean my crazy is getting stirred up?"

Bethany Anne cocked her head. "Not exactly. It means you've been cooped up too long. You need to get out. If you were back in Romania, it would mean you had been in your house too long and needed to go to the mountains for a little while."

Ecaterina agreed. "Yes, that is what I would do."

The vampire thought about the woman who had tended bar

and gone out to hunt, trap, and live on the mountain. She was a free spirit, and the other people on the ships probably needed a little R&R too. "Tell you what, we all need a little downtime. You aren't the only one who is probably feeling the need to stretch their legs. Let's figure out where we can anchor that has a good beach and is hopefully secluded. We'll tie both ships up and have a day or two of fun. Make sure we have a guard, but we all need to stretch our legs. Good idea. Also, if you want to move to operations, you'll have to train harder, be better, and generally get your ass back in gear. I haven't thought about you for ops because you don't train like you want to be on ops. Got it?"

Ecaterina assured her, "I understand, yes. Just do, don't whine." She opened her laptop again and jotted some notes. She would need to get organized so she and the others could enjoy some time off the ships. It was one of the most beautiful and expensive prisons in the world if you loved to be on the land as much as she did.

CHAPTER TWO

Miami, FL, USA

Nathan and Pete waited with Frank by one of William's armor-protected SUVs. Fortunately, there had been a set of keys easily available, since the mechanic had left that morning on a three-day stay-cation. He had met a woman at one of the clubs over the holidays and wined and dined her. Now, they were going clubbing around town for the next couple of days.

Three men waited for the Gulfstream to land and taxi over to them. Frank wanted to get the flavor of the new recruits, he'd explained. Nathan assumed he wanted to add another chapter to his book in process.

Lieutenant Commander Paul Jameson brought the plane to a slow stop. Nathan saw Paul wink at Frank and wondered what that was about. The door to the plane opened, and the steps descended to the tarmac. Beside him, Pete stood at casual attention, his time with John's group now ingrained in his posture. He was damn near a poster boy for Bethany Anne's Guards in his uniform with the elite patch on his shoulder. Nathan smiled as he remembered the conversation with the asshat back in New York. Pete had pointed to that patch and informed the troublemaker he wasn't getting into the group since he had a vote and had just voted him off the island, so to speak.

According to Ecaterina, there were five in this plane. A few others who had wanted to join decided to wait until this first group had gone through their paces and word about what they could expect got back to the pack and was disseminated.

Aboard the aircraft, Tim "Rocky" Kinley grabbed his duffel. The group on the plane had been told to bring the minimum since anything not allowed would be summarily dumped overboard. While he wasn't too keen on having his stuff thrown away, he figured it would be a small price to pay to get the hell out from under the Pack Council's laws. He had a temper. He wasn't one to simply randomly hurt people, but he had trouble controlling himself. With him being as large as he was, randomly punching people who pissed him off for fairly innocuous reasons had put a black cloud above his head. He'd had issues ever since he had gone through an impressive growth spurt at fourteen. Now, at six foot two, and weighing in at two hundred and twenty pounds, there were few people he really respected in his life.

The other four in the group didn't fit into pack life for reasons of their own, and so far, no one had asked why they had wanted out. It was understood that all of them would meet the vampire before too long. While Tim hadn't met her back in New York—he had been too far away to attend—he had been at the meet-up in New York with Gerry and Nathan. Tim wasn't a screw-off. He worked hard, and while he wasn't a super-smart guy, he wasn't a meathead either. He needed to be able to fit in with a group, and the only way to accomplish this, he felt, was joining a group of people so badass they would be able to put him in his place if he got out of control.

This vampire, by all accounts, would be able to make that happen. Now, whether any of the humans could was another matter. Hopefully, his anger wouldn't get him in trouble like it had in the past. May God forgive him if it did.

The co-pilot had unbuckled and opened the door for the guys. The man stepped back, and Tim started down the steps and looked up to see Nathan Lowell, the Queen Bitch's Guard Pete Silvers, and a middle-aged man with a grin and a notebook in his hand waiting for them. A black SUV was parked behind them.

Nathan Lowell was one man Tim would keep his emotions in check around. He hadn't personally dealt with the Were, but enough of the Wechselbalg community told stories about him that Tim would be cautious. He had watched Pete calmly shoot Terry in the kneecap from a distance and then toss him out on his ass at the meeting. He respected that, but Terry was just a fucking whiner. His inner wolf wasn't convinced yet of the young Were's martial abilities.

The older man was human. That he was in on this meant he must be a helper—maybe a librarian, or someone up the chain. Either way, he wasn't a physical threat, so he was dismissed.

The four other guys followed him out. Every one of them had alpha issues and couldn't adjust to being within the pack as it was, but none of them had tried to push Tim around. Enough stories had circulated that he was a hothead. He didn't look for trouble, but he sure as hell didn't back down from it, either. If they wanted a fight, a sneeze in the wrong direction would grant their wish immediately. No one had thought fighting on the Queen Bitch's personal plane was a good way to introduce themselves.

Each had his own duffel, provided at La Guardia. They were black with a blue patch, similar to the Queen Bitch's Guards' sigil, but instead of hair, the vampire skull had ears like a wolf. As a symbol, it wasn't very subtle. Maybe that was the point?

They formed up in a rough line in front of Nathan, who simply nodded to each as they arrived. He wore a green long-sleeved shirt and hadn't shaved in a couple of days. His green eyes evaluated them, and he appeared both at ease and ready to pounce if necessary. Pete, next to him, merely looked at ease.

Behind them, the plane's engines cycled back up and it started to taxi, moving a short distance away.

Nathan waited for the noise to settle. "Gentleman—and I use that term very loosely because if gentle is anywhere in your personality, I suggest you request a flight back to New York right now." Everyone enjoyed a small chuckle. A truly gentle Wechselbalg was rare.

Nathan continued, "I'm here to officially transfer you from the pack to Bethany Anne's group. Right now, the aircraft is refueling. When you get back on that plane, you will have formally renounced the pack ties you now enjoy."

Nathan smiled a little. "Well, maybe 'enjoy' isn't the right word to use, but you were under their protection, such as it was. When you step onto Bethany Anne's plane again, you will officially be under her protection and control. Don't mistake that last part. If any of her team makes the decision to toss your ass out, it will be tossed out. Until you make the team, there is no reason for Bethany Anne to believe your word over someone she has taken into the dark and come through the other side with, usually by killing the problems between points A and B. Don't make the mistake of thinking of any of her team as anything less than professionals who have been through hell and made it to the other side. They have probably seen and killed beings who would turn you human." There were laughs at that.

Nathan finished, "Welcome to the team. I hope to see all of you at the end of your training." He stepped back, and Pete moved up.

The young Were looked at each of them in turn, making sure he had their attention. "I doubt any of you will be turned human, God forbid." He got another small chuckle. "But I *will* tell you that you had better leave your B game here in Miami. When you get on the plane, Bethany Anne will own your ass. Since I am in charge of this group through the training, *I* will own your ass. Everyone know what this patch means?" Pete pointed to the patch on his left arm and got nods from everyone. "Good, then you know I won't hesitate to throw your asses onto the nearest helicopter, plane, or rowboat if necessary if you embarrass this group. I don't care if you make a mistake, since we all do. But you had better be running full steam when you make that mistake, do you understand?" He got five nods. "I'll get your names on the plane. I see it coming back over here. Grab your duffels and let's make history."

Tim was impressed. Maybe this Pete was someone to at least get to know, hopefully before Tim did something stupid.

Anton's Residence, Buenos Aires, Argentina

Anton grabbed one of his throwaway phones, looked back at the computer, which was open to a well-regarded social board for hookups, and dialed the number that started with the girl's measurements. Not a valid number, that was for sure. The female would need a forklift to carry those around if they were real.

The phone rang twice before it was picked up. "George is a dick…"

Anton replied, "Costanza was, but must you always be so crass?" Anton wasn't fond of the tv show, but he could appreciate the acting to some degree. The passphrase complete, he got down to business. "Have you figured out where the team that ruined San José for me is?"

The man was an operative for the American government who had been in South America too long. The agent succumbed to the idea that money was more important than his honor, and his lack of allegiance to his country replied to the question. "Not exactly. We know it was a Black Hawk that came in from the east. The pilot was good; he stayed as close to the floor as he could most of the way. Our first positive blip was about ten miles off the coast, so either they came in from a shore base or off a ship. My vote is from a ship since it's a cleaner solution than a base on land, but I don't have any information about any US assets in that area."

"Trust me, it isn't a US ship. The US doesn't have anything that could have handled the fight the way it went down." Anton heard a gruff grunt on the phone and decided to placate the American agent. "Stop beating your American chest. I'm not saying you don't have deadly people, but until you meet and beat a Nosferatu, you're nothing but a virgin. If you weren't a virgin, you would be dead. I want more intelligence; I need to know more about their operations group. Get some people who can deal with this. Earn your keep, and your retirement gets closer. Fail me, and your retirement becomes irrelevant. Make this happen, understand?"

The operative agreed, and they hung up. Anton went through the process of destroying the phone, thinking about where this Bethany Anne could be and what she could have with her. That she had flown in a military helicopter suggested she already had military contacts, which was a disturbing precedent. Maybe he needed to go back to his research group and see about pushing the two latest serum trials through?

He stood behind his desk and grabbed his coat. It was a balmy seventy-five outside, but he used the special lining as protection from the sun. Always be prepared. That philosophy had helped him stay alive for centuries.

When he finally took over the world, he would slap those little Boy Scout bastards who had used his phrase and make them pay tribute.

Miami, FL, USA

Lance read the number on his cell phone as he sat on a couch in Bethany Anne's home in Key Biscayne. Frank was on the other couch. He clicked the answer button.

"Hey, daughter dear, what do you have for me this time?"

Bethany Anne snorted on the other end of the line. "Can't I simply be a concerned daughter looking out for her loving dad?"

It was Lance's turn to snort.

He could hear her grin in her voice. "Okay, you got me there. I wanted to talk to you about Patricia."

"Oh, really? That's interesting, since I don't recall us talking about Patricia such that you might need to talk to me about her." He looked at Frank, who studiously ignored the byplay on the phone and kept writing in that strange language in his notebook. Great, now this would be part of the story.

Bethany Anne ignored his effort to redirect the conversation. "Can it, Dad. Get your dander up another time. How well do you know Patricia? Really know her?"

Lance considered the question. They weren't playing for a small local win here, but for all the worldwide marbles. His daughter had a point, dammit. "Well, not well enough to have a shotgun wedding, but well enough to know she'd have my back in a pinch."

"Dad, this will be considerably more than a pinch. Every one of my ex-military people has sworn their lives to what we're trying to accomplish. You will be forced to have the same talk with Patricia, and if she doesn't join in, I'll have to remove the information. Are you willing to make sure this happens, Dad? Because I'm not going to risk everyone in my crews' future because you have a good friend who can make your life easier."

"No need for theatrics, Bethany Anne, I get your point. I'm comfortable she's the right person, and I need her for more than merely making my life easier. But I do think she needs to have a chat with you to hash this out before we pull her in. Can you catch a flight up here when she arrives? I need her on the inside as quickly as possible."

"Probably. Just call Ecaterina or me when you've had your discussion. Who knows, I might be in the area."

Lance wasn't sure what she meant by that. He hadn't been

aware that she was planning on coming up to Miami from the *Polarus*. He would have to ask Frank about it later, or maybe Nathan.

"All right, she arrives in a couple of days. I'll let you know when it should happen. Pretty soon, I think." He told her goodbye and hung up.

He knew Bethany Anne wouldn't hurt her, but he did have to consider that Patricia might not see Lance as the same man she had respected for his efforts to protect his nation when she'd worked for him. If she disapproved of what he was working on now with his daughter, it might hurt more than he had thought.

He wasn't sure how bad it would hurt Patricia if Bethany Anne did have to erase some of her memory. Unfortunately, whatever she would say to Lance before that happened would stay with him the rest of his now-longer life.

CHAPTER THREE

The Queen Bitch's Ship *Polarus*

Gabrielle walked down the hallway to Bethany Anne's room. She had left Darryl and Scott moaning and groaning on the practice mats after throwing them around. Darryl had asked if something was bothering her since she had gotten more and more aggressive during the session.

Gathering her thoughts, she was ashamed to realize she had in fact allowed worry to invade her emotions while working with her team. Nothing too bad, but it needed to be addressed, and there was only one person who was even remotely able to understand her unique position.

She was a vampire who could have children.

In reply to Darryl's question, she told the guys to slap some duct tape on their boo-boos and swallow some Ben-Gay because they were a couple of babies. Scott merely laid on the mat and slowly raised one arm to give her the middle tent-pole answer to that statement. She had laughed it off and tossed each of them a towel. Earlier, she had worked out with John and Eric. They were as ready for a showdown with the Were group as she could make them.

She nodded to John as she entered Bethany Anne's quarters. Eric was walking around up top, and Killian, she knew, was up in his sniper position. She hadn't seen Dan yet today.

She knocked on Bethany Anne's inner door, and it opened a couple of seconds later. Ecaterina stood aside to let her in, then proceeded to leave the room. She called over her shoulder, "Sorry, got to run and get ready for a party." Gabrielle stopped to look at the smiling Romanian. She realized she hadn't really seen the woman smile in a couple of weeks. Party?

Gabrielle shook her head and closed the door. Bethany Anne sat on her bed, her legs crossed, and she raised an eyebrow at her. Her direct and often simple modes of communication were one of the traits she liked about this woman.

She was quick to get to the point. "I need to talk something out, and you're the only option here."

Bethany Anne thought about that for a split second, jumping into vamp speed to dissect the statement. Well, she *was* the only female vampire, and the ultimate boss. Typically, Gabrielle could talk to Dan about anything her Bitches needed, so this was probably a female vampire thing. She looked a little distressed, which was not very normal for the older—much older—woman. Bethany Anne sighed. "Children?"

Gabrielle nodded in agreement and slid into a chair against the wall. "You are not so naive for such a youngling."

"Process of elimination. Plus, I have to admit, I'm thinking about it, too. The ability to have children again took me by surprise, and I can't say I'm happy about revisiting this decision."

Gabrielle looked confused. "You have a guy whom you want to have children with? How did I not know this?"

Bethany Anne stuck her tongue out. "You know I don't, and stop trying to tweak me because I called you wank-bait."

The vampire looked at the younger woman. "It wasn't simply wank-bait. You also called me boner gypsy, jizz-queen, wank-conductor, boner barn, and penis harmonica."

"Dick harmonica, but who's taking notes?"

"Apparently, you are."

Bethany Anne tapped her forehead. "Alien symbiont, remember? He forgets nothing."

I didn't remind you of what you said.

Keep quiet. I might get to score again.

Hmmph.

Gabrielle's mouth twisted as if she had eaten a sour lemon. "I looked 'jizz' up. Really? Queen of sperm? That is disgusting."

Bethany Anne smiled. "Is that so? I figured that after five hundred years, you had tried just about everything. You have that tattoo, and all."

Gabrielle was quick to snap, "I am *not* five hundred years old." Then she got it. She hadn't told Bethany Anne her real age, and her dad, bless his black soul, had agreed not to tell anyone a very long time ago. "You are baiting me, but it won't work."

"Maybe not this time, but now I know you're less than five hundred." She winked at the older vampire.

Gabrielle put her hands to her temples and started rubbing. "You can be insufferable. Why can't you just let it go? Can't a woman have a secret or two?"

"I'm sure you have more secrets than I'm ever going to find out. For example, how many lovers have you had?" Bethany Anne asked.

She sputtered, "What? Why would I tell you such a thing? I am not a slut, but after a…few…years, a woman might acquire… companions. After a few…more years, they might exceed a handful."

"A handful at a time?"

"Not a handful at a time."

"Okay, four."

"It was not four. Only three." Gabrielle's face turned red as she stomped her foot. "Shit!"

Bethany Anne rolled around on her bed, cracking up. "My,

my, Gabrielle. Does Stephen know you have been quite the lucky lady?"

She pointed at her companion. "No. I swear, you had better not tell him, either. He would never let me live it down if I admitted to such a thing. Look at this, I come in here to bare my heart, and you pull this information out of me." Her eyes narrowed. "You are a very evil woman."

Bethany Anne got her laughter under control. "I'm simply curious. It's the natural predilection of females, and since I have lived such a chaste life—" Gabrielle snorted, and she glared at her. "May I continue? Since I have led such a chaste life, I'm trying to figure out what my future might be, and you are the only one I know who has been alive long enough to share. That you don't drives me a little nuts," she finished with a smile. "So, all of this is actually your fault for not sharing."

Gabrielle was about to tell the younger vampire off but realized she had come for a similar reason. "Okay, I get it. I didn't realize you have a decent reason for wanting to know my past. I never considered you might be thinking about your future. I merely thought you wanted prurient details."

"Well, some of those too." Bethany Anne smiled.

She rolled her eyes. "You are a handful, my Queen. Okay, I'll share more some other time, and yes, I have had in excess of ten lovers." Bethany Anne raised an eyebrow. "Okay, twenty." She raised the other eyebrow. "Forty, but that was over a very long time. There was a time back in Paris in the twenties I might have been considered some of those words you used."

"Really? The 1920s?"

"No, the 1820s."

"God, this is just like Ivan was talking about with Stephen. You have to confirm what century you two are talking about."

Gabrielle did her best impression of her father. "Indeed."

Bethany Anne sighed and sat up. "Okay, you've been fair. I

don't want to talk about this subject, so it's easier to pick on you. I don't know what I want to do about children."

"So, you understand my dilemma?"

"Maybe, but for you, I would think it could be both easier and harder. Easier because it has been a significant—but unknown—amount of time since you knew you couldn't have children, so why make a change now? On the other hand, you have a human lover, and within a few years, he will probably want children. Him knowing you can have them might make it harder for you as time goes by."

She sighed. "Yes, that sums it up nicely."

The younger vampire scooted to the end of her bed and draped her legs over. "How much do you care for Ivan?"

Gabrielle looked over Bethany Anne's head, gazing into the distance and focusing on nothing. "I don't know. Part of me misses him, but part of me forgets to miss him when we get busy. It is only when everyone is asleep and I am by myself that I think of him."

"So, to be blunt, you're lonely for companionship because it's not available, but it isn't a driving need in your life right now?"

Gabrielle wrinkled her nose. "It makes me sound like a user when you put it that way."

"Who's to say you aren't both users? I don't know if Ivan is pining away for you, either. The distance is probably showing you both that the relationship is nice but not a driving factor in either of your lives. You need to talk to Ivan and let him know you need some time. You don't need to keep him tied up if you truly don't want a relationship. It isn't like he wouldn't be willing to provide you a warm bed... Damn, listen to me! Using him as a convenient sex toy when you're in Romania sounds a little crass."

"But isn't that what men and women have been doing for centuries?"

"I don't know. *I* wasn't around, but *you* were." Bethany Anne's smile returned. "How many centuries has it been going on?"

"Ever since I've been alive." Gabrielle stuck her nose in the air. "Which is?"

"None of your business." She smiled, appreciating her companion pulling them out of the morose talk. "I'll call Ivan and let him know I'm too busy with the teams right now to continue a relationship at this time."

"Will you let me know how the call goes?"

She eyed the younger woman. "Will you continue trying to find out how old I am?"

"Yes," Bethany Anne told her bluntly.

Gabrielle sighed. "Well, it was worth a shot. I'll let you know about Ivan, even if I have to deal with your insatiable curiosity." She stood up. "Thank you for this, you know. I've never had a friend to truly talk to about these things."

Bethany Anne looked at her, puzzled. "Boys?"

"No. Well, yes, in a way. Matters of the heart. For vampires, such things can be used against us, and we don't forget leverage like information about who other vampires care for, so we don't share."

"Is that why you didn't talk to Stephen about it?"

"Oh, definitely not. It wasn't because he would use it against me. It is that he would laugh at me for centuries. At least one, that is, and I couldn't provide him proper guidance if he could throw this in my face."

Bethany Anne raised an eyebrow. "You mean, like three guys at one time?"

Gabrielle walked over to the bed, stuck her face six inches in front of the Queen's, and stated in a slow, measured voice, "I think I hate you."

Faster than the other vampire could react, Bethany Anne struck out with her lips and kissed her on the forehead. "No, you don't. You merely aren't used to having a girlfriend tease you. I'll get you past it, trust me."

Gabrielle stood, transfixed. The strike had been fast, the kiss was nice, and the comment made her heart glow like a fire on a cold night. She straightened slowly and looked down at the woman, who was smiling, a twinkle in her eye. "Yes, a girlfriend to tease me." She turned and walked to the door, opening and closing it without looking back at Bethany Anne. When she heard the click as it closed, she reached up and wiped away the tear rolling down her cheek. She hoped the phone call with Ivan went well.

Las Vegas, NV, USA

Jeffrey Diamantz and Tom Billings, the CEO and lead programmer respectively, looked at a large number of computer boxes sitting on the floor in Building One. They had talked for fifteen minutes about what designations they should use for them, then named them one, two, and three.

Building One was where ADAM would be constructed. Well, to be truthful, it was where the computers would all be put together, along with the critical kill switch. Building Two would be where they would house all the secondary computers and Internet connections, and Building Three would be for housing, showers, food, and tertiary uses.

The racks had arrived yesterday, and they'd had a crew come in the previous night to assemble the damn things. They didn't look like much—basically big-ass metal boxes on wheels. Both men had wanted to slap themselves in the head when Nathan had asked about moving the whole thing once it was proven to work. The original design had had them using computer server racks that bolted to the floor. Tom had suggested they use the much more expensive rolling racks and promised they would lock them in place. If and when they could move, they would have to shut everything down, move the servers, and bring them back online in the reverse order.

Of course, they would cross their fingers the whole time that somehow, they didn't kill the first AI in the world by doing it this way. That wouldn't look good in the history books.

Then again, if ADAM 1.0 was going to design ADAM 2.0, maybe he would have a better idea, although that was kind of like asking a brain surgeon to operate on himself.

They were looking at the server boxes around the room when they heard a vehicle stop outside. The brakes squeaked horribly. Tom looked at Jeffery, who simply shrugged. They walked out through the doors to find a dark blue jeep with an Air Force insignia on the door. One man stayed in the driver's seat while another got out of the passenger side.

Jeffrey took the lead. "Good afternoon, Officer…Billings?"

The blond-haired man closed his door and put on his hat, then reached out to shake Jeffrey's offered hand. "Yes. I'm from Nellis, as you might have guessed." He turned and shook Tom's hand.

"How can we help you?"

"I'm here to find out about our newest neighbor, who has purchased property and brought in a ton of computers right next to a large Air Force base. Plus, I understand our newest neighbor is bringing in a substantial amount of Internet and communications. I wouldn't want to mistake you for a foreign power trying to sneak a peek into our computer systems."

The blood drained from Tom's face, although Jeffrey was able to keep his composure a little better. Shit. Neither had considered what it might look like to the Air Force to drop millions of dollars on computer equipment and connectivity right on their damn flank.

Tom replied, "Ah, no. To be honest, we really didn't think about the fact that we were right on your fence line or how it would look. We needed a building fast, and this old machining area had the Ps we needed, or could acquire them fast enough to meet our timeline."

The Air Force officer was puzzled. "The Ps?"

Tom shook his head, trying to get his equilibrium back. "Yes, sorry—Power, Ping, and Pipe. Our company, Patriarch Research, has a new set of code we need to test, and it isn't something we want to do out on the wild and woolly web. The owners are pushing us to move forward fast. We thought we might have two years to test our research, but they gave us a bit less."

Officer Billings' face held a small smile. "How much time did they give you?"

"Two months."

Billings nodded as if he had expected that answer. "That had to grab you by the short and curlies. So how long did you look for a building?"

Tom looked at Jeffrey as if hearing it for the first time himself. "Two days…three, sort of." He turned back to the officer. "We had already used up five percent of our time, so we grabbed the first property we felt would work. Got our corporate overseer to approve the purchase, then started with the changes, including the power review, the Internet connections, the cooling, and the building modifications. We have the server cages inside, and a substantial number of computer boxes to go through."

The officer looked around. "What is it you're doing with all of this?"

Well, that was the rub, wasn't it? Jeffrey really didn't want to tell the man he wanted to create the world's first artificial intelligence, but if it ever came out that he had lied, he wasn't sure what his culpability would be. So he punted and turned to Tom. "Officer Billings, meet Tom Billings, our head of Research and Development."

Tom asked, "Nevada Billings?"

The officer shook his head emphatically. "Hell, no! Montana."

Tom shrugged. "No family in Montana, so probably not connected." He turned around and pointed at the building they had just come out of. "This is Building One. It'll house the main set of computers to run our Heuristic Internet Defense algorithm. We have no Internet coming into this building." He pointed to the next structure. "That's Building Two. It houses the Internet connections, and some servers to pull data from the Internet. We're using it to download everything we need, and then use sneakernet to move the data over to Building One." He jerked his thumb at the building behind them.

Officer Billings interrupted him. "Excuse me, but did you say 'sneakernet?' I'm not familiar with that term."

Tom pointed his finger down at his Adidas tennis shoes. "Sneakers, as in we are walking the data from Building Two to Building One using our feet. No connectivity between the two."

"Why wouldn't you have connectivity between them?"

Jeffrey winced internally. He hadn't meant for Tom to tell the truth.

His colleague shrugged. "Just a precaution. If the program doesn't work as we expect, we don't want it to do anything out on the real Internet. We operated the damn thing on the Amazon AWS system a couple of years ago and got a three-hundred-thousand-dollar data bill in ten minutes. That pissed the bean counters off." Tom turned to look at Jeffrey. "No offense."

He shook his head in amazement. "None taken." Instead of bullshit, Tom was baffling him with the truth.

Tom continued, "So, imagine what would happen if some idiot forgets to disconnect in time? Our Internet bill would make even the Kardashians wince."

Billings—the officer, not the research guy—was pretty convinced he didn't have any foreign terrorists on his hands, but rather a couple of bumbling scientists. He wondered why they hadn't been fired already. A three-hundred-thousand-dollar data bill? This made his daughter's seventy-dollar text overcharge pale in comparison. "What about the last building?"

Jeffrey took that one. "Building Three is for food, restrooms, showers, and cots. We only have a few weeks to get this done so some of us won't go home much. I don't want a bunch of ants in the computer rooms, so I'm being an ass about cleanliness."

That was something the Air Force officer understood and appreciated. "Okay. I hope you understand why we got a little nervous." Both men nodded in agreement. "I'll probably still stop by from time to time, just to make sure everything looks on the up and up."

They all shook hands. Jeffrey and Tom watched as the Jeep turned and left.

Tom looked at Jeffrey. "Is that what you wanted?"

He considered that. "No, but it was the perfect answer. How did we miss such an obvious problem?" He looked after the retreating vehicle.

Tom followed his eyes. "Maybe because we aren't terrorists who are wanted by the US Air Force and didn't think about what it might look like from their side?"

Jeffrey agreed, "Yeah, let's just hope ADAM 1.0 doesn't become Anarchist ADAM 2.0."

"There is that," Tom replied. They turned and went back into Building One.

CHAPTER FOUR

The Queen Bitch's Ship *Ad Aeternitatem*

Bobcat was deep in conversation with Chief Engineer John Rodriquez, who was on the *Ad Aeternitatem* for the meeting. It was held in a private room inside the superyacht. Bethany Anne had given him the authority to include whomever he felt was necessary to get the small super-craft project running, and Rodriquez was known for coaxing miracles out of baling wire and string. Well, if you didn't include the alcohol and cussing he considered necessary ingredients at times.

The chief engineer was talking. "I'm telling you, Bobcat, the thermal effects of that much speed will affect the people inside. You need to get a scientist who understands these metals better than you or me to run some tests. The design will probably work to cut down the wind resistance, but unless it has a way to ignore air…" He paused. "It doesn't, does it?" Bobcat shook his head. "Okay, then consider a rocket or a missile design. We can't have it long enough for three people stacked on top of each other, so we need to design it as a rocket fat enough to house three around a central axis. It can land on tripods that fold back into the body. Does it need stabilizing fins?"

Bobcat considered what he knew. "Doubt it. TOM's craft doesn't have much of that right now, so I don't see why we would."

Chief Engineer Rodriguez thought about it for another second. "Are we able to duplicate the propulsion system TOM's craft has now?"

"Not sure how we can fit that in, although I would sure like to." Both men smiled at that thought.

Bobcat sighed. "So you're telling me I'll need a rocket scientist, right?"

"Yup. I might be able to do a lot of things, but I am not a rocket scientist." They each reached for their beers.

"Looks like I'm gonna have to call Frank, then. I'll ask Ecaterina for the phone number. Wonder what kind of scientist I'll have to deal with?"

John looked at his companion. He had a guess, but he wasn't about to mess things up for the pilot by telling him what that was. He said his goodbyes and headed out to hitch a ride back to the *Polarus*.

Bobcat retrieved his cell phone and hit Ecaterina's number. It didn't take long for her to answer, and after a few seconds, she sent him Frank's number. He called and, surprisingly, the man picked up on the first ring.

"Frank, this is Bobcat. I was wondering if you had a few minutes?"

Frank's curious voice came back over the line. "Sure, Bobcat. What do you need?"

He smiled. "Believe it or not, I need a rocket scientist."

The older man laughed. "You don't ask for much, do you? Will any old rocket scientist do, or do you need a particular type of rocket scientist?"

The pilot hesitated. "Well, I didn't realize there were different types of scientists available. Do you have a catalog, perhaps?"

"Ah, no. I need you to give me an idea of what you need, and I will comb through the databases to find someone who might be available. Can you send me a request via email?"

"Sure, that would be easy enough to do. But will the emails be safe?"

"Just make it look like you're talking about someone from the show *Ancient Aliens*. It will be flagged as a false positive if anyone should actually read it."

"Okay, I can do that. Any idea how long this might take?" Bobcat was fishing for information. He was concerned he wouldn't get the craft done as soon as Bethany Anne might need it.

"I should have a good idea if anyone is available within twelve hours. I'll have more information within twenty-four, or at most, forty-eight hours. We might get someone in the next few days if they're available and I can pique their interest enough."

Bobcat felt a little of the tension leave him. "Frank, you are a lifesaver. I will buy you as many beers as you can drink the next time we catch up."

They said their goodbyes and hung up. Frank spoke to his now-dead connection. "Don't thank me until after you've worked with him."

The pilot turned and covered the designs he had been working on. Then walked out the door and shut it behind him. He ran into Chris in the hallway. They went upstairs, talking the whole time about the differences between the Sikorsky and the Black Hawk, and how each one handled. Bobcat was a little bummed at having to leave Shelly behind, but he knew these new craft were the future, and it *was* what he had signed up for way back in Miami—not that he would have believed Bethany Anne had she confided in him that he would be working with alien technology.

The Queen Bitch's Ship *Polarus*

Pete had to get Frank's help with passports for two of his guys, so that took some extra time.

He had gotten to know each of them on the trip down in the Gulfstream, and then on Shelly to get them to the *Polarus*.

The nominal alpha of this group was Tim Kinley. Pete found him smart, aggressive, and holding on to his patience by a thread. It hadn't helped that everyone was stuck in the plane waiting for Frank to get the passports pushed through. Pete had finally simply dropped the door and run everyone around the building a few times to get rid of some energy. Once they had the passports, they buttoned up and took off.

After Tim was Joel Holt. He was the fourth son of a pack leader in Virginia, and he didn't particularly like the family business. Pete figured he was the opposite of him, but where his dad had given him too much, Joel's dad had given him too little—too little time and too little attention. He wasn't sure his efforts to leave the pack life, and specifically his dad's pack, weren't a way to try to get a little attention from his father.

Rickie Escobar was next. Pete had talked with him for a while. He was funny, loud, and a bit of a cutup. The Guard wasn't sure if Rickie would make it past the first week. Not because he was weak, but rather because he didn't seem to take anything seriously. In the Guard, serious went to a new level or someone got killed. Not being focused led to deaths—your own, or worse, a teammate's.

After Rickie, Pete spent some time with Joseph Greggs. An intense and quiet guy, it was a little difficult for him to figure out the Were's reasons for leaving the pack. Finally, it all came together when the Guard had made a comment about the pack political system. It took ten minutes for Joseph to finally step down off his soapbox once he opened up that controversial topic. Pete wasn't very politically minded, so it wasn't a great stretch to admit he didn't have much to say about the subject, nor could he judge the merits of the other Were's points. However, Joseph didn't seem like a political nutcase so he would give him the benefit of the doubt for now.

Finally, the best conversation of the trip happened with Matthew Tseng. He was a rarity in America—an Asian Wechselbalg from immigrant parents. Typically, Wechselbalg from Asia—any of the countries in Asia—didn't come to the US. It had been rare enough that the Pack Council had watched them covertly for years to ascertain if they were plants. Strangely enough, the fact that the child of the couple wanted out of the pack put to rest the fears of a few council members who still considered his parents suspect after three decades.

Matthew had an easy demeanor and was fast as hell. They had played slaps for a while, and Pete couldn't win. The rest of the guys got involved, and even Tim had to admit the guy was preternaturally fast. He gave off a completely guileless vibe. If he didn't agree with something, he simply stated the disagreement. He never sought to prove his point unless you chose to discuss the issue further. Pete tried to answer some of his questions about TQB, and the more they talked, the more he seemed to...*fit*...in Pete's mind.

Tim stared out the window as they approached the ship. He was an adequate swimmer, but all this water caused him a little distress, increasing his anxiety. He heard Rickie say something about the size of the yacht being a compensation mechanism. None of the others laughed at his joke, and Tim heard the "tough crowd" comment under his breath.

That was when he spotted the sniper in a well-concealed location at the top of the large ship. As he looked around, he spotted others at strategic points. In his mind, it was a carefully orchestrated effort to look normal that would fool most people who did not see it from above. With a bird's-eye view, it was obvious that every person on deck had every other person within their line of sight. He had heard about the SpecOps feel from those who had been at the New York meeting with the vampire, but he hadn't realized how organized this team was. Tim wasn't a professional, but he had studied as much as he could on the Internet, and from what he could see, they weren't in Kansas anymore.

The Black Hawk touched down, and Pete opened the door. Two humans waited for them, an older fit man in a suit and a huge man who topped even Tim's height by four or more inches.

He fought back the desire to go over and slug the guy. His alpha personality was working overtime about something as simple as the man's larger body size and height. He had to get a grip, or he might end up thrown overboard. Pete had made sure to remind them Bethany Anne was now the final law and she absolutely could and would slap their heads clean off their bodies if they fucked up too much.

There was a saying that if you killed someone who needed it on land, they had a backhoe to bury the body. Here, there wasn't a need since the water would swallow you and no one would be the wiser. It helped Tim keep a tight leash on his anger.

Even Rickie was momentarily stunned and silent. Joel checked everything out, Joseph had his mouth open, and Matthew simply jumped off and looked around. Pete touched Bobcat's shoulder as he exited and closed Shelly's door.

Dan didn't try to talk this close to Shelly. He merely dipped his head in acknowledgment and waved to everyone to follow him.

They noticed that the big man waited and brought up the rear. None of them would somehow get "lost" on the way to wherever they were going. not that any had thought there would be a boat big enough to worry about getting lost on. Both Tim and Joel had seen another yacht with a helicopter not too far away. It was big, but not as big as the one they were presently on.

Everyone on the ship sized them up and then promptly ignored them once they saw the guys escorting them.

All the Weres wondered what they had jumped into and where the scary vampire was.

Dan took the new recruits into the large conference room and waved them all to chairs. Two more of the big guys with the same patches as Pete showed up, grabbed their bags, and took them away. One was white, and the other was black. A few seconds later, a tanned guy with the patch showed up and took a position in the back corner.

The middle-aged man went to the front and got their attention.

"Good afternoon, gentleman. My name is Dan Bosse, and I am the head of the military arm of TQB Enterprises. Previous to my present lofty position, I worked for the US Government for three decades. Half of that time was spent on special teams hunting young, vicious, mindless vampires called Nosferatu. Have all of you heard that term?" He received a bunch of blank stares. "Damn, what are your elders teaching you guys about vampires?"

Matthew raised his hand, and Dan called on him, "Yes, Mr. Tseng?" He was shocked the man knew who he was.

"Not to mess with them, and to run like hell if you know of one in the area."

Dan grunted. "Well, I guess I can't really argue that strategy. It's a perfect lead-in to the first part of my presentation. Eric, would you hit the lights?"

The lights dimmed, and the built-in LCD TV in the wall came on. "What I am about to share is not known outside of TQB Enterprises personnel. I have spent a large part of my life making sure the sacrifice of these men was never attributed to the UnknownWorld."

Dan went through a list of men, their ages, and their service records, ending with when and how they had died. It made an impression on each of the Weres, but their bias couldn't be broken that easily. These were humans—maybe tough humans, but they didn't have the stamina, strength, or speed of a Wechselbalg. It made sense that Bethany Anne would want to bring on a team of werewolves to help fight those things.

In fact, the werewolves reacted pretty much as John had called it a while back. They respected the deaths of the human agents but felt it wouldn't have happened to them.

The lights came on, and Dan got their attention. "What you are probably thinking is that if you were the ones fighting, you would not have died like these agents did. No amount of explaining or additional video will likely persuade you otherwise, so please raise your hands if you believe you can't be beaten by a human."

Dan looked around. "Mr. Tseng? You don't have your hand up." Everyone looked at him.

"I'm just cautious, Mr. Bosse. I'm willing to fight anyone you want me to, but I'm not willing to believe no human can beat me just because I've not met anyone who could." That got a little chuckle from everyone at the table. John calculated this one would probably be the toughest fight they engaged in.

"Fair enough. Unfortunately, the only vampires we have with us wouldn't be a good way to introduce you to a Nosferatu. The two who are on these two ships—both females, by the way—would have you on the ground so fast you couldn't learn anything, so you get the pleasure of going against the Queen's Guard. There are five of them, and five of you. One of the guards, as you already know, is Pete, so if any of you want to cry foul, we will put a human—if any of them are left—in for a second round."

Tim thought this seemed fair enough. Personally, he wanted a shot at the big guy— one who looked like he might last a couple of rounds.

They all left the meeting room, and Dan took them to the workout area. He gave them a change of clothes, and let them have time to warm up and stretch their muscles.

The Queen's Guard was doing the same thing while playing

AC/DC. It was weird to hear them screw it up and sing, "But Bethany Anne's got the biggest…balls of them all," and then laugh their asses off. Until the Weres knew differently, they wouldn't get sucked into anything that could get the vampire, wherever she was, pissed off at them.

Dan called Rickie up. "Mr. Escobar, you have the floor. Eric from the Queen's Guard will be your Nosferatu for this session." He looked at the new recruits. "Now, please understand that while most Nosferatu are mindless about attacking something to eat it, they don't lack intelligence, or at least cunning. If you permit an advantage, it is likely to use it. Do you understand this, Mr. Escobar?"

Rickie mouthed off, making a joke out of understanding the rules. "One Nosferatu coming up, and one Nosferatu going to go down." Rickie put his hands in the air as if this was a foregone conclusion. He noted Eric was using a strange walking motion that looked both painful to accomplish and reduced his walking speed by at least half. This would be too easy.

Dan spoke up one more time. "Is there anything you want to know about your Nosferatu, Mr. Escobar? Anything you want to make sure they can or can't do?" He stood there patiently, waiting for the Were's answer.

Rickie felt pretty cocky by this time. "Sorry, just need to know how long you want me to make this fight last? Like, should I allow him to last for at least a couple of rounds before he goes down?" He was smiling.

"That's your final question, Mr. Escobar? Yes? Okay, then the answer is you may win quickly or take your time, but remember, taking your time will merely give the Nosferatu time to keep after you. You may now try taking out the Nosferatu, Mr. Escobar."

Rickie's smile grew wider and he looked around, hamming it up for everyone. When he turned to face his opponent again, Eric shot him in the stomach.

Rickie went down, yelling in surprise. "Motherfucker!" The Guard jump-limped over to Rickie and used the 9mm to pistol-whip his head. He was knocked out by the blow to his temple. Everyone was stunned.

Eric stood up, jacked a round, and went to pick up his shell casing. Pete went over to Rickie and grabbed him by the shoulders. He looked at Joseph. "A little help here? He'll be okay. The shot was lead." Joseph helped move Rickie to a pad. Pete heard him mumble under his breath, "Still going to hurt like a motherfucker when he wakes up."

He answered him. "That's the point, isn't it?" Joseph realized there were five pads on the floor and five new Wechselbalg recruits. *Oh, fuck*, he thought.

Since Tim was the last one up, none of the guys got to see him ask for John. It wasn't even a fair contest. The Were might be big, strong, and fast, but unlike John, he hadn't worked out with vampires, nor had he been on operations against the Nosferatu. The fact was, the human was stronger, almost as fast, and substantially better trained and ready. Tim went down in the first five seconds. The guard didn't put his lights out until the third time. When he woke up, the Were would know he'd had his ass handed to him.

As Pete and John carried Tim over to a waiting pad, Pete called to Eric, "You shot him? Damn, that's cold, even for you, Eric."

Eric smiled. "Yeah? I bet he remembers to ask more pertinent questions next time."

Everyone chuckled at that. They all believed the werewolf with the mouth would use the experience to make sure he understood how the rules worked the next time.

It took no more than ten additional minutes before the Weres began waking up. By then, even the 9mm bullet was ejected by Rickie's body.

Dan wanted them all to see the wounds, so he didn't want any cleanup done until after the video viewing.

Once they were all awake and provided with water, it was a quiet walk back to the conference room. When Rickie woke up, Dan had gone over and had a private conversation with him. He'd grimaced but shaken his head.

CHAPTER FIVE

The second part of the meeting had them watching the Nosferatu video, Bill, and other rather bloody footage.

Dan didn't need to make the point that the first humans had been killed by Nosferatu. The men who had taken them out had beaten the Nosferatu. If the Weres weren't good enough to beat the humans, they would be Nosferatu dinner. It was sobering for the brash young men.

The picture of Bill in all his vampire glory was a little startling to everyone. There was one of the bogeymen, one of the vampires mothers used to get their boys to mind. It made an impression before Dan continued the video and showed them other attack footage.

At the end of the video, food was brought in, and Dan dismissed them to get into a fresh set of clothes.

Dan and John were pleased. While they hadn't planned on shooting anyone, it had been an object lesson every one of them would remember, and it had been only slightly painful for Rickie. It was more of an embarrassment, since he had been in more shock than pain when Eric pistol-whipped him into unconsciousness. He didn't feel much of anything until he woke up.

They were pretty tired by the end. Pete showed them to their rooms, and let them know the area was expected to stay as clean as it was at this moment. All cleaning would be done by them. He also mentioned they might want to get as much rest as possible. John Grimes, the big guy, was known to get new recruits up early.

He closed the door to their shared suite at approximately ten P.M. Four hours later, John Grimes came in banging a trash can lid to roust all their sorry asses out of bed. The whole Guard was with him, and he used this time to get them back into the gym and running laps with stop, drop, and give-me-twenty-pushups spread throughout the session. The Guards and the new recruits stopped at four A.M., and John told them they had fifteen minutes to be ready for breakfast.

Every one of the grumps and complaints John heard only caused his smile to get wider.

After breakfast and another session on Nosferatu training, John told the new guys to get ready for a sparring session. This time, all five were a little more cautious.

The time was ten A.M. Now came the final test.

Tim, Joel, Rickie, Joseph, and Matthew came out in their white workout clothes, and Pete came out in a black set with a patch on his shirt. Darryl, Scott, and Eric stood together, their arms crossed. Pete was the only guard who started stretching and warming up. John got their attention.

"Listen up. You guys are obviously a new team, and we are moving through this training operation for the first time, but that doesn't mean we won't train you to be ready to work together if something happens tomorrow. Because we *don't* know what will happen, I'm not comfortable that you guys can pull together and work as a unit. Therefore, you will decide who will be the lead. I don't know how a leader for a Wechselbalg team is chosen exactly, but since I don't care who it will be, I won't push for a particular choice. To make this as even as we can, the four of us will leave.

"Pete has decided he wants a shot at the leadership of the Wechselbalg, so he's going at it as well. The only rule we have is, any unnecessary or capricious damage will be counted against you, and it might take only one such display to get you tossed off the boat. How badly you act will determine whether we toss you off with a lifejacket or not, so don't fuck up. There are video cameras around the room. We will not take someone's opinion. If I can't make a decision, it goes to Dan. He will get Nathan's opinion, and if the two of them can't make a decision, it goes to Bethany Anne."

Tim spoke up. "Are you the lead for the humans?" He would feel a little better if he were beaten by the lead of Bethany Anne's team. At least that way, he could perhaps believe he wouldn't have lost to every one of those guys. He had watched all the fights before his and had been impressed with all the Guards, but had secretly felt he would have done better. John had dissuaded him from thinking he was as good as he believed.

John looked at him. "No, not anymore. Our lead is a female, and trust me, you don't want to go up against her by yourself. We often test the four of us against her. We've almost fought her to a draw, but we've never beaten her yet, so don't push yourself to try that anytime soon, Tim."

John looked at all of them, including Pete. "You guys need to figure this shit out for yourselves. The lead isn't necessarily the strongest. He's the one who will get you guys through the dark and out the other side safely while accomplishing the mission. Remember that as you discuss your choice." John turned around and waved to the other guys to follow him.

Team TQB wanted Pete to take the lead, but they couldn't do anything about that now. Nathan had explained that Wechselbalg would follow only strong people. It didn't mean they would follow the strongest physically to the detriment of intelligence or wisdom, but they couldn't and wouldn't follow someone who wasn't at the top as a fighter. It was built into their DNA. They, of course, didn't realize that was absolutely the truth. Their DNA *had* been manipulated to make them unable to follow weak leaders.

When Pete informed John and Gabrielle that he wanted to drive the new team, they had both asked him all the questions they could think of to make sure he was doing it for the right reasons. Both had been satisfied with his attitude and emotional stability. The vampire had spent eight grueling hours training him one on one, driving him to the end of his abilities and then kicking him while he was down. She'd asked him each time he was on the ground, his body mending the broken bones, dislocated shoulders, and minor cuts she had delivered with her swords, if he was willing to take this pain for his team.

Pete had to know, beyond anything these new recruits would dish out, that he was able to push through to the end. Gabrielle was finally satisfied he had what it took to accomplish this goal. If any of the new recruits could beat him, that person deserved the title.

She told him that if he threw his hat in to be the leader, he would stay on the new team. He would make his choice to make that team successful, whether from a leadership position or as a team member, just like in her group.

That evening, Pete consumed three normal dinners to get the energy he needed to recuperate from Gabrielle's training efforts.

The door closed behind John and the TQB team, and the Weres were alone.

Pete looked them all over. "Every one of you knows only one of us can be the one we all trust to lead us forward. I won't be pulling my punches. I won't be pulling anything that will stop me from making sure I'm the team lead. You had better not do it either."

He continued, "The six of us represent the first Were

Guardian team for Bethany Anne. If you were in New York for the meeting, you know I will not accept anything less than the utmost respect for her. For this reason, you will have to go through me to make team lead. If you believe anyone else, or you yourself, would make a better team lead, then let's get this discussion started."

The guys talked it out for a few minutes, then Tim made it plain he was throwing in. He was almost apologetic about it, but explained his inner wolf couldn't have it any other way. Pete didn't mind. Matthew, Joel, and Joseph all stated they would follow either of the guys. Rickie admitted that while he wouldn't mind trying for it, he was still nursing his injuries from being shot the day before. No one believed he was powerful enough to beat Tim, so it wasn't like he was giving up a good chance at the leadership position.

It really came down to Pete or Tim. The latter had thirty pounds and a couple of inches on Pete, but he didn't have his TQB training or the most recent training Gabrielle had put him through. Pain wasn't his friend, but he sure as hell knew it intimately, and had all the experience necessary to know what he could and would live through to make the position his.

Pete walked over to Tim and held out his hand, and the other Were took it. Both understood this wasn't personal. It was simply the way Wechselbalg decided things.

Bethany Anne was in her room. Three monitors had been brought in so she could view the discussions and the fight or fights. It looked like there would be only one, between Pete and Tim. The fight was piped over to the other ship as well, where Todd Jenkins and his group of Marines were also watching. Everyone wanted to know if this group could pull together and be something more than a bunch of unruly young Weres. This was a new experience, even for Dan and his group. No one had fought with Wechselbalg before. Thousands of miles away near Denver, Colorado, there was one other person watching this fight who wasn't part of Bethany Anne's group. Jonathan Silvers had been called, and had admitted he wanted to watch his son in his first alpha fight.

Jonathan was proud his son was fighting, yes, but he was prouder of the *way* he fought. Pete had taken a hammering early on. His opponent had the reach on him, but he got back up. Tim didn't want to know who could beat who up first. Both realized this wouldn't be a quick fight. Rather, this was a fight to decide the future. Only one Were would be left standing when this fight was finished. Many times, those who watched the fight cringed as a particularly hard punch or kick connected, with massive follow-ups.

Pete was the first to go down and barely rolled away in time. Tim held nothing back, but after the first five minutes, he didn't have any extra anger to harness because he was fighting to breathe after a particularly hard kick cracked a couple of his ribs. After fifteen minutes, they'd had to separate to give themselves a minute to heal. Surprisingly, Pete had the better healing rate between the two of them.

They hadn't started out as anything but two guys who needed to prove something to themselves and who had a desire to drive the future for Weres. Pete had a need to leave the kid from Colorado behind and step into the shoes of the man who would help lead his kind into the future. Tim knew he wasn't going back, and was striving to be the only thing he understood how to be—the one at the top.

Both were losing a little of themselves each time they connected or felt the brutal pain from wherever their opponent connected. Tim was bigger and he had the reach, but Pete was all well-tuned muscle and had been trained to strike harder and more accurately. Each man pounded the other unmercifully. Their faces were damn near unrecognizable. Pete's right eye had closed after successive blows. Tim would lean on his right side, trying to not put so much weight on his broken left ribs his adversary kept crushing with punches and kicks to stop them from healing.

By the twenty-fifth minute, there wasn't one person watching who didn't respect both men. Pete had an appreciation for Tim he hadn't had when he walked into the gym that morning. The older Were couldn't believe anyone could take that much damage and still remain standing.

Pete stopped dancing around and set his feet. "Was that the best you've got, Tim? Can't you put anything else together? I can go all day doing this shit. What are we at—twenty, thirty minutes? Ready to go for an hour, or are you ready to stop doing the fucking tango with me? Let's end this. It isn't that I don't respect you, but there is no fucking way I trust someone I don't know to move the Wechselbalg forward for Bethany Anne. We have more to accomplish than you know, and I will never quit, I will never give up, I will only finish my mission. *Ad Aeternitatem*."

Tim wasn't sure what those last two words meant, but he recognized them from the patch. He grunted his agreement and walked up to Pete and settled into position.

Pete began, "I called it. You go first."

His adversary didn't say a word, merely reared back and slashed down to hit Pete in his half-exposed face. He stumbled, but straightened and moved back into position. It was his turn, and he used it to deliver a solid uppercut that reached Tim barely before the block. The Were's head snapped back, and he took a couple of steps away before he shook his head and got back into position.

They went on like this, exchanging blows that came with increasingly less power and accuracy for five more minutes. The strikes would have put most humans on the mat. Todd's group of Marines all had their mouths open at the sheer ferocity of the two men going at it like gladiators of old, no quarter asked, and none given. No one doubted these two guys would be some scary people to meet in a dark alley.

Pete's left eye was slowly closing, and Tim's ribs had been damaged again. He spat blood as they grinned at each other.

Tim spoke through thoroughly cracked and swollen lips. "For a skinny fuck, you've got a really good right hook." He threw another downward slashing punch, but Pete was able to block most of the damage and kept it away from his face.

"There's only one problem with my right hook, Tim." He shifted back into position.

"Yeah, what is that?"

Pete let loose a lightning-fast left that connected solidly with his opponent's jaw. Tim's eyes rolled back in his head, and he dropped to his knees and then slammed down on the mat.

The Guard stood straight and looked down at the man he had just bested. "My left hook is even better."

He gazed at the four other Wechselbalg. All of them had stopped everything but breathing as they witnessed the two guys pummeling each other. They recognized the sheer determination that pushed them through pain and injuries that should have caused them to drop to the mat forever ago. "Any of you guys want a piece of this? I've got all day. We are the Guardians. We don't stop, we don't quit. We do not know the word defeat. We will move through the darkness, we will defeat our foes, and we will never leave our people behind. Anyone who can't deal with that, step over here and let's discuss it."

Joseph, the quiet one, shook his head. "Hell, no."

Pete knelt and grunted as he started to lift Tim. "Come help me take our team member to medical. It seems he ran into a wall."

The man mumbled, his words easily heard by the Weres, but he was unable to move his body. "No, a fucking freight train kicked my ass. As soon as I can move, I'll buy you a… Shit, I have no money." Then Tim dropped back into unconsciousness.

The team all smiled as they helped their new lead carry him to medical.

The Queen Bitch's Guards lifted their beers to the monitor and exclaimed in solemn voices, "To Bethany Anne's Guardians!"

Back in the United States, in a very pricey bedroom in Colorado, a man stood with tears sliding down his face.

Two hours later, Pete had his new team of Guardians running through some of the same workout routines he had learned from John. Tim was right there with them, and Pete told him they would keep their bloody clothes on. He wanted everyone to realize how fast Wechselbalg Guardians came back from what would have put humans in the hospital, and he and Tim were the poster boys for that as they walked through the hallways. If either one of them had cleaned up, it wouldn't have been as pointed an example.

The workout room door opened and the six guys looked over, expecting to see John or maybe Dan Bosse come in for a follow-up.

Instead, some who had seen one of them before felt their internal warning signals go off the charts. Two vampires had just entered the room.

CHAPTER SIX

<u>Key Biscayne, FL, USA</u>

Frank went looking for Lance and found him in the kitchen making a sandwich. Looking up, the General asked him if he wanted one.

"No, thanks anyway. I need to get your opinion on something —or rather some*one*."

"Okay. Can we do this while I eat this roast beast?" Lance tossed a jalapeno chip into his mouth and grabbed a beer. "Want a beer?"

"Yeah, actually. That sounds good." Frank sat on the barstool. His body had continued to get healthier, and he figured he was probably biologically in his late thirties about now.

"Foreign or domestic?"

"Foreign. I feel like living on the wild side." Lance grabbed a Heineken and set it on the bar, closing the refrigerator after putting the roast beef in the meat drawer.

He continued, "Okay, time's a-ticking. Who's our candidate for craziness today?"

Frank gave him a funny look. "Do you know what I'm about to ask?"

The General swallowed his bite. "No, but you rarely ask me about anything related to people, so this has to be out of the ordinary." Taking another bite of his sandwich, he twirled his finger in a universal "get on with it" gesture.

"Bobcat called me asking for a rocket scientist." Frank pulled the tab off the can of beer.

Lance snorted as if to ask, "Really?"

Frank answered the unasked question. "Yes, a real rocket scientist."

"Okay, what's the problem?"

"Other than that those chips are God-awful loud?" Lance grinned. "He has a bit of a stigma attached to him."

"In what way?"

"Like the tinfoil-hat-wearing type."

"Okay, explain more while I crunch as loud as I can."

"Has anyone told you what a pain in the ass you are?"

"Outside of my daughter? Not too many can get away with it when you're a general."

"It might explain your poor table manners." Frank took another swallow of his beer.

"If I remember correctly, I was making my sandwich and eating in the normally prescribed location to eat, namely the kitchen. You followed me down here, and are now harassing me in the aforementioned eating area. I believe you are actually showing less decorum than I."

Frank considered that for a couple of seconds. Dammit, he was right. "You're still an ass-munch." Lance laughed at him. "Okay, Marcus Cambridge was with NASA for about three decades until he got kicked out for political reasons, then SpaceX grabbed him. He lasted three years before they also showed him the door."

"What for?"

"Apparently, as he gets older, he's been getting more and more blatant about his belief in UFOs—to where he is airing his point of view more often, and it's getting him into political hot water. Being so vociferous about his views in public does not sit well with the establishment."

"So, what's the problem? Does he have the skills we need?"

"Oh, his skills and knowledge, and even his research are what we need badly. The problem is, do we need a tinfoil-hat scientist working on our team?"

Lance put his sandwich down and pushed his beer to the side. He clasped his hands together and rested his elbows on the countertop. "Let me get this right. You came down to the kitchen, interrupted my lunch, and criticized my eating habits to ask me whether a scientist who believes in UFOs is appropriate to work on a UFO, right?" He grinned at his companion.

"Yes, but he's... Well. Oh, dammit. You're right. I'm letting others' opinions of him cloud my judgment. He's right, but doesn't have proof to back it up. I've got proof that he's right, and I'm letting others persuade me that believing in the truth and speaking it without evidence is a problem." He stood from the chair and grabbed his beer.

Lance picked up his sandwich. "Where are you going?"

Frank called back over his shoulder, "Packing for Orange County, California, to go speak to the guy."

"Need backup?"

"Not fucking likely, ass-munch."

Lance chuckled and finished his sandwich. Ten minutes later, he noticed a missed text message from Patricia. She was arriving in…he checked his watch. Too soon. Oh damn.

He called William but was unable to raise him, and then remembered he was supposed to be off. Tossing his trash, he grabbed the keys and jumped in one of the SUVs. He made very good time to the airport and was pulling up outside the terminal when his phone chimed with a text message saying she had landed.

Two hours later, Lance pulled back into the driveway,

listening to gasps of surprise from Patricia as she saw the expensive surroundings and caught the smell of the waterway so close by. She had commented as they went through the security post at the beginning of the subdivision, and made another when he pulled onto their street. Finally, when he had to open the gate to enter the driveway, she simply shook her head in amazement.

This was absolutely unlike the General Lance Reynolds Patricia was familiar with. He was a gruff man who wasn't into large displays of wealth. "Is this yours?"

Lance laughed. "Hell, no. It's my... Well, it's the property of the primary owner of the company I help manage. She's out of the country..."

"She?"

Now, why did that sound like he had just said something wrong? "Yes, *she*. As in female. What is it with you ladies? You want females to move to the top of the chain, but when a man works for one, it becomes an issue?"

"You are in her home."

Well, taken out of context, she kind of had a point. Damn women and their logic.

"Sort of her home. This house and the one next door are used as a base of operations when she and her team are here in the States, although I'm working to find a much bigger and better facility. When she's here, there are nine to eleven people spread between the two houses. Right now, there are three of us using them."

"Where is she now?"

"God only knows. She told me she might be in the area and drop in. I think she's on her yacht somewhere near South America. Who the hell knows? It isn't like she alerts me when she needs to move around."

"Why so many people? An entourage?"

Lance snorted, turned off the car, retrieved Patricia's luggage, and opened the front door. "Not exactly." He stepped aside to let her in. While she was admiring the large entryway, her attention was drawn to Frank as he came down the stairs. "Patricia, let me introduce Frank Kurns, one of the three employees living here at the moment."

He held out his hand. "Pleased to meet you, Patricia. Love to chat, but I have to catch a flight to California to pick up a rocket scientist."

They shook hands, then she watched as he hit the button to open the gate. An Escalade waited to take him to the airport.

Lance closed the door and took her to one of the bedrooms made up for visitors. It wasn't overly large, but it did have its own full bathroom, TV, and computer setup. A large red rug set off the darker gray and white color scheme. Patricia admired the furnishings, which had a very European flair. "I would love to meet the decorator. This is lovely."

The General, remembering his last comment about Ecaterina to Patricia, decided to let that opportunity pass him by because he really did want her help.

"I'll have to ask who did the decorating for you. Are you hungry?"

She turned and smiled. "Something light would be nice. I'm planning on seafood tonight, and you're picking up the tab."

Did he just get stuck with the bill that easily? Well, he *had* asked her to fly out. "Okay, seafood tonight, and there are snacks in the kitchen."

"Did Frank just say he had to go pick up a rocket scientist?" They walked to the kitchen, and she sat on the same barstool he had a few hours before, getting comfortable after setting her purse beside her.

"Yes, the team needs his expertise to build some craft with new technology from one of our…acquisitions." He grabbed some snacks and put out a couple of bowls. Patricia raised her eyebrows and held out her hand. Lance handed her the bag, and she got her own chips.

"So, are you messing with the military-industrial complex, then?" She popped a chip in her mouth.

"Not really. Well, we don't have any plans to in the near future. Too early to tell for farther out." They would have to eventually, but no reason to bring that up right now.

"So, tell me more about what you're doing. I have to tell you, between you calling me from Las Vegas, DC, and now Miami, it seems like you're into a lot. I thought you were leaving to settle down."

Lance grabbed another beer and a Sprite for Patricia. She wasn't a big drinker. He handed her the soda and popped the top on his beer. "No. Where did you get that idea?"

She looked at the can and back at him. "Perhaps a glass and a little ice?" She smiled.

"Sorry." He reached for a glass and turned to the refrigerator to fill it with ice. "Basically, it's just us guys here right now. I've completely slipped into bachelor habits." He handed the glass to her with a napkin and a straw.

Patricia tried to process his question about why she had thought he would settle down. She had watched Lance spiral into a depression after his daughter disappeared. Having opened that can of worms, she now had to admit she had assumed he was checking out of life, in a way. He waited for her to answer, not making it easy on her.

"Lance, we've worked together for a long time. I watched as you withdrew more and more into yourself last year after your daughter left. I guess I simply thought you wanted to go off and be by yourself once you quit."

He took a sip of his beer and thought about what she'd related. "That's a fair assessment if you don't know the rest of the story. I guess I *did* withdraw into myself after Bethany Anne left."

"What's the rest of the story?"

Lance set his beer down. "Before I answer that, let me ask you a quick question, Patricia. What was it you fought for when you were part of the military? Was it the flag? Was it Congress? Was it the country? Was it the rest of us near you?"

She took a couple of chips and nibbled on them to give herself time to consider his question. "I actually entered the service because I needed a job and a way to get an education. I have to admit it wasn't for the ideals so many people espouse. In the end, I was there because of those who were around me, you and the others. Of course, I needed the job, but it really wasn't for the ideals, and certainly not Congress." Patricia laughed at that.

This was about what Lance had expected. While they'd had telling conversations over the years, he knew she didn't have a super-strong nationalist focus. Patricia was more of a live-and-let-live sort of person. How could he get her involved and prove to Bethany Anne she was a legitimate prospect for the team?

He tried another approach, hoping to find a reason that would indicate to his daughter that what his gut told him was true. "Patricia, who do you love? Who would you be willing to fight and die for? Friends, family, loved ones, maybe the dog down the street?" Lance smiled when mentioning that option. Patricia did have a soft spot for animals.

She poured the Sprite into the glass. Patricia had to answer the question, but she wasn't willing to tell him the truth. "I have one or two people I would be willing to fight and die for, or at least die beside. But I don't have any family left, so that isn't going to work. Why do you ask?"

Lance sighed, one part agitated and two parts frustrated. "Because what I'm involved in is literally life and death, not only for our nation but also for the world. For you to be a part of this with me would give you access to secrets that could be harmful."

She bristled. "Lance! You know I have top security clearances. Why would you think I couldn't be trusted on the outside?"

He turned the beer in his hand, trying to figure out the best way to say this. "Patricia, I'm not worried about you sharing secrets with others. I am worried about you having secrets that would cause others to want to harm you."

That surprised her. She hadn't expected she might be in danger if she worked outside the military. "Why would I be in harm's way?"

"I would like to say I'm involved in the dog-eat-dog corporate world, but the truth is the other team doesn't mind getting their hands bloody in this competition. I'm not willing to get you involved if you don't understand the danger."

"How are you going to tell me what the danger is without letting me know more than I should know?"

"Well, that's part of the problem, isn't it? I have to let you know enough to understand that being part of what I am part of is dangerous. You have some protection by being with the group, but if you leave the group with this knowledge, the other team might come after you for information you don't even have. We aren't only going up against corporate interests, but potentially political and…other interests. Any or all of them might come after you for completely different reasons, believing you have the key piece of info they need."

Patricia sat back in her chair, playing with nonexistent lint to give herself time to think this through. "Lance, what are you involved in?" She looked at him with seriousness in her eyes. It wasn't often she dropped the facade of being a secretary and spoke to him directly as a concerned friend.

Lance wiped his face with his hand, looked steadily back at her, and smiled. "Patricia, I am more alive today than I have been for the last ten years. I would love to have you as part of my team to move this forward. In fact, I will even admit I need you terribly. I am completely overwhelmed, and the job isn't going to get any smaller in the future."

He had no idea he'd just spoken the three words Patricia had been waiting to hear: "I need you."

They continued talking for another half-hour, but she was

already sold and was only waiting to make sure Lance felt he had pitched her well enough. Finally, she put a hand up to stop him from continuing. "What's the next step?"

Lance stopped with his mouth open, closed it, and pulled out his phone. He started texting a message, then looked at Patricia. "I asked the CEO to interview you now."

"What? Just like that? She's going to drop in to talk to your potential new secretary?"

He put his phone away. "Patricia, I'm not hiring a new secretary. I am hiring my right-hand man—or woman, in this case— for my team. There won't be a person I rely on more to help me accomplish everything I need to do. Therefore, you had better believe the CEO is anxious to make sure you are the right hire."

Patricia was a little taken aback. A woman who owned two expensive houses, one yacht somewhere near South America, and who knew what else would drop whatever she was doing and come talk to her? She had always thought she wanted to feel important. Now, she wasn't so sure it was a good feeling.

A yippy-dog sound issued from Lance's phone, and he picked it up and looked at the incoming text. "Well, it looks like the CEO is available and will be here probably in the next five hours or so." He looked at Patricia. "Care to have dinner now?"

She closed the chip bag. "Oh, sure, feed me cheap chips before you take me to an expensive seafood place. You just wanted an inexpensive date, you bastard!" They laughed. She handed him the chip bag. "Why do you have the CEO's text-sound set to a yipping dog?"

Setting the bag down, Lance looked at his phone and started texting again. "Her executive assistant wasn't happy about something done to her involving a frozen drink, so she's trying different ways to get back at the CEO. She hasn't heard it yet, so I'm leaving it on my phone to figure out a way to help the carefully laid revenge happen. There, I asked her to make sure she wouldn't arrive sooner than five hours. That should give you at least an hour or so to get your appetite back, depending on how far away you want to go." He looked up at her. "So, how hungry are you, and how much of a view do you want?"

Rancho Santa Margarita, CA, USA

Marcus Cambridge stared down at his phone in disbelief. He had just hung up from a conversation where he had been asked if he was available to meet for an interview in just a little over an hour. The man, a Mr. Frank Kurns, had explained he had tried to reach him earlier in the day but had been unable to, so he had hopped on an airplane and flown across the country from Miami. Just to see him.

Marcus didn't know what to do or even what to feel. He had been out of a job for the last three months, ever since SpaceX had fired him. Oh, sure, he had friends back at NASA and SpaceX who felt he could get re-hired if he would only stop talking about aliens and UFOs, but he was too old to not express his beliefs. It didn't make any sense to him why everyone wanted to ignore the possibilities and not discuss them in public.

Unfortunately, he'd separated from his latest wife after the SpaceX debacle. She hadn't wanted to be with a man where she had to worry every day he'd start talking about aliens again and get fired from yet another job.

She had enjoyed the little dinners around Orange County until she'd realized people were whispering about him—and therefore her—behind her back. Quite simply, she could not stand the idea that she was the butt of jokes because of his beliefs.

He sighed. He wasn't really sure what to make of Frank Kurns, but he had invited the man to his house. It was the only appropriate thing to do. Wasn't it?

Marcus usually relied on his wife to answer these types of questions for him. At six foot two and only a hundred and ninety pounds, he was your typical tall, beanpole-thin bookish scientist who often forgot where he left his glasses even though they were on top of his head.

He would take a shower first, that was it. At least he could be clean for the interview.

Miami, FL, USA

Patricia and Lance came back from a seafood place located on top of one of the buildings on Miami Beach. The view had been fantastic, and the seafood was actually pretty good. He knew they could have found better food in other restaurants, ones that didn't rely on the view to acquire patrons.

But she was looking forward to seeing the sights, and he enjoyed being able to provide the view for her. He had even put this dinner on his own credit card, although he knew Bethany Anne wouldn't mind him charging it to the company.

The meal had become more than a simple recruitment effort. By the time it was finished, he wanted to be the one to have paid for it, and so he did.

They found themselves back in the kitchen, where they had been when she first arrived, and hadn't been there two minutes before they heard a noise upstairs. Patricia looked toward the ceiling. "Did we miss someone coming home?"

Lance looked up and considered the location. "I think the CEO must have been closer than I thought. It looks like your interview is about to happen." He hoped Patricia would be able to remember the dinner after her talk with Bethany Anne.

CHAPTER SEVEN

Rancho Santa Margarita, CA, USA

Marcus sat on the couch in the living room, staring at his reflection in the dark screen of the tv until he heard the knock, then he stood and went to the door, his shirt a little wrinkled. He couldn't find where the iron or ironing board were stored—another one of the little things his wife used to do for him. He opened the door.

A middle or maybe late thirties gentleman stood on the porch. He opened the door a little wider and stuck his hand out. "Frank Kurns?"

The man shook his hand. "Yes, I'm Frank. You are Marcus, correct?"

"Yes, I am. I'm sorry, won't you come inside?" He stepped back, giving him a little more room to enter, and closed the door behind him. "We can step into the living room here and talk. Does that work for you?"

Frank looked around the house. While he wouldn't say it was terribly dirty, it was certainly in disarray. Books were on every flat surface he could see—metallurgy, chemistry, mathematics, space, a rare biology volume or two interspersed between them, and others he didn't recognize stacked everywhere. "Certainly. That would be fine."

The two men seated themselves, Marcus on the couch and his visitor on a loveseat. Frank started the conversation. "Mr. Cambridge, I represent a company that is looking to do research on very difficult-to-understand metals and propulsion systems which will eventually relate to both atmospheric and above-atmosphere craft. I have been asked by the project manager responsible for three-man trans-atmospheric craft to acquire, and I quote, a 'rocket scientist' for his project team. After due diligence, I decided you might be the individual he needs."

"Mr. Kurns—or may I call you Frank?" Kurns nodded his agreement. "Okay, Frank. Before we go too far, I have to tell you I am a little set in my ways. I don't need to go through this process if all you or the team is going to do is ask me to leave when I start talking about aliens. I'm not sure if you've done much research into my last two positions? I ended up getting tossed out of both because I have certain beliefs that are not universally held as truth, and they embarrassed those I worked for. Usually, enough so that whatever benefit I bring to the team isn't sufficient to overcome the embarrassment, and they toss me."

Frank thought for a minute about how to answer his question. "Marcus, I'm aware of why you were fired from SpaceX and NASA. In fact, I took some advice from a general I work with in regard to your situation and the comments about your 'tinfoil' beliefs. I can assure you that if you are hired, you will not be fired for those beliefs. But I will have to ask some questions related to them to get a better handle on why you think what you do, and how it may—or may not—affect your responsibilities based on what our research already knows."

Marcus sat back on his couch, relieved to get this part out in the open. Ever since his last wife, Martha, had left him, he had felt a little adrift. He had even, for a few days, wondered if he should simply let go of his belief that there were others out in the universe. That this man had flown all the way across the United States to talk to him even after knowing this about him left him feeling vindicated, at least for his professional capabilities since they were willing to overlook his personal beliefs. "Of course, that only makes sense. What is it you would like to know?"

Frank opened with the obvious question. "Why do you believe in aliens? Do you have any proof of their existence?"

Marcus smiled. There was an easy response, although not one which usually provided any sort of answer to that question. "The absence of proof doesn't prove the absence of truth. I have never seen an alien. I have never seen an alien UFO, and I have never been visited in the middle of the night or had an alien stick their finger up my butt." They both grinned at that. Actually, Frank was a little relieved to find Marcus had a sense of humor.

He continued his questions. "How can you believe so firmly without proof in something that has ruined two jobs, one of them with arguably the leading space company in America? And, if I understand my research, your last wife left you over this same set of beliefs, right?"

Marcus shook his head. "She didn't exactly leave me over that. Truth be told, I think she holds some of the same beliefs herself, but she wouldn't acknowledge them in public where people could ridicule her. Unfortunately, I was willing to do so, and the ridicule directed at me splashed over onto her. She couldn't handle it, and decided to seek other pastures. Note, I didn't say greener pastures, merely other pastures."

"Okay, that explains your wife, but what about your contemporaries? What about the other scientists?"

"Those bastards? They wouldn't believe something unless a committee had already blessed it and it had two articles peer-reviewed in a professional journal. Finally, someone would have to replicate the results in a third-world country with subpar capabilities before they would believe it."

Wow, Frank thought, this guy was still a little hot under the collar about the situation.

He wondered how Marcus would take his next couple of questions?

Patricia turned around in the chair, hearing footsteps—obviously a female's from the clacking of the heels—in the entryway. The woman coming through the door with a smile on her face was the last person she had ever expected to see.

"Bethany Anne?" She was confused. The woman before her certainly looked like Bethany Anne, but wasn't she dead? "You're the CEO?" She looked at Lance, who was smiling, and turned back, confusion etched on her face.

Bethany Anne came up and hugged her. "Yes, but I can't run the whole operation, so I had to shanghai my dad to run and organize the business side. Now he tells me he can't get along without your help, so here I am to make sure we get you on board and keep him happy. Why don't you come upstairs with me so we can talk about it without the old fuss-bucket getting involved?"

Patricia turned toward the General, a questioning look on her face. "Lance?" He smiled and waved her toward his daughter.

"I'll be fine right here, Patricia. I'm not going anywhere. Besides, if you girls don't take too long, we still have time to go out for drinks afterward." That helped settle her feelings and concerns that he would be there for her when this was all done. She hopped off the stool and went with Bethany Anne.

Patricia followed her through the suite's doors, and Bethany Anne closed them behind her. She looked around in amazement. "This has to be one of the most beautiful rooms I have ever been in. You have simply got to tell me who your decorator is."

"Decorator?" She looked around the room. "The lady who

helped me do the whole house is named Ecaterina, and she's from Romania."

Patricia's eyes narrowed. "Ecaterina? I have that name right, correct?" Bethany Anne was quick to pick up on the other woman's annoyance.

"Yes. She's helping me with a lot of different jobs around the company, sort of like what you will do for my dad. Why, do you know her?" She was sure the visitor had never met Ecaterina, but it was obvious she was familiar with her name.

Patricia tried to hide the annoyance she felt. "No, I've never met her. Lance has mentioned her a couple of times on the phone. He happened to use her as a joke I think he was pointing my way. Honestly, I should be upset with him, not her. No wonder that slimeball didn't tell me who helped decorate downstairs. I swear, I will get that man back if it takes all night."

Bethany Anne was starting to understand the situation. What she had here was a case of a woman loving a man who had no clue she cared about him. How very typical of her dad to not know how a woman felt about him. Unfortunately, that wouldn't be good enough for what they needed to accomplish.

"Decorators aside, Patricia, you have to understand there's a lot going on, and for you to be involved could be dangerous—"

"Yes, Lance already told me about the danger. I haven't been told what it is yet, and honestly, I'm not even sure how you're involved. Why did you disappear? Why did he not know where you were for months? Don't you know how much pain you put that man through? My God, I feel like I want to slap you right now."

She paced the room, her aggravation growing with each step. "It was awful watching Lance slowly deteriorate in front of my eyes. Watching the life of someone I have cared about for so long just draining away and not being able to do anything about it." Bethany Anne was pretty sure the woman didn't realize what she had just divulged.

Patricia continued, "He might be willing to follow you across the world and do God only knows what, but if you want to know the truth?" She stopped to look Bethany Anne in the eyes. "The truth is I will follow Lance, not you, to the ends of the Earth. I have been with him, I have worked with him, I have cried for him, and I would have died for him if it would've helped him get through his pain." She sat down on the small couch at the end of the bed. "Damn, did I just admit all of that out loud? In front of his daughter?" She sighed. "What am I going to do with myself now? I'll just hop on the nearest plane and leave Miami. Maybe I can get a waitress job back in Denver."

Bethany Anne cocked an eyebrow. "Why do you believe anything you just said is a problem?"

Patricia looked up at her. "Isn't it obvious? Lance is on a mission. I am assuming that mission is because he loves you, whether he understands the bigger picture or not. He's more alive right now than I have seen him in months. Hell, probably years."

Bethany Anne studied the older woman. My God, she thought, am I about to play Cupid? "Why do you say he's more alive?"

The visitor threw out her arm. "Have you seen how young he looks? It's like he went and got a damn facelift and a tummy tuck or something. I thought being seven years younger than him would give me an advantage, but I'm not so sure anymore. And look at you! My memory might not be perfect, but you are definitely looking substantially better than the last time I saw you. What did you do, get a breast lift? And you have got to be working out like crazy. How did you become the CEO of a major organization? Weren't you working for the government or something? I feel like I've gone down the rabbit hole here and I can't stop shooting my mouth off."

Bethany Anne walked over to a Victorian-era chair and sat down on it facing Patricia. "I can understand that you feel overwhelmed. I can deal with the fact that you don't know me well enough to trust me, and you place your trust in my dad. Understand, however, that he does not have an unreasonable trust in my mission. Nor, I believe, will you, once you understand what it is and see the proof for yourself. But your trust in Dad is not misplaced. If it wasn't for the fact that you will see unbelievable things in the near future, I would let you stay ignorant and blissfully happy. Unfortunately, I don't have the time to drop in here and give you an update every time you need it, so this will be your one big interview and brain dump into the reality of the situation. You will have to make a decision tonight."

Patricia tried to smile and bring a little levity to the conversation. "Can we get this done before I lose the chance to go get drinks with him?"

Bethany Anne smiled back at her. "I can make this happen quickly, or it can last for the next couple of hours. It all depends on how quickly you can believe in something."

"Really? What is it you want me to believe?"

From down in the kitchen, where Lance was nursing a beer, he could hear Patricia scream, "Oh, my God." He flinched a little, guessing his daughter had decided to show her something vampy. He took another sip, trying to calm his nerves as the discussion upstairs continued.

An hour later, he heard one set of steps coming down the stairs. He walked around the bar and met Patricia at the bottom. He was hoping she remembered her meeting with Bethany Anne, but he had prepared himself for the fact that she could have had some of her memories wiped.

He was a little puzzled at the look of admiration on her face. She had stopped on the last step, and her eyes were at the same level as his. She reached out and grabbed his head, planting a kiss on his nose. He looked at her, confusion written on his face.

She smiled at him. "What? Was Russia or China or even the terrorists not enough for you, Lance? You had to decide to take on aliens as well?" He felt the relief wash through him. She had passed Bethany Anne's tests.

"Well," he grumped at her, "there are vampires to deal with." Patricia shuddered. He had seen that reaction before, usually from anyone who'd had an up-close view of his daughter when she had gone all evil dead woman on them.

"I am perfectly willing to let Bethany Anne handle the vampires, if that is okay with you? Saving the world is enough for me."

Patricia stepped around Lance and started for the door. He turned to watch her as she walked with more of a perk to her step than she'd had when she arrived, he thought. In fact, he would admit that as she reached the door, everything seemed a little perkier than he remembered. Had she been working out since he had left the base? He grabbed the keys and followed her out the door, admiring the view.

CHAPTER EIGHT

Rancho Santa Margarita, CA, USA
Frank had started to like this scientist. "Marcus, I have at least one, maybe two more questions for you. You might be able to answer them together. The first one is, if you were tasked with finding proof of alien life in another solar system, how would you do it? The second one, which is the corollary, is how would you confirm if aliens had visited the Earth?"

Marcus stood and went to the window to look up into the night sky. "Well, that's the crux of the argument, isn't it? If one were tasked with finding alien life in another solar system or another universe, how could we even know unless the aliens were far more advanced than we are? For example, right now here on Earth, we send out radio waves to communicate at a distance. Do you know the speed at which radio waves travel? No? Actually, radio waves travel very quickly through space.

"They are a kind of electromagnetic radiation, so they move at the speed of light, which is a little less than three hundred thousand kilometers per second. The reason it takes so long for radio messages to travel in space is that space is mind-bogglingly big. The distances to be traversed are so great that even light or radio waves take a while to get anywhere. It takes around eight minutes for radio waves to travel from the Earth to the sun, and four years to get from here to the nearest star.

"Do you know how many stars there are for us to check in the galaxy? If we use a pencil and figure out the answer on the back of a napkin, the number is more than a hundred billion. Remember, the nearest star is four years away using light speed or, in this case, radio waves.

"Back in January of 2015, scientists discovered a couple of potential Earth-like planets around a red dwarf. They were named Kepler-438b and Kepler-442b. They sit at about one thousand, one hundred light years away, so we would have to assume the alien civilization on either of these two planets was sending out radio waves at least one thousand, one hundred years ago. Or that, in one thousand, one hundred years, they will be able to receive our radio waves."

While Frank usually considered himself pretty good with numbers, the size of the numbers Marcus threw around was a little overwhelming.

"So, either alien civilizations have been sending us messages for centuries—or actually probably more like tens of thousands of years—or they have somehow visited us and left clues behind. Have you ever read the *Foundation* series by Isaac Asimov?" Marcus sat down again.

Frank shook his head. "No, I haven't. Why?"

Marcus sighed. "It makes this next concept a little easier to understand. Someone your age might have difficulty trying to figure this part out."

Frank smiled. He wondered what Marcus would think if he knew his real age.

"In the *Foundation* series, there was a plotline where a protagonist put different pieces of information the farthest possible distance away from each other. Conceptually, most people were looking at two different edges of space. Think of it this way: if you stretched your arms out, you would say the largest distance was between the tips of your fingers, correct?"

Frank agreed that sounded right.

"Most of the people in the book thought the same thing, but the reality was he wasn't talking about distance in miles, but a different type of distance. He had put the information at the core of civilization, and then at the far edge of civilization. Does that make sense?"

Frank thought about the statement for a few seconds. "So, in this case, he wasn't talking distance in miles, like you say, but rather the farthest distance between two types of belief?"

"Essentially, yes. So, the equivalent when looking for proof of aliens would be to look at the farthest distance away, considering a hundred billion stars and the distance and time it takes for radio waves to travel, or look right here on Earth. Since I can get to most places on Earth much easier, I think I would start here."

Frank couldn't help it. He was naturally an inquisitive person, and he loved to acquire new knowledge. This conversation with Marcus was causing his mental juices to flow. It took him a couple of minutes to realize he was so caught up in the story and logic he failed to remember the obvious. He didn't need to look across the Earth for proof of an alien's existence. He had a damn spaceship on one of Bethany Anne's superyachts.

Frank looked at the scientist. "I know from reviewing your information online—I have access to some of the government's databases—you have no other family. What we're doing is beyond top-secret. What would it take for you to be willing to go away and research alien life without compromising a top-secret mission? In our case, you would never be able to publish any of your information. Actually, all things considered, you probably *will* be able to, but it will be decades in the future."

"You mean after I'm dead?"

"Not necessarily, but that decision will be at least ten to twenty years in the future. We have unbelievable medical coverage, so I feel comfortable in suggesting you will probably still be with us."

"Young man, maybe from your perspective, death seems to be in the future somewhere, but at my age, the damn thing seems to be right around the corner, waiting for me."

Frank considered how to get Marcus to come with him willingly without divulging too much information. The worst that could happen was he would go public with something he told him. Considering he was already believed to be a crackpot, that probably wouldn't hurt Bethany Anne's team right now—but it could potentially be used in the future once more of the truth came out.

He sighed dramatically. "Marcus, I need a rocket scientist. I need a rocket scientist in the worst way. Your personal beliefs in aliens and UFOs will not affect your professional relationship with any of our team. I would like to offer you the chance to work on a superyacht that is presently off the coast of Central America near Costa Rica. We have need of your engineering skills as well as other capabilities you bring to the table. There will be a nondisclosure agreement, but you probably guessed that already. That's normal in your line of work, correct?"

"Of course. Nondisclosure agreements are standard in the industry, although I have to say I'm not fond of them from a scientist's perspective. But since I'll never be published again in any peer-reviewed journal, I don't think I'll be giving up much."

"Okay. This project will be at least two to three months, minimum. I will authorize one and a half times your previous salary plus all expenses there and back and a small per diem if you are off-ship. Unfortunately, if you have any pets, they will not be able to go. Do you?"

"No, of course not. I get lost in my studies too often to take care of any animals. Without a wife, I sometimes can't figure out what I need to do for myself. By the way, what do we do for food on the ship? Do I have to cook for myself?"

Frank smiled. "No, of course not. There is support staff in charge of cooking and cleaning."

The scientist stood. "Someone will cook for me again? Why didn't you tell me that in the beginning? I'd be willing to go for free just for someone to cook. I can't cook worth a damn, and I hate my own food. But since you've already told me what the pay will be, you can't go back on that." Marcus seemed like a child waiting for Christmas morning.

Frank laughed. "I wouldn't dream of it. What will it take to get your house ready for you to leave for a while?"

Marcus looked around, "Honestly? Not a lot. I'm sure I can get Martha to come by once a week to make sure everything still looks good, the mail is dropped off, and the lawn is done. I have the lawn service on automatic payment, so it will continue to look good and the HOA won't get after me."

Frank considered that now would be a good time to have Patricia on the payroll. He could simply hand this whole situation off to her, and it would magically get done. Honestly, he could completely understand why Lance was so interested in her coming on board. "When do you think you can be ready to go?"

"How fast do you want to leave?" Marcus asked.

"Yesterday would be a good time," he answered truthfully and stood.

The scientist put up a finger and walked away around the corner, down the hallway, and disappeared into a door at the back. He was gone five minutes before he came back with a backpack and a laptop bag. "I have nothing better to do tonight. Let's go." Frank laughed and headed for the door.

No time like the present to continue saving the world, he thought.

Anton's Residence, Buenos Aires, Argentina

Anton considered the information he had received from his

CIA contact in Costa Rica. It didn't make any sense for the helicopter to be based on land, at least as far as he could tell. That put the helicopter on a rather large ship. After discussing the potential possibilities with his subverted contacts in the local military, they came to the conclusion that it would have to either be a military vessel or a well-financed individual. Anton didn't believe it was military. No one from Michael's family would use the military in this situation.

He knew about the agents, of course, but even they didn't use military ships for this. That left a private vessel. There weren't very many that could house or hold a Black Hawk helicopter. He sent out requests to information gatherers in South America to be on the lookout for a large yacht that had a Black Hawk helicopter on it, feeling confident he would have his answer within a few days at most.

From there, he considered, he would pull together a strike team to take over the yacht, preferably after he had pulled Bethany Anne off. It would decimate their ability to protect themselves from his team. He would add a couple of vampires for good measure since he wanted to keep this boat intact. Maybe he could do the same thing and create his own floating base. He wasn't sure why he hadn't thought of that before; it made perfect sense. Anton hated admitting an adversary had a better idea than he had come up with on his own.

No matter. Once he took the yacht, all would be right with the world again. He started pulling together the contacts to acquire a couple of cigarette speedboats. He picked one of his throwaway phones up to make a call.

Nathan looked down at his phone but didn't recognize the Texas number. He considered ignoring the call, but it wasn't like he was too busy. He clicked the answer button. "Hello?"

"Mr. Lowell? This is Ben, one of the, ah, workers you helped get a job? From the Miami group?"

Nathan remembered Ben. He was one of the hackers Bethany Anne had saved from the "terrorists," and had changed his name to work for Nathan's company in Texas. "Yes, Ben, what can I do for you?"

"Um, Mr. Kurns—the man you had me talk to a few weeks ago—said I should follow up with you on a request I made to him when we talked."

Nathan could hear Ben's hesitation about continuing this line of conversation. He wondered how long it had taken him to get the courage up to call him. "Certainly, Ben. What is it you would like to know?"

"Actually, I had asked Mr. Kurns if I could meet the lady who saved me from the building back in Miami."

Nathan was a little shocked. Of all the questions he had expected the man to ask him, meeting Bethany Anne wasn't at the top or even in the middle of the list. It wasn't even *on* the list. "I'm sorry, Ben, I'm a little confused. Why do you want to meet her?"

There was a pause on the other end of the line. "I keep asking myself the same thing. While I agree she is very attractive, she is also scary as hell. I don't think a date is the reason I'm trying to reach out to her. It almost feels like a need to close a loop. Does this make any sense? Somehow, I feel like I can be of more assistance to her than what I am doing here. I need to make amends in some form or fashion, and until I get to ask her and she tells me she doesn't need my help…" He didn't finish his thought.

Ben had been considered the best at his former company, now owned by Bethany Anne. There was a back channel for conversations between Nathan and the head of the company. Lance had overall responsibility, but approved of Nathan handling their questions. Therefore, the main project leads still routed their questions to the Were. Nathan asked about Ben and Tabitha every two weeks or so. Both received glowing reviews, and Ben had accomplished even more than anyone had expected. Now that he had reached out to him, he didn't feel like he would be poaching if he took him away from the company.

"Ben, tell me what you know about the hacking activity from China, please."

For the next hour and a half, they discussed the particulars of the Chinese hacking situation. It was obvious to Nathan, a world-class hacker himself, that the man had skills he could use effectively. While they talked, he opened a chat program to discuss how quickly Ben could be moved to Miami. His Texas manager didn't want to let him go, but Nathan pulled the "do I have to get the CEO to call you for this?" card and his manager agreed the absolute earliest was at the end of the following week, but he would really appreciate at least three weeks.

Nathan told Ben to go ahead and finish out his next week, and to expect to get a call and airline tickets to come to Miami within three weeks at the outside.

Ben wasn't old in nerd years. Computers and computer code plus a little bit of caffeine from time to time were his existence. It wouldn't be hard to move him to Miami.

After hanging up with Ben, Nathan called Ecaterina. He had been trying to stay busy, keeping her and her situation out of his thoughts. His last conversation with his girl on the *Polarus* hadn't gone too well, and he had gotten the full brunt of the Romanian woman's anger. Unfortunately, he knew enough of her language to understand every word.

He was happy to not be stuck on a boat in the middle of the ocean with her at the moment. He didn't care how large the boat was; it wouldn't have been large enough. While he understood her desire to get involved, his personal desire to keep her safe had made him say a couple of stupid things. He had known they were stupid before he spoke, but unfortunately, he hadn't been able to stop his mouth in time.

When she had suddenly stopped talking to him and made a face he hoped never to see on her again, he had realized his need to keep her safe had created a sudden need to keep himself safe from her. When your woman could very literally gut you or shoot you from a distance, being in Miami while allowing her to cool down on the ship had seemed to be an intelligent move on his part.

Now work called, and he had a need to talk to her. He sure hoped he didn't get an unreceptive response.

CHAPTER NINE

<u>Constanta, Romania</u>

Stephen went into the kitchen and opened the refrigerator, grabbed a packet of blood, and pulled it out. He opened the packet, poured the contents into a mug, and put it in the microwave. A few moments later, he drank it without making a face.

The bell on the door rang. This wasn't a normal doorbell, but rather an old-fashioned one made of iron he had installed over a hundred years before. Anyone coming to the front door would reach up and grab an old rope and pull. Pulleys would then guide the rope to ring the bell deep in the house. Stephen rather liked the sound since it reminded him of the past. He walked out of the kitchen and up to the front door, sensing there were vampires on the other side.

He could hear their murmurs and their concerns. With one of the voices being female and the other two male, he was pretty sure who he would find on the other side.

Stephen opened the door and smiled at the three individuals on his front stoop. All three were anxious and not sure what to do, and he stood there looking at them expectantly. Finally, the young lady spoke for the three of them. "Excuse me, is this the house of Stephen?"

"Yes, it certainly is. How can I help you this evening?"

"Would you let Stephen know Claudia and her brother Juan and her friend Scott have arrived? We will be happy to stay out here until he admits us to his home."

The three had been arguing whether or not they should act as if they had an invitation to his home or act subservient, as would be expected of a Forsaken relationship. Stephen opened his front door wide and stepped back. "Please, make your way to the front room and be seated."

They walked through the front door to the sitting area on the left. Claudia and Juan took a couch, and Scott took the chair across from them. Their host closed the door and followed them. "Would any of you care for a drink? Do any of you need blood?"

Claudia looked a little relieved. "Yes, we would all appreciate at least a little blood. We have been concerned about whether or not it was permitted to drink in Stephen's lands."

"I understand. Please understand that the blood I will give you will be reheated from packets." Stephen noticed a small look of distaste flash across Scott's face.

"I'm sure that will be more than adequate, and thank you very much." Claudia glared at Scott. Stephen tried to hide a smile as he went back to the kitchen, prepared three more mugs of blood, and brought them back to his guests. After they finished their drinks, he collected the mugs and returned them to the kitchen.

He walked back into the sitting room and took another one of the chairs, and all three of them looked at him expectantly.

"Now that you have had refreshments, what can I do for you?" Juan was the first to understand they were speaking to Stephen himself.

It took only seconds for the other two to catch up. Claudia's face reddened in embarrassment. "Forgive me, Stephen. I did not understand you were the one answering the door. We would never have presumed to request you serve us as you have."

He laughed. "Please understand I don't operate here in Europe as you are used to with the Forsaken in South America."

All three vampires sat back in their seats, a little more at ease. Claudia continued the conversation. "When I spoke with Ecaterina from Bethany Anne's retinue, she said you might be able to provide safety for us in Europe within your house's protection?" Stephen noted that Scott had a visceral reaction to Bethany Anne's name. He was trying to be polite, but the visitor was starting to get on his nerves. He realized his Queen wouldn't have a problem with Scott's reaction, especially if he had been close to Clarita, but Stephen was from another age and could be counted on to react to facial expressions if they continued for too long.

Stephen answered, "Yes. It would not be a problem for you to live in Europe. Obviously, this permission is predicated on you rejecting the Forsaken creed regarding humans. Please be aware" —he turned to look directly at Scott—"that we in Europe operate under the authority of Bethany Anne. I will brook no disrespect of my Queen. Is this understood?" His eyes didn't leave the man's face.

Claudia wanted to slap Scott. He had been their biggest problem ever since they had left South America. While Juan was Claudia's brother and had changed to a vampire to help her cope many years before, Scott was Juan's friend, who had found a mother figure in Clarita. He had been hit particularly hard by her death. She hoped he didn't ruin this opportunity for safety with an outburst caused by the emotional pain he was still working through.

Juan spoke up. "Stephen, could you explain Bethany Anne's role in the UnknownWorld to us? Our experience in South America is not very helpful in understanding what is going on. In fact, without my mother explaining that she was under attack because of Adrian, we would probably have thought it was an internal political issue with the Forsaken."

Stephen spent the next three hours explaining the true history of vampires and how Bethany Anne fit into the new changes coming about. He was circumspect when explaining how she became a vampire, but he did give them enough understanding to realize their brother Adrian started the whole situation by killing Bethany Anne's mentor back in Washington DC.

Claudia and Juan could understand the anger she must have felt. Scott, however, did not want to hear any justification for killing his mother. Finally, in a fit of disgust, he stood up, walked to the front door, opened it, and slammed it behind him as he walked out into the night. There was a moment of silence as Claudia and Juan sat on pins and needles, clearly concerned about Stephen's reaction.

He looked at the door Scott had just closed. "Well, I suppose that could've been handled better. Fortunately, whatever he might have to say about Bethany Anne I won't hear or need to take action on. I suppose that was the most mature response he could come up with."

Stephen was not like the powerful vampires either of them was accustomed to working around.

They continued talking into the morning, waiting for Scott to come back. Sometime later, Ivan came in and introduced himself. He was a little despondent and not his typical cheery self, but seemed to enjoy the conversation with Claudia and Juan—particularly Claudia.

Stephen knew a phone call had occurred between Ivan and Gabrielle. He would need to call his daughter and find out what was going on later.

Finally, Ivan went into the kitchen to make himself a late snack, which was where he was when the trouble started.

. . .

San José, Costa Rica

Special Agent Matthew Burnside walked into the San José Police headquarters. He was part of the Office of Asian Pacific, Latin American, and African Analysis and frankly wasn't supposed to be talking to anyone right now, including—he looked down at his hastily written note—one Superintendent Rodriguez.

Unfortunately, he had gotten a call early this morning from someone with enough pull in the Military Affairs group to drag his ass out of bed to ask the superintendent some questions.

He typically dealt with ongoing political volatility, military security, and the many and varied leadership changes. With all the unstable economic situations that occurred on a regular basis down there, he often wondered why he'd left California. It was rare he did anything more than read reports and occasionally make a few phone calls. Being called up to run out into the field wasn't something he did, but this meeting would be about all the supposed drug murders that had occurred in the last couple of weeks. Matthew had read the many newspaper reports and understood that something was very fishy. He had even read the reports about the so-called Death Angels who had protected the city, and the helicopter that flew at night.

Matthew introduced himself to the attractive brunette secretary at the front of the building. She was immune to his blond hair and told him he could wait in the second meeting room down the hall and to the left. He had only sat there, smelling the old cigarette smoke, for about five minutes before an attractive, maybe early-forties lady with black hair and glasses stepped in and introduced herself.

"Hello, I am Superintendent Rodriguez of the San José Police. I am one of the officers in charge of the task force for investigating the missing persons and murder cases. How can I help you this morning, Agent Burnside?"

Matthew decided simply asking for what he wanted was the

best way to move forward. "Pleased to meet you, Superintendent Rodriguez. I have been asked to obtain information related to the most recent murders and the paramilitary group using a Black Hawk helicopter. We would like to understand why you worked with them, and where they might be at this time." It took Matthew approximately five seconds to realize he'd completely fouled up with the lady. Her pleasant expression quickly morphed into one he recognized as barely contained anger.

Her voice was clipped and angry. "Just like that? You want information related to our problems without so much as 'we are sorry for your deaths?' Did you know two of my close friends were killed during the troubles? Now, all you want to know about is a paramilitary group operating in my country? This is what you came here to talk to me about? No other items of note? I don't recall seeing any American agents at the funerals. Perhaps you *were* there, and I didn't recognize you?" Matthew understood really quickly where he had gone wrong.

He felt bad as he told her, "No, Superintendent, I was not there." What a clusterfuck, he thought. No wonder that dick hadn't wanted to take this meeting himself. If no one from the agency had even sent condolences on their losses, how were the two groups supposed to continue working well in the future?

Superintendent Rodriguez stood up. "Then you will understand if it takes me some time to finish with my personal grieving before I spend any effort tracking down a paramilitary group responsible for saving many more of our lives. Once I finish my grieving, feel free to reach out and contact me again to see if we can help you. Good day, Agent."

The superintendent left the office, barely stopping herself from slamming the door in his face. Matthew thought about it for a moment and opened the door quickly. "Superintendent?" Rodriguez turned. "Would you happen to know the name of the reporter who was helped that first night?"

"Giannini Oviedo." Rodriguez turned away and continued

walking, obviously not willing to answer any more of his questions. It wasn't until she reached her office and was able to think clearly again that she realized she had just given away an important name, and the American agent would follow up on it.

Shit, she thought, she needed to get Giannini on the phone quickly.

The Queen Bitch's Ship *Ad Aeternitatem*

Bethany Anne was on TOM's ship, looking into the Pod-doc at the dog she had decided to name Ashur, not quite believing her eyes.

TOM, he's big.

He really is a very beautiful dog.

And big.

That, too.

So, what are the readouts telling you?

They are telling me we will have an interesting canine.

Define interesting.

Well, something out of the ordinary? Something unexpected? Something—

TOM, quit your bullshitting and tell me what's going on.

Okay, just trying to bring a little levity to the news.

Duly noted, and you failed miserably.

Wow, tough crowd. Okay, all kidding aside, we have a superdog.

TOM, "superdog" isn't very helpful as a description. Give me something to work with.

Well, as you might expect, he has increased speed and strength, his bones are tougher, his skin is tougher, he's obviously bigger all the way around, and, of course, he's white. Not exactly a good color for hiding at night.

True. Any chance we can change his hair to black?

Are you kidding?

Um, maybe?

Well then, answering from a scientific point of view, we certainly can change it. The nanocytes can alter the pigment-producing cells, but it would probably take a few weeks for the color to completely change as the hair grows. The Pod-doc had to deal with some genetic abnormalities and select various recessive genes. In the process, we got white hair.

Well, good to know. No need to do it right now, but if he goes down again, remind me we had this conversation. I'm sensing you left something out. Give.

Well, this time, it isn't actually anything bad. There are two particular nuances I hadn't expected. The first is a substantial ability to act as a conduit for the Etheric. The second is his modified mind.

What do you mean by "modified mind?" I don't want to release a huge, vicious animal with mental instability.

No, no. I don't think he has any mental instability. Actually, from the research you and I did previously, dogs have intelligence that equates to maybe a two- to three-year-old human child. I'm guessing this dog's intelligence is a touch higher than that estimate.

Bethany Anne was getting frustrated with TOM's insufficient answers.

How much higher than that?

I can't really say at this time. It might only be one or two more years, or we might have something that increases over time. It's not like I have a lot of research to work with here.

She continued to study him. The dog was certainly beautiful with his white hair, and she was curious what his eye color would end up as. She turned to the right and slipped through the Etheric back to her room on the *Polarus*. They would pull Ashur out of the Pod-doc pretty soon.

God only knew what they would find when they did that.

Bethany Anne walked out of her suite into the conference room, following a knocking noise. She found Bobcat banging his forehead slowly against the wall. She stopped walking and stared at him. He continued to hit his head for thirty seconds straight before she interrupted him. "Bobcat, why are you damaging my wall?"

Startled, he turned to see her staring at him. His forehead was red, and he flushed with embarrassment.

He sighed. "I left William in Miami to keep an eye on the assets up there. Over the holidays, he hooked up with a lady and requested a three-day leave to go out with her. His three-day leave ended two days ago. I need his help down here on the project, so I called Miami, but I got no response. Ten minutes ago, I got a call from an unknown number, and I answered the phone." Bethany Anne raised an eyebrow at that. He should not have answered an unknown phone call for security reasons, but it looked like she needed to get to the bottom of this first problem before she introduced and reprimanded him for the second. "The nice gentleman on the other side was actually a sheriff. It seems William got left high and dry two nights ago at a bar by this woman. He then proceeded to drink away his pain. I don't remember if I shared this with you, but William can't hold his booze."

Bethany Anne nodded. She had heard the stories about William and drinking. For such a large man, he didn't do very well in bar brawls, but since he was so large, he was a natural target. She winced, thinking about what must have happened.

"So, how bad is it?"

"Well, he should only be nursing a headache by now, but the fact that he did it in the first place causes me some serious concerns. I think it might have been a poor decision to leave him alone up there. He doesn't have a focus now that the SUVs are done."

Bethany Anne thought about that for a minute. "I can see your point. He's driven by challenges, and we haven't given him any new ones. He hasn't been down here with us, either. Ask Ecaterina to have our legal representation get him out of the clink and put his ass on a plane down here as soon as possible. Make sure he understands he is going to work this fuckup off."

Bobcat's shoulders slumped a little, some of the tension draining from them. Bethany Anne spoke again. "Mind you, he's *your* teammate, so you're going to work this fuckup off as well." He nodded. He understood it always went uphill as well as downhill within Bethany Anne's group.

She turned around and left him to deal with getting William down there.

CHAPTER TEN

San Andreas Island, East of Nicaragua

Both the *Polarus* and the *Ad Aeternitatem* had arrived near San Andreas Island during the evening. William had been flown down to the island the previous night and was waiting to be picked up. Personnel on both ships were looking forward to a little R&R and enjoying themselves over the next couple of days. Ecaterina had made sure both ships would be properly protected while personnel got a chance to play in the sun and the surf.

Both ships made quite a splash with the locals. Some of the smaller yachts came out occasionally, and people waved as they took their time checking out the sleek lines of the ships. A couple of the ships' personnel had to ignore the requests from the boat bunnies who were trying to get on board. Although they smiled, they explained to the attractive ladies that the owner of the ship would not permit anyone on board and they were very, very sorry about that. One particularly attractive woman broke a couple of hearts with her pout.

Ecaterina had talked to Nathan the previous night, and both had had something to say about how they had acted. He admitted he had gotten a little bit too protective, and knew he had to rein in his efforts in that regard. She conceded that she would try to understand his protectiveness and remember it came from a good heart. They agreed to make up for their missed time the next chance they got. Both finished the phone call with smiles on their faces and anticipation in their hearts.

Bethany Anne, Ecaterina, and Bobcat planned on taking one of the boats over to the pier to pick William up. John and Eric would go with them as their protective detail. The vampire wasn't happy her father had escaped from his detail, but she understood all four of the Queen Bitch's Guards needed to be on the ship when the Wechselbalg arrived. She would get even with the old man as soon as she could.

It didn't take long to get to the pier, tie up, and locate a taxi. Ten minutes after their arrival, Bethany Anne got a phone call from Gabrielle. She asked if it was okay to bring the boat back and start ferrying over those who had shore leave due. Bethany Anne didn't mind. If she got stuck on the island, they would go to a restaurant for a while and relax.

When they caught up with William, he had the good grace to be embarrassed as Bethany Anne dressed him down. She let him know in no uncertain terms that the next time he failed and got drunk, he not only wouldn't remember doing the drinking, he would probably not remember the last few months of his life. He understood the security breach he had caused. Yes, he had been lonely, and having the woman shaft him so publicly at the club had been embarrassing, but he agreed the proper response would have been to go home. Bethany Anne sent William and Bobcat off to find the machines he would need to help fabricate Bobcat's design. The two ladies then went to find outdoor spaces Ecaterina would enjoy exploring. John and Eric had to keep up with them as best they could.

By the time the party made it back to the pier, their boat had returned and was available. They met Chief Engineer John Rodriguez, Gunnery Officer Jean Dukes, Todd Jenkins from the

Ad Aeternitatem, and two others from the *Polarus*, the five of them dressed as any tourist might be. Bethany Anne waved to the group as they passed and her group proceeded back to the *Polarus*.

"I'm not feeling good about those guys over in the corner," Todd muttered to Jean Dukes under his breath. She looked around the room, acting as if she were looking for shipmates, and spied the men Todd was talking about. She turned around. "Why, because they're Middle Eastern?"

The three of them had split off from the other two crewmen from the *Polarus* and found a bar.

Todd smiled. "Well, while that certainly could be a problem, it's not my main issue. My main issue is that they keep looking pointedly at us, as if they were trying to pick a fight."

Jean started to turn back to the men in the corner but was able to stop her natural confrontational response. Fortunately, she never went anywhere without packing heat. She hoped Bethany Anne was as good as her word from the original introduction. She might have some explaining to do pretty soon.

The chief engineer arrived back at his chair and sat down smiling, bringing two beers with him. He set one of them in front of Jean. "Come on, Jean, we're off the boat. Let your hair down a little bit." He raised his beer to Todd at the same time, and then took a swallow as if to show them how it was done. John looked over her shoulder, and Jean turned to follow his eyes.

The three men Todd had been watching were coming right at them, obviously looking to talk to them. She heard Todd adjust his chair on the floor, probably to get a better angle in case he had to get up quickly. Jean turned her chair casually and rested her hands across her chest, one of them near the shoulder holster under her light jacket.

The three men disregarded her, one of them paying attention to John, who had stood up, and the other two looking at Todd—not a bad decision when you considered how big he was. The man in the middle, probably early middle-aged if Jean was judging correctly, spoke to them.

"Are you three from the big yacht, *Polarus?*"

Todd didn't like the question or the looks on their faces. Had it only been the three of them, he probably would have tried to defuse the situation by lying and simply leave. But he was aware there would be multiple parties coming onto the island, and he needed to deal with this situation only once. He spoke to the man in the middle while keeping the other two in his peripheral vision. "Yes. Why do you ask?"

"Because we knew the previous owner, and our boss would like to have a word with you."

Todd waved his hand at their table. "Not a problem. I was hired by the new owners, and would be happy to talk to him. Or is it a her? Either way, invite them over."

The man shook his head. "I don't think so. Our boss doesn't visit dives like this." He looked around the somewhat seedy bar and adjusted his coat with his right hand, showing the butt of a pistol stuck in his waistband. "He would prefer the three of you come to him."

Todd shook his head, a smile playing on his face. "I don't think we'll be visiting him today, tomorrow, or anytime in the near future. In fact, I'm sure my boss would be very upset if we allowed anybody to force us to go somewhere she wouldn't want us to. She is very adamant about rudeness like that."

Jean had a hard time keeping the smile off her face. She inched her hand a little closer to her pistol. Fortunately, it had nine shots, and there were only three men. She was having an equally hard time not making a comment after being ignored as a second-class citizen by those morons.

"Your boss is a woman?" The man turned to the side and spat

at Todd's feet. "How do you pull your pants on each morning, allowing a woman to tell you what to do?" He nodded to the man on his left and then to the man on his right. Both moved their hands near their waists. He turned back to Todd. "Which is it going to be? Come with us willingly, or don't leave this place?" Jean noticed that a couple of patrons had quietly grabbed their beers and stepped away from her party.

She turned her mouth slightly toward Todd. "Todd, are we going to dance soon or not? This conversation is pushing my patience."

Todd chuckled a little bit. "Jean, I would love to dance. You lead, or me?"

The man in the middle turned back to her and reared his right hand back as if he were about to slap her. As she replied, "Me," she kicked out, breaking the kneecap of the guy on the left. He screamed as he fell. Todd shoved his chair back and swung a hard left into the gut of the man on the right. Jean pulled her pistol and aimed at the middle guy, who had his own pistol out. Her shot beat his and holed his forehead, splattering his brains over the patrons behind him. His shot missed, but she heard the sound of it hitting someone behind her. Todd finished cracking the man nearest him over the head and laying him out. When Jean went quickly to the man, grabbed his knee, and stuck the pistol between his eyes, he stopped cussing and paid close attention. She muttered to herself, "Dammit, I've never studied their language."

The man's eyes were crossed, staring at the barrel touching his forehead. "I speak English, I speak English. Just get me a doctor. You will not have any problem from me. This was his idea." He nodded his head in the now-dead man's direction. "We had friends on the boat. He lied. We don't have a boss who wants to know anything about you." Jean put her gun away and made sure Todd was okay. That was when she heard John behind her.

"Can I get a little help here?" She turned to find John

Rodriguez leaning off his chair, his hands covered in blood, trying to stop the flow.

The color drained from her face. Pumped up on adrenaline, she had forgotten about him being behind her. Todd was already speaking into a phone, getting help. Jean reached across and grabbed a cloth napkin. Moving quickly around the table, she tied a tourniquet as best she could. It didn't look like the bullet had hit any major veins in his leg, which was a huge blessing. Well, she would soon find out how her new boss reacted to violence.

John was moved back to the *Polarus* within twenty minutes.

Jean stayed to speak to the police. Once she got back to the *Polarus*, she made sure John would be okay, then she went to Bethany Anne's suite. She wouldn't wait to be called on the carpet like she had in her experience in the Navy. John and Eric both nodded at her and let her go in.

Bethany Anne was working at the conference table. She looked up as Jean entered and asked her chief gunnery officer, "You wanted to talk with me?"

Jean replied, "Yes, ma'am. I wanted to give you my version of the events that happened this evening."

Bethany Anne's face scrunched in concentration. "Didn't Todd already provide the report to Dan? Did you have something to add to that?"

Jean's mouth opened, shut for a second, and opened again. "Yes, ma'am, he did speak to Dan, but I wanted to make sure you understood why I felt it necessary to fire my weapon."

The vampire put her pen down, stood slowly, and walked around the table to stand in front of Jean. "Do you have your pistol on you?" John and Eric looked at each other. Neither had considered the fact that Jean might bring a gun near their boss.

Jean nodded that she did and handed it over to Bethany Anne, who had her hand out in a "give me" gesture. The vampire pushed down on the top bullet in the mag to see if it went down, made sure the pistol was still on safety, and handed it back. She walked back around the table.

Sitting down, she grabbed her pen and looked up at Jean. "I would have kicked your ass if you hadn't reloaded. Is this understood, Ms. Dukes?"

Jean smiled and was just able to stop herself from saluting. "Yes, ma'am. I completely understand, and my powder will always be dry." She turned to go, and John winked at her. Her smile was bright enough that he might need shades, he thought.

Bethany Anne spoke up, her head still looking down at her notebook. "Boys, make sure you never take away Jean's guns for my sake, understand?" Both men told her they understood and went back to their jobs.

Las Vegas, NV, USA

Tom Billings watched as Jeffrey drove up in his car and he and his two children got out. Jeffrey reached into the front seat and pulled out two sandwich bags and an iPad. Tom called, "Is it National Bring Your Children to Work Day and I didn't get the memo?"

Jeffrey smiled. "I'm not sure if it had anything to do with it being National Bring Your Children to Work Day, but when my wife hands me an iPad and two already made-up lunch bags? I got the memo. I'm just going to put them into Building Three and make sure they're okay, then we can discuss transferring the data. Give me ten minutes." Tom waved at him as he and the two kids went into the housing area.

Closer to twenty minutes later, Jeffrey caught up with him in Building Two. Tom was sipping his second cup of coffee as Jeffrey grabbed his first. "So, have we confirmed how we're going to move the data?"

Tom agreed, "Yes. I've installed three hot-swappable arrays both in here and in Building One for ADAM. We'll be able to load up the hard drive, yank it out, sneakernet it over to Building One, and plug it in over there. It won't require any special mounting or drivers to be loaded each time; the system automatically recognizes and connects. Hopefully, we'll be able to do this as fast as we can load up each hard drive and transfer the data."

Tom marked a line across his list, crossing off one detail accomplished. "Okay, so what data will we start with?"

Jeffrey sat down across the table. "Do we have any ideas yet where to go? Do we start with history, science, ethics?"

Tom scratched his head with his pencil. "I'm not really sure it matters, at least not at this stage. We need to get the program a good foundation of information so that when it wants to dive deeper, ADAM at least understands enough to classify what area of knowledge it needs more data for. So, I'm for giving it a foundational understanding of the cosmos at this time and allowing selective uploads at a later date. Plus, we aren't running the system right away anyhow, are we?"

Jeffrey scratched his chin thoughtfully. "True. I don't want the system trying to make heads or tails of the world with a minimal dataset, so let's load as much as we can—say the equivalent of a college education—before we go any farther."

Tom looked at him, thinking back to what he had said a minute before. "Ethics?"

Jeffrey nodded. "Sure. Ethics is the basis of all reasoning. It's the one area where artificial intelligence breaks when someone considers Asimov's Three Laws. The Three Laws are too simplistic to work for an artificial intelligence. For example, the First Law states the robot may not hurt a human, or through inaction allow a human to come to harm. But how do you tell the artificial intelligence what a human is? I suppose we could classify a human as Homo sapiens, but what would we do with edge cases? Even if we decided to classify humans by our DNA, at what point is the DNA not human anymore?"

Tom was a little surprised. "What do you mean, at what point is DNA not human anymore? Like, if someone is a mutation?"

Jeffrey smiled. "No, I'm not thinking X-Men here. I'm asking, what about a dead person? Their DNA is human, but between helping a human who is alive with the right DNA and a human who is now dead, I don't want the artificial intelligence to get confused. Or what happens if the human is recently dead and they could, through action, be revived?"

Tom stood, taking his empty cup over to the coffee pot and filling it again. "This day hasn't started, and I'm already getting a headache."

Buenos Aires, Argentina

"Come in." Anton hated waiting for the knock on his door. He could hear anyone approach his office, and thought it was a waste of time to wait. His butler stood there with a small envelope, and Anton waved him over. Jackson approached the desk and put the envelope on it, then, turning, he left his office and closed the door behind him.

Anton picked the envelope up and opened it, taking a few seconds to read and then reread the information it held. He smiled. It seemed there was a large yacht that had been seen with a Black Hawk helicopter on top near Costa Rica. Perfect.

Now all he had to do was track down the name, and he would have what he needed for the next part of his plan.

CHAPTER ELEVEN

<u>The Queen Bitch's Ship *Ad Aeternitatem*</u>

TOM, are we ready to do this?

Well, I can't answer for you, but I'm certainly ready to crack this thing open and see what we created.

I never realized you had a little bit of Dr. Frankenstein in you, TOM.

Doctor who?

Wrong character, although I can see a resemblance between you and Doctor Who as well.

Who the hell is Doctor Who? I'm asking about Dr. Frankenstein.

Bethany Anne grinned. She loved it when she could confuse the alien. Mind you, since he understood so little of Earth popular culture, it wasn't much of a challenge. But she would take her little joys where she could.

Never mind. Let's get this show on the road. Tell me what I need to do to open this.

TOM took her through the quick routine, and Bethany Anne popped the lock manually to open the Pod-doc. He had made sure the canine would still be asleep when the door opened, and it was five minutes before the dog started to come around. The big head lifted off the bed, and he looked around until he spied Bethany Anne. He wagged his tail in recognition and took a couple of sniffs of the air. She talked quietly to the dog, scooped him up, and set him quickly on the floor. While not concerned that he could maim her, she had no desire to have those claws scratch her skin.

The dog got up…and up and up. The top of his ears reached above her waistline. She mumbled under her breath, "I sure hope we have enough meat."

TOM, are you sure the dog won't affect my ability to translocate?

No, I am not a hundred percent sure. You have to give me points, though. I was right. We did make it to Miami and back.

Yes, but I had to drink five packets of blood when I got back. You know how much I hate that stuff? I about threw up on the fifth one. That shit is disgusting.

Well, technically, you didn't have to drink all five. You only required one.

Yeah, but if I hadn't drunk the rest of them, my energy levels would have been too low to do anything in a pinch.

Stop being a little baby. This is going to be okay, trust me.

After Bethany Anne grabbed Ashur by the scruff of the neck and translocated to her bedroom on the *Polarus*, she didn't feel any reduction in energy level. That was strange. She knew he was supposed to have an affinity for the Etheric, but this was beyond her expectations.

Ashur growled and looked around in confusion. "It's going to be fine, Ashur. You had better get used to this stuff." He stopped growling, walked over to a couple of pairs of her shoes, and sniffed. Her nose wrinkled, "Oh, that's gross, Ashur! How can you smell those? God, you're going to be as embarrassing as a guy. If you sniff any of my unmentionables, your ass will go topside." He stopped sniffing the shoes and looked at her, tilting his head as if considering what she had just told him.

She went to the door and unlocked it, then opened it and waved for Ashur to follow her. He looked around one more time as if he was confirming what he was seeing and followed her out the door, his head held high.

Bethany Anne and Ashur headed over to the gym. She didn't meet anyone in the hallways, which was unique. The dog sniffed everything continuously. She told him to sit while she went to go get a couple of towels. As she came back, the door opened and Gabrielle stepped in. He growled. "Stop that!" Ashur swung his head back to Bethany Anne and continued growling, a little more forcefully this time. Bethany Anne dropped the towels. "No fucking way..." The closer she came to him, the more he growled and showed his fangs.

Gabrielle backed up. "You two have something to discuss?"

Bethany Anne's eyes turned red, her fangs elongating. "There is nothing to discuss. There is only one alpha, and this puppy is about to find out—" That was when Ashur drove his hind legs into the ground, catapulting himself at the woman in front of him who wouldn't submit. He had been curious before and had tagged along, but when the second woman showed up, he couldn't allow any doubt as to who was the head of his pack.

He was snatched out of the air and dropped hard on the ground, the breath in his lungs exploding out of him. He tried to turn over and gain a grip with his strong legs but found himself up in the air again. This time the woman held his back against her, his feet aimed away.

Gabrielle stayed near the door. "Why are you holding him in the air like that?"

"Because he has nails and teeth on the other side." Bethany Anne tossed Ashur casually to the floor, where he rolled and flipped until he hit the wall with a thud. He took a second to get his bearings and growled in Bethany Anne's direction again.

Scott's head popped in beside Gabrielle. "Who the fuck let Cujo on the ship?" When the vampire pointed in Bethany Anne's direction, he continued, "This is the German Shepherd from the park?"

"Yup."

Scott shrugged. "Don't pick up any cats. I'd hate to see what they turn into." His head disappeared.

Bethany Anne muttered under her breath, "Everyone's a critic."

Ashur growled louder, and Bethany Anne hissed and walked in his direction. She stopped controlling the malevolence her body radiated when angry, and he backed up one step for every step she took toward him. Finally, his butt was against the wall. He dropped down, his belly on the ground, but he still had a look of rebellion on his face. Bethany Anne moved into her fastest speed and got her face six inches in front of his, daring him to try something.

So he did. With his haunches pressed against the wall, he attacked, aiming to take a bite of her face. Bethany Anne slapped him upside the head, and his whole body flipped ass-over-appetite three times. He wound up on his back with her holding him by the neck, her red eyes and fangs staring him in the eyes. He whined, giving up trying to best her.

She let him go and he turned back over, staying down. "If you try that shit with me again, Ashur, I will bitch-slap you from the front to the back of this boat, and it is one long fucking boat." She walked back to pick up the two towels while he stayed two paces behind her.

Gabrielle remained glued to the door. "Remind me not to get into a pissing match with you."

Bethany Anne smiled at the vampire. "You tried, remember?"

She thought about their swordfight when Bethany Anne had her fangs on her neck. "Yes. No need to revisit that again."

They laughed together and walked out of the gym. Bethany

Anne wanted Ashur to get accustomed to the ship and let the people get accustomed to him. If he was going to cause any trouble, she wanted to get it over with now.

Fortunately, it seemed one trial for dominance was all he needed. He only snapped one time when Eric was going to pass Bethany Anne from behind while she was talking to Dan. The Guard jumped aside and laughed off the adrenaline charge, then continued toward the gym where Pete's group was working out.

Hmm…it seemed Ashur had her back. Good to know.

San José, Costa Rica

Giannini Oviedo wasn't a tall woman at five foot two, but if you believed the talk on the streets, she easily topped six feet. Given that her articles discussed two of the attacks from personal experience, the only reporter who had been an eyewitness to the events, she had the respect of those at her newspaper and the people on the street.

Presently, she was cleaning her living room. She had decided to stay home for the day and take care of some normal challenges. Even her best friend had been a little embarrassed when he learned she had been saved by the *Ángeles Oscuros* the night he wouldn't join her on the street.

She had the only pictures, as dark as they were, of the team that had been in the fight at the park. The rights for printing the images had provided enough income to pay her rent for the next three months. Now, if she could use the acclaim from her exploits to move up the reporting ladder at work, she would be golden.

The sharp tone of her phone ringing snapped her out of her woolgathering. She took a look at the phone number, realized it was her contact from the police, and hit the answer button. "Good morning, Superintendent. How are you doing?"

Rodriguez' voice was crisp, but she sounded annoyed. "Good

morning, Giannini. I'm well, thank you. I just had a visit from an agent of the American intelligence group based here in our country. Unfortunately, I wasn't thinking, and because I was angry with the agent, I mentioned that you were the one who had the information they might need. Expect them to call on you, or at least one man, sometime this morning. Watch them. I'm not happy they have come here asking questions and expect us to lie down for them. Sometimes Americans lack common courtesy." There was a heavy sigh. "It could be I am merely upset and not thinking clearly, but he didn't give me a good feeling. My meeting may have been with a low-level contact and safe, but take care of yourself, okay?"

Giannini thought it wasn't often Rodriguez came across as caring on the phone. She was usually a very prim and proper police superintendent, so Giannini felt a little warmth at the effort on her behalf. "Of course. I will pay attention and make sure I don't close my front door should they want to talk. Do you believe I should just close up and try to meet them elsewhere?" The pause on the other end of the line was telling.

"No. I don't think he intends any harm to you, but if you feel bad after he leaves, call me back, and we will see what we can do to help you. Your articles have been beneficial, and I appreciate you telling the story of our lost brothers and sisters who died fighting those beasts. For a reporter, Giannini, you're not so bad." Her smile came through the phone. "Call me later and let me know how it goes, okay?"

"Of course, Superintendent. I will be happy to do so." They said their goodbyes and Giannini hung up.

She had finished cleaning her living room and was working on her kitchen when there was a knock at her door. Quickly, she set aside the dishrags and dried her hands. She walked to the front door and looked through the peephole to see one man standing there. He definitely looked American. She called through the door, asking who he was. The visitor answered that he was with the government, and would she mind providing some additional insight to questions regarding her articles?

Giannini noted he failed to say what government he belonged to. Mind you, she thought, he might not want to advertise that the Americans were looking around for something out in her hallway. She cracked the door open a few inches. "Yes? What questions can I answer for you?"

"May I come in, ma'am?" If she hadn't known what nationality he was before, his vernacular would certainly have given him away.

"I'm sorry, Mr.—" Giannini left the question hanging.

Matthew wanted to kick himself. "Matthew Burnside. I apologize for not saying that a moment ago."

"Mr. Burnside, I'm sure you understand why a single lady would be concerned about allowing a strange man to enter her home, yes?" She noticed the flush on his face.

Matthew looked up the hallway and down to the other end. He certainly wouldn't push his way into her home, so he had to make a decision about whether to ask his questions there in the hallway, or perhaps try to meet her at the police station or her workplace. Both of those places would probably garner him more attention than his boss would prefer. "Yes, I can understand that."

He proceeded to ask her questions related to both nights when she had had interactions with the SpecOps team. He paid close attention to any details about the helicopter she could provide, and the makeup of the team. He was surprised to learn two of the team members had been female. He asked her the same question in three different ways to confirm this answer, and she was adamant she had seen two women in the group.

"And you say they carried a dog back to the helicopter at the end?" He continued to write notes in his little book. It had become uncomfortable to hold in his hand and write, so he had pressed his book against the wall next to her door.

Matthew had called his contact after his previous interview with the police failed. The contact on the phone had asked if he needed backup for this conversation in a tone that suggested he had no spine. He had rejected the help, so he was a little relieved to be able to acquire some information that had not already been provided in the newspapers. After his debacle with the superintendent, he used his best manners and tried desperately not to offend this contact.

He said his goodbyes after making sure Ms. Oviedo understood his appreciation for taking the time to answer his questions, went downstairs, and exited her building, turning left. He hadn't made it one block before a dark-haired American man a little taller than he was stepped out from the side of a building and caught his attention. "Matthew?" He walked over to him.

"Yes, who are you?"

The man gave his name and the name of the contact who had rousted him out of bed. Matthew frowned. "I told your boss I didn't need any backup this morning."

He put up both hands. "Hey, don't jump my back about this. I was told to come down here in case things didn't work out. All I need to know is whether or not you got the information?"

Matthew nodded. "Yes. She was very cordial, and was willing to give me extra information that wasn't included in her articles, not that there was a lot available. Her editor allowed her to print almost anything she wanted. I have a few bits of information, such as the team makeup, but not a lot that we're going to be able to use directly at this time. I'm sure we'll get reports. We will be able to correlate her information with something out in the field and make a match."

"So, this information well is dry?"

Matthew wasn't sure he liked how this guy phrased his question, but it could be he was just tired and was getting rubbed the wrong way by having someone sent as a backup when he hadn't needed it. "Perhaps Ms. Oviedo will remember something in the future, but I feel confident she's told us everything she knows or remembers right now. Maybe something in the future will jar her memory."

The man looked up at Giannini's building as if he knew she lived on the third floor and was looking right at her window. "Maybe something will." Matthew said goodbye and continued to where he had parked his car.

Up in the apartment, Giannini stepped slowly away from her window, concerned by what she had just witnessed.

CHAPTER TWELVE

The Queen Bitch's Ship *Ad Aeternitatem*

Marcus Cambridge felt a little overwhelmed. He was in his stateroom on the *Ad Aeternitatem*, and his whole world was upside-down.

There really *were* aliens, and he wasn't able to tell those who had fired him to go fuck themselves.

Okay, maybe he should clean up his language, but to be proved right after years and years of ridicule had stirred up a lot of emotions in him. He had met Bethany Anne, and she alone would have been mind-boggling.

The infinitesimally small nanocytes that must have modified her body at a genetic level would be worth decades of research. The fact that people labeled her a vampire was, in his opinion, an example of inaccurate associations with folklore. A more accurate take would be that the ignorant from a thousand years ago hadn't had the scientific knowledge to recognize the opportunity.

She was a human with gene modifications, although he had to admit, her glowing red eyes and ability to grow fangs were pretty damn scary. It was a good thing he still had good bladder control for his age. Now, he was about to see an actual UFO and put his hands on it. He had a meeting with the project lead, Bobcat, the one who had asked for a rocket scientist and forever changed his life.

Marcus hoped he would never have to go back to California. At least, not because he got fired. As a scientist, he was in heaven.

He had been fired from the National Aeronautics and Space Administration, the most advanced governmental space exploration agency in the world. He had been fired from SpaceX, one of the preeminent commercial space exploration companies in the world, only to find himself involved with a group that was centuries ahead of either one of them. While he might not live to see it, his name would be vindicated in history. Even from the grave, he would have the last laugh.

He smiled, the first genuine smile he had been able to produce in months. Life would be interesting until the day he died. He got up from his bed, grabbed a light jacket, and decided to be early to the meeting with Bobcat.

Five minutes later, the pilot entered the conference room with a smile on his face and rolled-up papers under his arm. They introduced themselves to each other, and Marcus found himself liking the down-to-earth project head. Unlike a lot of others who, in his opinion, only cared about due dates and how to stay within budget, Bobcat worried about results and safety. Actually, he was more worried about safety, results be damned unless the vehicles got his people from point A to point B safely.

Marcus quickly found himself tasked with understanding how to move a rocket type object with completely new propulsion systems and gravity-defying capabilities. Then they debated the materials necessary to accomplish this feat. They discussed that the second version would do everything the first version would, plus go into space.

Marcus looked around, and Bobcat asked him what he needed. He answered, "I'm looking for something to drink. Maybe some soda?"

The pilot had the first look of alarm Marcus had seen on his face. "Please God, tell me you're not a Pepsi drinker?"

The scientist looked at him strangely. "No, why? Well, I could drink a Pepsi if I had to, but my preference is either Dr. Pepper or Coke."

Bobcat exhaled. "Because the boss is strictly a Coke person. She believes Pepsi…well, let's just say Pepsi is the devil's brew. It got so bad that her personal support specialist had hidden a couple for those in the group who liked the drink, and Bethany Anne found them. I wasn't here at the time, but I understand half the ship woke up to her screams after Bethany Anne put two frozen Pepsis against her skin while she was sleeping. Now, I'm not sure what Ecaterina will do, but I don't think we've heard the last of the little war between the two women. The Romanian has bigger balls than I do, that's for damn sure."

"Why, what do *you* drink?" Marcus was enjoying this little story and curious which direction Bobcat went, Coke or Pepsi.

"Beer."

"No, I mean for breakfast. What would you have for breakfast if you could drink anything?"

Bob just looked at the man. "Beer."

Marcus smiled. "I sense a certain consistency to your answer. Am I to presume you only drink beer?"

Bobcat smiled back. "No, I drink coffee as well. But you did specify I could drink anything."

He laughed at that. "Okay, you got me. Getting back on track here, what do you think our budget is for this project?"

The pilot laid his hands down on the drawings. "I don't want there to be any misunderstandings with this answer like we just had on the beer thing, so let me make it quite clear." Bobcat paused, "We. Have. No. Budget."

He grabbed a pen and drew a downward-pointing triangle on a piece of paper. Quickly, he labeled the left tip of the triangle time, the right quality, and the bottom point cost.

"They always say you can have something high quality really fast, but not cheap. Bethany Anne is all about high quality and really, really fast. She doesn't give a damn about the cost so long as we get it done by yesterday. Make sense?"

Marcus looked down at the piece of paper Bobcat had just written on. "I feel like I just found the end of the rainbow and dug up the pot of gold. My man, we are going to design, build, and make history."

Bobcat glanced back down to where the scientist was looking. "True. Unfortunately, no one will know about it for a while."

"Yes, but they'll know about it in the future, and I hope to still be alive and able to shove it down their throats." Both men laughed.

Bobcat looked up at Marcus, a glint in his eye. "Want to see a real alien spaceship?"

The Queen Bitch's Ship *Polarus*

Ecaterina knocked on Bethany Anne's door and walked in when the vampire called out to her. Her boss was reading on her laptop in bed to get a better understanding of some of the businesses her father was reviewing, specifically those related to blood disorders. She looked up. "What's up?"

The Romanian woman sat down on a chair. "I just had a conversation with the San José Police Department contact. It seems we have a potential issue with our reporter down there." Bethany Anne closed her laptop and gave Ecaterina her undivided attention. "Some agents from the United States are looking into our efforts to clean up the city a few weeks ago."

The vampire frowned. "Well, that's a real pain in the ass. I wonder how Michael's team would have dealt with this? Never mind, Frank always did it, and we've been trying to keep him off the radar. It looks like we need to get him involved again."

"Yes, I talked to him. He informs me the situation has already gone too far for him to do anything in the short term."

Bethany Anne put her elbow on the laptop, resting her chin in her hand. "Why do I get the impression I haven't heard the rest of the appeal?"

Ecaterina told her, "Our police contact has requested our help in trying to extract the reporter. That is what you call it—'extract,' correct? Anyway, she wants us to help get her out of the city and away from the American agents."

Bethany Anne pondered this for a minute. While she had no direct connection with the reporter, she had liked her spunk, and the articles she had written had helped calm the city down. "Okay. We don't forsake our own, and while she doesn't know much about us, she *has* been helpful. Let's get Gabrielle and the team together and send some people with Bobcat and Shelly to San José to pick her up. Who knows, maybe she can be helpful to us at the same time?"

Her assistant went to the door, opened it, and called to Darryl, who was on station, requesting he grab the rest of the team for a quick meeting.

Five minutes later Dan, Gabrielle, and the team were in the meeting room with Ecaterina and Bethany Anne. It seemed like it should be a simple decision to fly to San José, grab the reporter, and fly back.

But once the team understood they would be working against who they presumed was the CIA, it caused a few concerns on the parts of Darryl and Scott. Gabrielle had no issues with it, as one might suspect. She glanced at her two team members and asked them what their concerns were.

Darryl gazed at her. "We're talking about operating against American interests. I recognize we might run into some bad people from time to time, but how can we be sure this team is bad?"

Gabrielle replied, "Why would a simple snatch cause a problem?"

Scott replied, "It isn't grabbing her and bringing her to the *Polarus* that's the problem. It's what occurs if we have to get into an altercation or a firefight."

Ecaterina put her phone down on the table, the noise catching everyone's attention. She hit the play button, and everyone was able to listen to the voice of the contact from the San José Police Department. It was obvious she was emotionally disturbed after her meeting with the American, and it was hard not to feel empathy for the person behind the voice.

Gabrielle spoke into the silence. "In my country, not too many decades ago, we had a government that was only successful by hiding the truth. Reporters, both those who are highly valued and those who seek the truth, make some governments unhappy. These reporters are just as valuable to a country as other agents who might be working for the government in a foreign country. Remember, this is her country, and the United States has no right to hurt a reporter who, may I remind you, told stories about what we did. I am not suggesting the United States is trying to harm her, but something is going on that causes her to be concerned for her life. All we have to do is pick her up and bring her here. If no one shoots at us, we obviously won't shoot at anyone else. But might I ask what you would be willing to do if someone *does* shoot at us?"

The look that came over Darryl's and Scott's faces told Gabrielle all she needed to know. Darryl spoke for them both. "If someone shoots at us for a simple taxi ride? I doubt they have our best interests at heart, and unfortunately, whether they know it or not, they would not have the world's best interests at heart. I would—*we* would—have to defend ourselves." Scott agreed.

Until then, Bethany Anne had stayed quiet, but now she rapped her knuckles on the table to get everyone's attention. "Let's get this out in the open. My focus—our focus—is to protect the world. Without the world, it won't matter if you're from the United States, Germany, Romania, Costa Rica, Russia, or China. You get the idea. Unfortunately, we will ruffle feathers. When you ruffle the feathers of really powerful people, they come after you. We will certainly have issues with some people *in* the United States. What we will never have is issues with the people *of* the United States. I don't believe every person in the United States government, or any government across the world, can be said to focus on their peoples' best interest. Some will, some won't. However, we are focused on saving the Earth.

"Up till now, your fights have been easy. The Forsaken and the people associated with them have simply been in a different country. Realize that we will have enemies who have no clue about the UnknownWorld. They will want what we have; they will want TOM's ship, they will want our technology, they will want me, they will want Frank, they will want my dad, and they will want you. Some of those who choose to fight us will believe right is on their side. Unfortunately, I can't agree with that. There will be people, possibly the President of the United States and others, who may decide they are better prepared or possibly consider themselves or their role better positioned to accomplish the effort of saving the world."

She paused and looked at each of them in turn. "I won't begin to question how well-meaning they might be, the same way I wouldn't question how well-meaning China might be, or Russia might be, or Great Britain might be." As each foreign country was mentioned, the men at the table realized they had introduced their sense of nationalism into the meeting. If the United States held all the cards, there was no way Russia or China would play along. Their only chance to accomplish the goals quickly was remaining as neutral as possible. The fact that Bethany Anne and most of her team were Americans was already a potential problem for the future.

John spoke into the quiet. "As for me, *Ad Aeternitatem*."

Eric spoke next. "*Ad Aeternitatem.*"

Darryl glanced at Gabrielle. "Sorry." He looked at Bethany Anne. "*Ad Aeternitatem.*"

It was Scott's turn. He nodded at Gabrielle. "I apologize. *Ad Aeternitatem.*"

Dan nodded at Bethany Anne. They'd had this conversation a while back on the tarmac of a small airport in Miami.

He chose to send Gabrielle, Darryl, and Scott with Bobcat. Two hours later, after the extended tanks were filled, the team left to fly to San José. Ecaterina called the contact to let her know the approximate ETA.

Constanta, Romania

Scott was walking off his anger, and he had walked for the last hour and a half, since he had a lot of anger. While he wanted to blame this Bethany Anne for Clarita's death, when he was honest with himself, he realized it was Clarita's fault, as well as that bastard Adrian's. Adrian's for killing someone, and Clarita's for trusting that sick bastard in the first place.

It was merely easier to blame Bethany Anne than put the blame on a woman who had pulled him out of the depression he had been in for most of his life. He stopped a couple of hundred yards from the house and looked at the stars, trying to make the world right again. He stood there, silent, still working out his issues when he heard the crunch of steps on pebbles—people walking down a small trail and coming in his direction. He turned slightly and crouched in case he was outlined against the night sky.

His hearing was superb. Unfortunately, what he heard were plans to rush Stephen's home and attack and kill everyone inside. There was a small argument about simply "blowing the fucking thing apart" and a scathing retort asking how the original speaker would confirm Stephen's death. What if he were underground? Would the "blow it up and let God sort out the remains" guy like to try to remove all the rubble to find a door, only to figure out their quarry had left by another route days before?

Scott had heard enough. He moved silently toward the house, staying in a crouch. He managed to get halfway back when he stepped around a bush and put his foot squarely on a branch, making a resounding crack. That did it. He was screwed on the sneaking part, so he decided speed was the best choice and took off running for the front door.

He heard a commotion behind him and some yelling. Well, if nothing else, he and his siblings would be able to mount a defense inside the house instead of being caught unawares. Maybe Stephen had a good place to run to and then escape from inside the house. He was only twenty feet from the door when he heard a rocket go off behind him.

Stephen could hear someone approach the house rapidly, and he stood and focused his attention on the door. Alerted by his actions, Claudia and Juan turned to look in the same direction. While Scott should be back sometime soon, they hadn't expected him to run for the front door.

Certain they could hear him inside, Scott yelled, "We are under att—" The rocket-propelled grenade hit him square in the back, driving him into the door before exploding and ending his life.

CHAPTER THIRTEEN

Stephen covered his face as the front door was blown into his house. Chunks of debris rained down from the ceiling above, and Claudia screamed.

He became calm, as cold as ice. No one in the UnknownWorld would attack him except one of his brothers. Anton would be his first guess, but he wouldn't rule out any of them until he got a name—and he would, by God, have a name very soon.

Ivan ran in from the kitchen. Stephen reached over and grabbed Claudia by the arm, pulling her up from the chair and out of her stupor, and pushed her to Ivan. "Ivan, please take Claudia down to my bedroom. Take her through the door. You know the one I'm talking about, yes?" Ivan nodded. "Good. You two step inside and lock it from the inside. You will be safe there until I take care of this."

The Romanian man grabbed Claudia's hand and pulled her gently in the direction of the stairs. She finally caught on to what was happening and became an active participant, quickly leaving the first floor for safety.

Juan and Stephen looked around and saw Scott's body in pieces in the foyer. Both heard rapid steps approaching. Stephen spoke. "Come with me. We can defend much easier from the kitchen." When they arrived there, he reached under one of the cabinets and flipped a lock mechanism, then reached down to open a cabinet door and retrieved a pistol, tossing it to Juan. "These are loaded with silver and will deliver quite a painful lesson not to intrude. Are you good with using that?"

Juan agreed. "I am good with using this and most other things you can provide me." Stephen pulled out two short swords and tossed one to him.

"That's all I have up here. I wasn't as prepared for a frontal attack as maybe I should have been. When we finish with these asshats, I will be sure to rectify that immediately."

Bobcat was about half an hour outside San José when he received a call from the ship. Gabrielle heard him say, "Roger," before he turned to get her attention. "We have the coordinates of her building. It seems she is concerned about them coming back right now. Additional agents have met up with someone she saw earlier, so she's going up to the roof, and we'll grab her from there. We have a rope ladder in the back. Have the guys set it up in case we need it."

Gabrielle passed the instructions to Darryl and Scott, who got busy. Fifteen minutes later, the pilot turned to get her attention again. "I just got word we were pinged. They'll know we're on our way, so this might be a hot landing." She nodded in acknowledgment and caught Darryl's and Scott's attention again.

"We'll have to pick our contact up off the roof, so I don't want either of you firing any shots. I understand you both are fully on the team, but there is no need to push your feelings on this matter right now. I will handle the situation, understand?" Both men nodded in understanding.

Gabrielle unhooked her sword belt from behind her back and

set it aside. If she had to move quickly, she doubted the sword would be beneficial. Fortunately, she didn't expect to have to behead any Forsaken this time.

Bobcat saw they were attracting attention from those on the street and in buildings below. He hated not knowing how high up their permission for this operation went. If they didn't have the high-level authority to fly over San José, this operation might get pretty dicey pretty quick.

Matthew Burnside was frustrated with his job. He and three other agents had been detailed to go back to talk with Giannini Oviedo at her apartment and "respectfully request" she come with them for additional questioning. He wasn't sure how he could respectfully request anything. When four foreign agents showed up at her door, it would be nothing less than intimidating to the woman.

Five minutes from her apartment building, he received a phone call from the CIA agent in charge. "Burnside here." He listened intently to the man on the other end of the line. "What do you mean, there's a Black Hawk coming at us? Who the hell is sending a Black Hawk? You mean the group from the other week is back?"

Matthew could feel the eyes of the other agents in the car staring at him as he listened. "Look, we aren't black operatives here. Our job is research and support of information, which we then move up the chain. The fact that you're asking us to do field operations is outside our normal purview. What the hell do you want me to do against a paramilitary group? Hell no, I will not grab or snatch a woman illegally. Look, you do your job, and I'll do mine. We'll make it work. Fine. We're almost there, and we will ask her gently to come with us. Yes, I will tell her the other group is coming after her, but that's all I'll fucking do. We aren't going to commit a felony just because you have your panties in a twist about talking to this woman. Yeah, well, bite me." Matthew stabbed the end button on his phone. "Fucking prick."

He turned to the guys in the back seat of the car. "I'm sure you heard that, but we have the paramilitary group or who we suspect is them coming after our contact. We need to rush upstairs and persuade her to come with us." One of the agents in the back asked a question. "What? No, this is not a snatch-and-grab. I'm not committing any felonies for some dick over in Operations. You know as well as I do that if something goes wrong, he will disappear and we will be left holding the bag, so we do this politely, and we do this legally." He pointed at a building a block and a half down on the left. "That's her building. Park in the first spot you can find and let's go."

They were able to find a place to park a half a block away. As they got out, Matthew spotted two more agents coming from the other direction who met them at the front door of the building. He stared at them. "Who the hell are you?"

"Backup." Matthew glared at them, but neither offered him any more explanation.

He shrugged. "Fine, we'll go get the lady. You guys can stay out here." His group entered the building with the two agents tagging along behind. He couldn't force them to stay, so he simply ignored them and kept going up to her apartment.

When he approached the door, he turned and looked at his team, including the two new guys. "Hey, she's a little sensitive about strange men and her apartment. Why don't all of you back off about fifteen feet?" The two new agents took a few steps back. It was the most he could hope for, so he ignored the rest and turned and knocked.

He got no response, so he knocked a little louder the second time and waited. Nothing. One of the two agents came up beside him. "Is this the right place?"

Matthew looked at him with annoyance. "I was here only this morning. Yes, this is the right place."

The agent took one step back. "Good to know." He pivoted on his left leg, using his right to kick the door at the doorjamb. It slammed open.

"What the hell?" But there was no one there to yell at. The agent had already entered her apartment, and Matthew was pushed aside by the second man. By the time he and his team got in, the other two walked back from what must've been her bedroom.

"She isn't here. Are you sure she didn't leave the building?" Matthew thought the question was directed at him at first before the other agent answered.

"We didn't see her leaving through the front door, and we have her car staked out as well, so unless she decided to leave by the back door and walk, she's still in the building somewhere."

Matthew watched this byplay when he realized a new noise was coming from outside. He stepped closer to the window and pushed aside the drapes when he recognized the sound. "Guys, we've just run out of time. I hear the helicopter approaching." The two strange agents stared at each other for a few seconds as if they were communing telepathically.

The first one looked at the second. "Roof?"

"Roof." They ran through the front door, heading God knew where to get to the roof.

Charlie, one of his agents, asked Matthew, "Should we follow them?"

Matthew sighed. "Probably, but I'm not too enthusiastic about getting between those two and whoever is flying up above. This time it looks like we're team backup. Let's go." He led his team out the apartment's front door and told Charlie to close it as best he could. They went in the same direction as the two other agents, assuming there would be a way to get to the roof wherever they ended up.

He had almost caught up when they found the way to the roof. In fact, he was only a few feet behind them when they burst through the door.

The agents turned to look to the left, so that was where Matthew looked as soon as he came out of the door.

A Black Hawk helicopter dropped a rope ladder to a woman waiting for it at the far edge of the building, maybe sixty feet away. Two huge guys in black and a woman were in the back of the helicopter. He flinched as two shots were fired from beside him and noted one hole in the body of the helicopter.

He rounded on them and yelled, "What the fuck? You're shooting at a SpecOps group, you idiots."

Agent One crouched. "They bleed like the rest of us. Boss said to bring back that woman, and that's what I intend to do."

Matthew turned back in time to see the woman in the helicopter drop fifteen feet to the roof and then toss the first woman over her shoulder. Both agents had been caught unprepared. The helicopter turned toward the next building over and the black-clad woman ran, carrying the reporter. The first agent raised his pistol and fired twice before he went down, a slug through his shoulder. Matthew looked at the helicopter. A man with a rifle he would swear had a barrel opening as big as his arm stared at him, so he threw his hands in the air since he didn't want anyone to mistake him for one of the stupid idiots who was shooting. The second agent yelled over his shoulder as he started to run toward the women, trying to get a better shot, "God, you desk jockeys are a bunch of pussies." He had just raised his pistol to fire when he crumpled to the ground, shot in the leg. Matthew looked back at the helicopter to see the guy with the rifle elevate it.

Matthew and the second agent watched in awe as the woman, encumbered as she was with the reporter, jumped the distance between the two buildings. It had to be at least twenty feet. On the other side, she stood and wrapped her arms in the ladder, still holding the reporter. The helicopter lifted, taking the women away. Matthew assumed they would drop down as soon as they were at a safe distance.

Gabrielle heard the bullet hit Shelly. Staying there and waiting for the woman to climb the rope ladder wasn't an option anymore, so she yelled over her shoulder and told Darryl and Scott to hold their fire, she would be right back. With that, she jumped down to the roof below and grabbed the reporter, threw her over her shoulder, and pointed at the next building over, hoping Bobcat would understand. Sure enough, the Black Hawk helicopter moved in that direction.

She checked her energy levels, as she had been instructed by Bethany Anne and TOM. There was no time like the present to pull from them, so she streaked toward the side of the building, the lady screaming as if they were headed to their deaths. Gabrielle kicked off the building with everything she had, which ended up being just a bit too much. She cleared the side of the building easily and almost hit a chimney. Fortunately, she was able to land, but her leg crumpled beneath her. She turned at the last moment so her back hit the ground, protecting the reporter. Scrambling to her feet, she pulled the woman up and grabbed the rope, slinging an arm through the ladder. She told her passenger to put a leg in a loop, then, grabbing her around the waist, she flicked her head up, trusting one of the guys would see it and tell Bobcat to move. Sure enough, Shelly lifted off a few seconds later and took them away. She looked at the reporter, who was staring at her. "What is it?"

The woman screamed her question, not realizing Gabrielle could hear her just fine. "Why are your eyes glowing red?"

Gabrielle was trying to come up with a suitable response for that when the woman suddenly drew in a ragged gasp of air. "You're bleeding!"

She followed her gaze down to her leg. Sure enough, she had been shot. No wonder she had lost her balance on landing. "So I am. Let's hope I don't faint from blood loss, shall we?" Gabrielle smiled at her as the woman realized her protector might suddenly fall. At least it got her mind off the question about her eye color.

Bobcat located a parking lot with enough room six blocks from the building and lowered Shelly slowly enough for Gabrielle and Giannini to jump off the rope ladder. The ladies grabbed it and pulled it away from the helicopter so the pilot could land. Both Guards jumped off. Darryl helped Giannini get onboard, and Scott handed the vampire a blood packet. She ripped it open and downed the contents quickly, hoping the reporter didn't notice.

Gabrielle stared at Scott while she was drinking. When she finished, she wiped her mouth. "I thought I told you guys not to shoot."

Scott grinned at her. "No, you asked if we understood. That is not the same as asking if we agreed." Scott took the ladder from her so he could roll it back up and they could board the helicopter. "Besides, I will not be the one to tell Eric we failed to get you back in one piece." Scott turned to jump back on the helicopter. Gabrielle took a second to ostensibly wipe any remaining blood off her face, along with the tear that had formed in her eye. Seconds later, Bobcat had them back in the air and was heading east.

On the helicopter, Giannini caught her breath after all the

excitement. She looked around and recognized Darryl as the man who'd helped her that first night. He was smiling at her when she slapped him. "That is for pinching my butt." Then she leaned over and kissed him. "That's for saving my life."

Darryl decided not to correct her for the pinching misunderstanding.

They flew back to San Andreas Island, where they made sure Giannini was safe in a nice hotel, with clothes and enough money to stay for a month, Darryl having been nice enough to volunteer to take her shopping on the company's account. Gabrielle exchanged contact information with the reporter. She liked the woman, but didn't think allowing a reporter on the *Polarus* was a good idea just yet.

Giannini wasn't sure what to make of the team and the rescue. She created a journal in a secure Dropbox folder on the Internet and put in her notes and all of the conversation she could remember. She wasn't sure she had seen the red eyes, but she had absolutely seen the woman's leg heal quickly. She had been lucky to meet them back in San José, and now she was beyond lucky to have been introduced to them again. They hadn't requested she not talk about them, but Giannini wouldn't spoil her chance at a bigger story by burning the beginning of a professional—and maybe personal—relationship too quickly.

She sent a quick and hopefully untraceable message to her contact in the police department and sat back to enjoy the paid vacation for at least a day. Maybe two, she decided.

Dammit, what a clusterfuck this had turned out to be. He could hear the sirens in the distance. He turned and walked back down the stairs, grabbing his men who had been in the stairwell. "Let's let those jackasses answer the questions this time." They made it to their car before the police drove past them. As seven cops jumped out of the police cars and ran into the apartment building, Matthew's group nonchalantly drove down the street and left the scene.

Matthew Burnside was hot, angry, and flushed. When the phone call came from the agent in charge, he didn't wait for a statement before he tore into him about bringing black operatives in on his operation with instructions to shoot to kill. His people weren't cattle to be used and abused. The only question that made it through his tirade was one regarding the status of the two other operatives.

He explained he didn't know, didn't care, and wasn't about to figure it out. Those two had unnecessarily endangered a foreign national, started a firefight with a SpecOps team in broad daylight, been shot for their troubles, and had last been seen bleeding on the top of a building with San José police coming in from the first floor. They were welcome to jump to the other building, as he had seen the SpecOps woman do.

Then he listened to the question coming at him. "What? Yes, she jumped between the roofs while she carried another person. If your super-duper special agents can't jump as far as a woman carrying someone can, they deserve to sit in jail for being pussies. Yes, I'm sure it was a woman. She dropped about fifteen feet from the helicopter, slung the reporter over her shoulder, and took off in a sprint. And yes, she jumped between the buildings. I don't know—maybe twenty feet or more.

"Look, I'm not hopped up on drugs and shooting people. Your people are damned lucky they didn't let loose with the guns on that helicopter. They are incompetent. Yeah, you heard my ass just fine—incompetent. I don't give a shit what you want. This is going up my chain, and they can decide how to deal with this clusterfuck. No, you don't get to decide what 'need to know' is.

When you drop unidentified agents into what should have been a normal and simple request to speak to someone, you lost that prerogative. No, which part of 'I don't give a shit what you think' did you fail to hear? Yeah, good-fucking-bye to you too." Matthew wished he could slam his cell phone down. He exhaled in frustration. "What a prick!"

CHAPTER FOURTEEN

Juan had never been the best fighter. While he could handle humans and even Weres without too much trouble, he was a very solid middle of the pack when fighting other vampires. It didn't help that he considered himself more of a lover than a fighter.

He could see at least three Nosferatu, but they looked different than those he was familiar with. These showed too much intelligence in their actions, and two of them wore what looked like shrapnel-based suicide vests. Those clowns hadn't expected Stephen to go down easily and were using the serum. Juan didn't know how many vials existed in Europe, but there weren't any more available in South America. At least, according to rumors, there weren't.

Juan hadn't believed he would live forever. Claudia, who had been his rock and his reason for living before her sickness, had been unable to find any joy in her extended life. This was because the other vampires in South America had rejected her. Oh, they thought she was attractive enough, but they shunned her non-Forsaken opinions. It had taken three months for him to see that if no existing vampires were going to accept Claudia, then he would see if Clarita would change him so he might care for his sister in un-death as he had in life. Clarita had explained he wouldn't truly be dead, but Juan figured without the sun, what was life? He couldn't let it stop him from following Claudia and becoming her rock in turn. Once Scott had joined them, he could almost enjoy his life again. Scott was dead now, his body destroyed moments before in his last act, trying to warn them.

Now it was his turn. Juan knew that if those Nosferatu made it close enough to Stephen to explode their vests, the shrapnel would tear his body apart and no one would stand between his sister and these *malditos*. Crouched behind a couch, he held the pistol in his left hand and a short sword in his right. Stephen was behind the kitchen counter. Juan admired the vampire, who smiled like he was enjoying life. Maybe he could learn something in his last few seconds of existence.

"Stephen!" The older vampire looked at him. "They have the special Nosferatu. Do you know what those are?" Stephen nodded. "There are two with shrapnel vests, and we can't stop them from going off. Either they blow them, or if we kill them, they automatically explode." The other man's smile slipped a bit, recognizing a bad situation. Juan lowered his voice. "Take care of my sister and tell her I loved her, okay?"

Stephen's smile disappeared, and he started to say something, but Juan had already made his decision and started his personal charge toward the front of the house where three Nosferatu waited for him. Stephen decided he would not allow him to attack without support. His Queen would expect nothing less from one of her subjects.

He had barely stood when a pair of massive explosions rocked his front chamber. Debris, steel shards, and ball bearings rained through the opening. Some of the ball bearings ripped through Stephen's body as the concussion lifted him and tossed him back against the wall. A splinter of wood at least a foot long impaled his chest, piercing his left lung. He spat blood and left bloody streaks as he slid down the wall, his legs unable to keep him upright. With an explosion that size, Claudia's brother had to have been killed instantly.

His pain was indescribable, more than he had felt in centuries. He stared at nothing for a minute, trying to get his mind to focus. He hoped Ivan had been able to get into the secret room with Claudia. The future was looking pretty grim for him at the moment.

Ecaterina was wiped out. The trip and R&R for the last couple of days on land had been what she had needed. Now if Nathan would only find a way to get back down here, life would be complete again.

Ashur sat on Bethany Anne's bed, damn near taking it over because he was so big. He was a beautiful dog, all white with striking blue eyes. Ecaterina was sure he understood their conversation and was actually taking it all in. The vampire had a hand on his back and was petting the dog unconsciously while she reviewed information about her companies and the reports no one had realized had been coming in until the General had talked to Jeffrey, Patriarch Research's head guy.

Ecaterina closed her laptop, resting her eyes. Bethany Anne spoke. "Hey, why don't you go to sleep early? I won't need anything for a while, and it looks like all that sun and fun has wiped you out."

She hated to admit it, but she had gone overboard just a bit. Wearily, she stood up and grabbed her laptop, then opened the door to go back to her room. "Open or shut?"

Bethany Anne looked up from her computer. "Hmm? Oh, leave it open, please. Oww, *fuck*." Bethany Anne bent over in obvious pain and distress, her hand clenching in Ashur's fur.

Ecaterina's eyes opened wide, and she yelled over her shoulder, "*John*. We have a problem."

She heard the men racing from their posts as she dropped her laptop on a nearby chair and darted around to Bethany Anne's side. Based on John's experience, she thought it would be safe to touch her back but not a good idea to grab her hands. Ashur whined slightly, whether it was from the vampire pulling his fur so hard or a sympathetic connection, she didn't know.

She placed her right arm across Bethany Anne's back. "What's wrong?" She looked around, not seeing any blood.

"Stephen…" She gasped. "Stephen has been hurt. Blood! I need blood *now*."

Eric called from the door, "I'll get it!" and rushed over to the small refrigerator in the meeting room. Opening the bottom drawer, he grabbed three bags. He wasn't sure how many she needed, but it was rare for her to need more than one or two. He raced back into the room.

TOM!

I feel it, Bethany Anne. It's the connection we made to Stephen when you healed him. Something has seriously hurt him, and we are feeling it across the Etheric.

Is he at home?

I can't tell, but he's supposed to be there.

In her pain, Bethany Anne had trouble thinking properly.

We'll have to go to his house. We have to translocate there, TOM.

I don't know how much energy that much distance will take, Bethany Anne. We might not make it there, or we might make it and collapse. That would be bad if someone with even a simple pistol up and shoots us.

Can't. Be. Helped. What about pulling energy through Ashur?

There was a second's indecision. **That will increase our chance of success significantly. Pulling Etheric through him would mitigate how much you have to access. Of course, all three of us could disappear forever.**

TOM, I won't forsake Stephen. I've got his back.

I've got your back, Bethany Anne. For better or worse, I wouldn't have it any other way.

Clamp down on this pain, okay? I can't think.

The pain lessened, and Bethany Anne was able to take a breath. She let go of Ashur and sat up, feeling Ecaterina's arm across her shoulder. Eric held three bags of blood, and she took the first one, ripped off the top, and downed the contents. "Swords and pistols *now*." John didn't ask what was going on, just ran into her closet and grabbed her weapons and her protective vest. She downed the second and third packets.

"Leathers?"

Bethany Anne hated to waste any time, but if she got there and wasn't able to protect herself and fight, it was stupidity in action. "Give me everything."

John brought them in. She stripped right in front of them, John holding out each piece when she needed it. He flicked clothes as fast as he could since her dressing speed was incredible. When it came to a fight, her team was all business. "Stephen has been attacked. I'm going to try to translocate from here to his house. TOM says Ashur should make it doable, but if you don't hear from me in an hour…well, it's been a good ride, right?"

She shoved her pistols into the holsters, and John reached out and grabbed her face in his two very large hands. He pulled her forehead toward him and kissed it. "Come back to us, boss. You got that?"

She nodded. "Ashur, let's go." He jumped off the bed. Bethany Anne grabbed a fistful of hair as he landed, and the two of them disappeared.

John stared at the place she had just been. "She had better fucking be all right."

Eric put an arm on his big friend's shoulder.

Stephen knew the vampire approaching him, or at least knew of him. He coughed up blood as he spoke. "Terence. I've always heard you were a prick."

Terence was a little less than six feet tall and had a mustache that had gone out of style in the 1970s. "Ah, Stephen! A pleasure to speak to you, especially as this will be the only time." He looked around at the destruction. "Kinda messy, Stephen. I rather expected you to have better taste." When he waved in another vampire, Stephen turned his head to look at the new arrival.

In better times, or at least with blood, Stephen would be okay. Right now, he was bleeding from too many small holes. It took most of his energy to stop the bleeding, and there was nothing left to help him fix his body.

Stephen's lips parted, his fangs trying to grow. "Reginald. How very surprising to see you here." He coughed up more blood, then reached down and pulled up a piece of his shirt, using it to wipe his chin clean. "So, dear old brother is behind this attack?"

The well-built man in front of Stephen was easily three inches above six feet and wore an Italian-made suit. He tried to step around the piles of debris, blood, and body parts to get closer to him. "Stephen, it is very good to see you. Yes, your brother sends his regards, and wishes you would have simply stayed asleep instead of cavorting with that bitch Michael created." Reginald used the side of his shoe to move a hand missing two fingers away from where he stood.

Stephen smiled. "That 'bitch' will take my dear brother's heart. That cock-sucking prick has officially signed his death warrant." He coughed again.

Reginald barked a laugh. "What? You have truly lived too long if you believe a new vampire, even one created by Michael, will be able to hurt David." He looked around, spying a head in the corner, "Oh, who is that? I don't recognize him."

Stephen turned his head, following Reginald's eyes. "His name was Scott. Yet another death you will answer for."

Reginald shook his head. "Please, Stephen. There is no one here to hear you blather on. I get it, I get it." He glanced at the older vampire, "You are letting me know revenge will be yours because your Queen will avenge you."

He squatted, trying to keep his pant cuffs off the floor, and was now eye level with Stephen, careful to stay outside his reach. "You need to grow up, old man. Your belief in vows and trust is not only old-school, it belonged to times and countries that don't even exist anymore. Funny, Hugo told me the same thing when he died, and do you see me running? No? Of course not! Why? Because revenge only happens when those delivering the revenge have power. You don't, your Queen doesn't, and David even has the mighty Michael sealed up, waiting for his own death. There is no one to avenge you. Your family is dying quickly. Your kind and your beliefs are almost caput, *finite*, ended."

He stood. "What would your precious Queen say if she could tell me something right now?"

Reginald watched as his face scrunched in concentration, looking into the distance behind him, then the vampire spoke, "She would say you are a cock-tip sucking, stinky fudge-loving, fucking retarded cluster-duck shitfaced ass-jacker. No, wait, sorry. That was cluster*fuck* shitfaced ass-jacker." Stephen's face relaxed, and he smiled at the intruder.

Stephen found the look on Reginald's face priceless. Now he understood the phrase so well. "Really? Your Queen has quite a limited and base vocabulary. You really want to follow a bitch who talks like that? Are you sure you haven't lived too long?"

He smiled and pulled his legs up to push himself back against the wall, sitting a little taller. He coughed once more, wiping his chin. "Yes, quite sure. I would have been happy to have died in service to my Queen, but I have been informed she isn't finished with me yet."

"Really? Are you daydreaming now, Stephen? Too much blood lost?" Reginald sighed and spoke to Terence. "It is sad. I had hoped for a different outcome. Let's finish him, find out who else is in this place, and then burn it."

The three bullets that blew Terence's head apart sounded like one solid thunderclap. Reginald flinched at the sound but stopped when a deep and dangerous growl emanated from behind him.

Stephen's smile was malicious, holding no love for the vampire in front of him. "Reginald, it's time I introduced you to my Queen, Bethany Anne."

Ivan sat with Claudia in the darkened room, a small chamber maybe ten feet by six feet. Stephen had shown him the multitude of ways to exit his house a few weeks back, but right now, his decision was to wait. There was no way he would be able to outrun any vampires waiting outside since they would hear him. It would be best if Stephen won and yelled to him from the other side of the wall to return. Right now, not even Stephen could open the door to this room. There was a back way out, but it was frankly small, and until it was light outside, it wouldn't be any help.

Claudia had been weeping, Ivan trying to give her support by patting her back. She leaned into his arm, seeking a connection and something to help her. Scott had been killed in the massive explosion, and then all had gone quiet.

She buried her head in Ivan's chest, reaching around to pull him to her. He hugged her back, an unconscious response on his part. He replayed the last conversation he had with Gabrielle, which hadn't gone well. She had some emotions over the changes that had been made to her, and would need time to deal with what they meant. Further, she wasn't planning on moving forward on the personal side with him for a while. She had been locked into Bethany Anne's team, and Nathan was going to work with her dad on the intelligence side, so she wouldn't have a lot of time to fly back and forth to Europe.

Ivan hadn't tried very hard to dissuade her from her decision. He cared for her, but it seemed something had happened to her physically that had her shaken up. He was a firm believer that if you let the bird go and it came back to you, it was yours to keep. He merely had to let the bird go. He told her he would wait, that nothing needed to be decided right then. Finally, he had gotten her to agree to talk again in a couple of months. He knew she didn't believe anything would change, but he needed even the faintest amount of hope to get through his own feelings.

Now he had a very passionate woman needing his attention, concerned she could die at any moment.

Claudia mumbled something into his chest, and Ivan looked down. "Excuse me?"

She took her mouth away from his chest and spoke loud enough for him to hear. "Hold me. I'm scared."

His protective instincts kicked in and he held her tightly against his chest.

Reginald remained very still. The growling came from about ten feet behind him. He was pissed he had allowed himself to trust Terence's assurance that the area was clear. The fool had paid for his mistake, and Reginald tried to figure out a way to turn this situation around.

A woman's voice spoke behind him. "You know, I can almost see the little gears in your tiny pea-brain turning, trying to figure out what to say and how to say it to get yourself out of this situation. Here, let me help you understand."

As long as she kept talking, Reginald would only get smarter and have more time to turn this situation around. That was when both of his kneecaps exploded, the shots fired simultaneously. He dropped to the ground, screaming in rage and pain. "This is a very expensive suit, bitch!" She fired again and the elbow he had used to try to sit up vaporized.

He lay on the ground in shock and watched as a beautiful woman with black hair walked around him. She holstered two pistols, pulled a sword from her back, and cut through Terence's neck, severing what was left of his head. He lost her when she went into the kitchen.

Her voice called, "Stephen, anyone else to worry about, and would you like this cold or warmed up?"

Stephen smiled. "Oh, I can last long enough to have it warmed up. I will enjoy this so much more with warm blood, and I don't think we have anyone else in the house."

Reginald gritted his teeth. Two kneecaps and an elbow would be a fucking trial to heal. His plans had never gotten him shot before. He wasn't a quick healer, and couldn't afford to get into a battle where he relied on his healing abilities.

Now he was screwed, his kneecaps slowly regenerating but his elbow not even starting to heal yet. He lay there on the ground and saw the hand with the missing fingers. For a moment, he considered whether eating it would help him heal any faster.

The microwave dinged, and he heard the crunch of boots as the woman came back into his vision and walked over to Stephen, handed him a mug of blood and then quickly yanked a large splinter from his chest. The vampire only grunted and took the blood slowly as if he were drinking a spot of tea.

Reginald bared his fangs, thinking about the blood in the cup. He heard growling. He arched his neck backward and looked behind him, coming face to upside-down face with a large, angry-sounding, all-teeth beast. He closed his mouth and turned his head back to the woman, who had stood and now walked over to where his feet lay at odd angles. He decided to negotiate. "I've got knowledge you need, so I can be useful. We can bargain."

The woman's smile was not very regal. She looked beyond angry. Actually, she looked vengeful. He was looking into the eyes of someone who would kill him as easily as breathe. "Oh, I don't think we will be bargaining for anything, Reginald. What we are going to do is play a game. This isn't an ordinary game. I'm going to sit here and do everything I can think of to make you scream in pain. Then I'm going to heal you enough to do it some more. The only way I will stop is if Stephen asks, very politely, for me to do so, but I have to admit, I have already done more than you believe possible, little Reginald."

"What…what are you talking about?" He did not like his chances if Stephen would be the decision maker on when his pain would stop. What happened to women not liking torture?

"You see, I am the Queen, and my subjects are never forsaken. Just a few minutes ago, I was near Central America when you hurt my subject. Not powerful, Reginald? How many vampires do you know who can travel seven thousand miles in a second?"

He didn't believe any of this. He *couldn't* believe any of this. If she wasn't lying, then what was she? Suddenly, his neck felt the pressure of a sword tip, and he heard a whisper. "You aren't paying attention, Reginald. Penalty box for you." He screamed in pain when she flicked her sword, cutting off his left ear. Then she was back beside Stephen again, helping him stand up.

Bethany Anne made sure he was able to remain upright on his own against the wall. "Hold on. If Reginald is going to make so much racket, let's make sure we have a little time." She moved her sword to her left hand, drew her pistol, and shot both his kneecaps again. His screaming went up an octave. She holstered the pistol. "Just making sure he can't walk for a few minutes."

He nodded, deciding that explaining Reginald was a slow healer was inconsequential to Bethany Anne. Stephen knew this side of his Queen. This side was death, and Reginald wouldn't leave this house alive. Stephen would bet all of his wealth on that outcome.

"I guess the room at the end of the hallway was acceptable, my Queen?" he asked. Bethany Anne smiled at him, making him feel ten times better.

"Yes, it was. I appreciate the extra blood packets in the room. It was a nice touch, and it would have been harder had they not been there. Thank you."

Stephen's own wounds were starting to heal. Bethany Anne checked a couple of them, tsking to herself.

TOM, can we move this along?

Maybe a little. I still don't want him having too much blood.

Bethany Anne cocked her right elbow and put her hand, her wrist to the outside, in front of Stephen's mouth. "Bite." It wasn't a request, it was a command.

He sank his fangs lovingly into her wrist, pulling the blood and energy into his body. It took only seconds for him to feel the change, his healing speeding up. "Stop." He retracted his fangs, breathing harder from the excitement that overcame him when drinking from her wrist.

He wouldn't make the mistake of ever trying to grab her wrist against her will again.

"Ivan?"

"He and Claudia are in a safe room beneath us. I showed him how to get out a while back. They are fine right now. I'm not sure how much of what we are going to do to Reginald Claudia needs to see."

Bethany Anne thought about that. "Her brother and her friend?"

Stephen shook his head. "Dead."

Bethany Anne pursed her lips. "Well, if it was me, I might want a little of my own back. I'll find them in a few minutes and ask her. She doesn't have to come up here."

Stephen, his voice dry, barely whispered, "It was David."

Bethany Anne cocked her head. "What was David?"

"David, my sibling. He is the one who set this up. He has Michael."

Bethany Anne turned back to Reginald. "Really? Why, isn't that nice to hear, Reginald? Quit. Stop your fucking whining, you cunt-lipped ass-jacket. Crying? Really? The big bad Reginald who kills vampires and isn't afraid of revenge is crying? Guess what? Hugo called, and he is waiting to discuss his death with you. Tough shit, he has to wait until I'm done with your ass. Where is Michael, you fucknut? Oh, growing a pair, are we?"

Bethany Anne walked over to Reginald's feet. "See here?" She snapped her fingers. "Reginald, pay attention! This gets worse. I'm going to tell you a children's rhyme used in America. Ever heard of 'This little piggy went to market?' No? Let me teach it to you. This little piggy went to market," Reginald screamed as Bethany Anne sliced through his leather shoe and took off his small toe. "This little piggy stayed home." She sliced through the next toe, cutting it off. He tried to move his legs, but the pain from his knees was too intense. "Want to tell me where Michael is, or shall I continue teaching you the children's rhyme?"

Reginald was only too happy to explain where David's castle was.

Fifteen minutes later, after a couple of texts to John, she took Ashur and followed Stephen's directions to get Ivan and Claudia out of the hidden safe room.

Bethany Anne walked up to the wall the hidden door was installed in. She could hear noise coming from behind it, so she put her ear close to listen more intently, then stepped back, rolling her eyes. Ivan had apparently gotten over Gabrielle's phone call pretty quickly. Why was it that every time she needed to have a discussion with a woman, Ivan was playing hide the sausage with her?

Bethany Anne spoke loudly. "*Gott Verdammt*, Ivan. I can't leave you alone for one fucking minute before you're having sex. You fucking dick." She smiled as she heard the two of them start scrambling around. She waited thirty seconds until the noises, with the occasional squeal of pain as they stepped on a toe or something, stopped.

Ivan's voice called from behind the wall, "Is that you?"

"Who the hell else do you think would speak to a fucking wall this way? Open up before I get pissed and come through it. I'm getting impatient here, Ivan."

She heard a snick, and then a three-foot-wide portion of the wall opened toward her. Smiling, she stepped aside and looked into the room to see a disheveled Ivan and a woman with messed-up hair and eyes still red from crying. His shirt had the buttons in the wrong holes. She eyed him up and down. "Ivan, I think you have some explaining to do. If not to me, then maybe Gabrielle? Two months? Really? Did you last two days? You and the slut need to clean yourselves up before you come upstairs." She turned to go, then stopped and turned around. "By the way, slut, do you want a piece of the person who killed your friend and your brother before he expires?"

Claudia said no. She had figured her brother was dead, but to have it brutally laid out was almost too much. The woman turned back around and left.

She walked out of the room and sat on a bed. "Who is that bitch?" She looked up at Ivan, who was lost in his own thoughts and looking miserable. "Ivan." He jerked and looked at her. "Who is that bitch? And Gabrielle? Who is she, and why do you need to talk to her?"

Ivan walked over to her and sat down. "Gabrielle is Stephen's daughter. She was my girlfriend until she called and asked for a timeout. Well, maybe I asked for the timeout."

"You were dating Stephen's daughter? Oh, God, I just screwed Stephen's daughter's boyfriend? How much worse can my life get?" She put her face in her hands. "Who was the bitch?"

"That's Bethany Anne."

"Oh, fuck my miserable life."

Miami, FL, USA

Across the Atlantic, Frank sat at the kitchen table, his head in his hands and his shoulders slumped, staring at the laptop in front of him. Nathan came in to grab a cup of coffee but stopped on his way out. Frank hadn't noticed him, so he pulled out a chair next to him and sat down. "What's wrong?" He didn't move. "Frank, what's wrong?"

Kurns looked up then, noticing the Were for the first time.

"I missed it." His right hand swept across his laptop as if that were the answer to Nathan's question.

"What? What did you miss?" They all knew Bethany Anne had survived a dangerous translocation to Romania to help Stephen and Ivan.

"David. My system recorded a conversation between Anton and David a few weeks ago. I had the information, and somehow I missed it. Nathan, I've never missed anything like this. What's going on? Is my brain aging out? Am I becoming unfit?" An edge of desperation mixed with despair came through his words.

Nathan set his coffee on the table. "Tell me what happened and we'll figure it out. I haven't noticed you becoming a fumbling old professor, so don't give up on me, Frank. Otherwise, I'll be relegated to hacker status for the group." Nathan's voice trailed off. "Fuck us."

He noticed the change in his companion's demeanor. "What? Fuck us why?" His voice inched toward normal as he caught up with Nathan's obvious concern.

"Frank, what if someone has hacked us?" The two men stared

at each other, alarm rising in their eyes. Nathan's chair made a scraping, keening sound as he pulled it around to sit beside Frank, who turned his laptop so they could both read it.

Frank's funk evaporated as his fingers moved quickly over the keyboard. Both men were lost in concentration as they tried to track down a possible digital attack they hadn't noticed.

Lance and Patricia stepped into the room and saw them deep in conversation, using words neither one recognized. The general grabbed the keys to one of the SUVs, and they left to get a bite to eat.

Two hours later, Frank sat back and muttered, "*Gott Verdammt*. How the hell did they find that?"

Nathan stood and stretched his back. "I don't know, but they were able to stop the email from getting to you. The data was still on the server where it was recorded, but something intercepted your email and returned the acknowledgment. You never received the email and the other server doesn't look compromised, so we have some sort of man-in-the-middle attack. Your email didn't include much to go on, so I doubt they understood the content, and so far, the firewalls held. We need to upgrade that system. It doesn't look like the attacks have stopped yet. They're subtle, not brute force."

Frank leaned back and sighed. "Yeah. I suppose as often as I do this to others, I shouldn't get upset when it's done to me. But can you imagine what we might have done if I hadn't missed this?"

The Were shrugged. "Coulda, woulda, shoulda. Can't think like that right now. What we need—" His cell phone rang. It was Stephen's number. He stabbed the speaker button. "Hi, you're on speaker with Frank and me."

Bethany Anne's voice came across the speaker. "Hi, guys. I assume you've heard the situation report from the *Polarus* team?"

Nathan replied, "Yes. What do you want us to do?"

"I need you two to find out everything about David's properties, particularly this old castle that is right outside…hold it…" She pulled the phone away from her face and spoke to Stephen. He provided the name of a small town, and Nathan wrote it down. When he heard her put the phone back to her ear, he broke into the conversation. "We got that. So you want a detailed reconnaissance and other info how quickly?"

"Yesterday. Stephen is almost healed. He and I will make a fast sneak attack before David understands his effort to kill Stephen failed. John might be a little upset." Nathan's laughter interrupted her. "Okay, John's head will blow off like a massive volcano, but between Stephen, Ashur, and me, we'll get this first part done. I'm not trying to take the bricks apart, merely get Michael free. Once we have him, we'll probably have one mean and righteously pissed Patriarch on our side again. It could really change our tactics, especially if I can kill that sonofabitch David in the process."

Nathan thought about how calm the UnknownWorld had been without Michael around. "Sure we couldn't rescue him but keep him on ice? Life has been nicer without his shadow over everything."

He heard her sigh. "Nathan, I get that. I really do. I'll take care of Michael. He owes me big right now, and I could use some additional information he can provide before we move forward."

Nathan asked, "You know Carl is dead, right?"

"I did, but how did you? Reginald was pretty free with his information when I spoke to him."

They heard Stephen snort in the background. "After you pulled his arm off."

Maybe, the Were mused, Bethany Anne *was* the right person to talk to Michael. He had wondered if she was ignorant or merely insane when they first met. He figured if anyone might be able to rein her in, it was Michael. Now he worried more for Michael than he did for Bethany Anne. Those two made a hell of a couple. Oh, holy crap. He hoped *that* never happened. *Please, God in heaven, don't let those two become a couple.*

She brought his wandering thoughts back on track. "Ignore Stephen. How did you know about Carl?"

Frank jumped in. "Because we just heard a conversation recorded by a system I had in place between Anton and David talking about it. Here, let me play it." He played the recording on his laptop speakers, Nathan holding the phone to the device.

"When did that happen?"

Frank admitted, "A couple of weeks ago. I thought I had failed you by not uncovering this quicker, but the reality is, we have someone aggressively hacking us and the email informing me of the recording was blocked. I'm sorry, I should have figured this out more quickly."

There was a pause while Bethany Anne thought about what she had heard. "Well, it gives us a few hints. That we aren't looking for Carl changes the rules of engagement a little. There won't be anyone at the castle we can't shoot, and we need to find something that constrains a non-corporeal body. Michael will be inside it. Better late than never with the info, but find and get rid of whoever or whatever is attacking us."

Nathan jumped back in. "What if it's governmental?"

Bethany Anne's response was immediate. "Get rid of the attack, and fuck up their computers and operations. If it takes a more personal discussion, let me know. Until we figure out if ADAM will come online, we can't have this bullshit interrupting our efforts. I'll take them on the same way I take on anything else—find their nuts and kick them so hard they have to swallow to speak. Your priorities are my castle information and then these hacking activities. Do you have enough resources, guys?"

"I've got someone coming in—one of the hackers you caught in Miami."

Her voice was surprised. "Really? I'm going to get a plus in my karma column for not just killing people indiscriminately? That's a nice surprise."

Nathan smiled. He had to add, "You'll be even more excited to learn that he wants to meet you."

This time there was a pause on the line, if only for an extra second. "Like a date, or just a meeting?"

"He requested a meeting, but I think he wants a date." Frank looked at him like he had just provided more information for his book.

"Ahhh, you know what? I don't give a fuck. It's not like my dance card is full right now. See how he does with you, and if he isn't a slimeball, you can set up a dinner meeting. Let's see what happens when he finds John and Eric hovering over me."

Nathan smiled. He doubted John and Eric would matter. Most geeks simply rolled with the punches, especially if a beautiful woman was involved. He had to get Ecaterina involved in this. The story might become a chapter in Frank's book, after all, if they could actually swing something. Maybe a little payback for a frozen Pepsi in their bed? "I'll let you know after I've worked with him some. I have to tell you, I'm going to let him know dating you isn't a good idea. Not that I figure he'll listen to me. Sorry."

She retorted, "It *isn't* a good idea. I could eat him for dinner, and that's literal, not sexual. He could get shot or tagged as an information source, so make sure you try to scare him away. But we're all living on borrowed time, so if he has the 'nads to ask me out, he will probably get a yes. I hear Ivan coming so get back to me on Stephen's phone with the info. I want to be gone within the hour." She hung up.

Frank was already pulling data.

Ivan looked like shit when she spoke to him. "What's going on with the slut bunny? Is she okay with all the deaths, or do we have a horny zombie down there?"

Ivan started to interrupt her but realized she was trying to get his mind back in the game. "She's in shock right now, but Claudia is made of pretty stern stuff if it doesn't require violence. She isn't a violent person."

"Okay, you two talk to Stephen and figure out where she can stay before the sun comes up. I'm surprised we haven't had anyone official come out this way yet."

Stephen spoke up. "We are pretty far away from any populated areas, and most people fear my home and don't come here without an invitation."

"I must have surprised the hell out of you." She smiled at the vampire.

"Yes, that is true." Stephen looked at Reginald's remains. "I'm going to call a cleanup crew. They will take all the remains, then come back and fix the house. I'll have Scott and Juan cremated so we can hold a service for them after our discussion with David." He paused and looked at Bethany Anne. "And by discussion, I mean decapitating that arrogant ass and burning his body, in case anyone is curious." His eyes were angry.

Bethany Anne shrugged. "Works for me. I might want some questions answered, but I won't lose any sleep if they aren't." She pointed to the fridge. "Do we have enough extra bags? I can't let Michael drink from me. I'm not sure what that would do, so it's probably a bad idea."

Stephen went to the fridge and pulled out ten bags. "I brought in a lot for our extra company, so we might be a little overstocked right now."

"Really? How many bags?"

Stephen looked back in the fridge. "I don't know. At least twenty-five? Why?"

Bethany Anne walked into the kitchen and looked around

Stephen at the blood sitting there. "Because desperate times call for desperate measures." She turned and looked at Ashur, who lay calmly on the couch. "Stephen, how much do you trust me?"

Stephen pulled bags from the fridge and put them on the counter. "With my very existence, my Queen. It is a vow that apparently is only relevant for countries that do not exist. *I* believe it was not misplaced." He continued pulling bags out. "By the way, what is a shitfaced ass-jacker?" He asked the question exactly as if he wanted to know the weather the next day.

"Hmmm? Oh." She pulled her attention away from Ashur, who had been watching them intently. "It's a drunk guy who sticks his dick in the wrong hole and claims to the girl afterward it was all a mistake. So don't be one, okay?"

"Not to worry, I never miss." Stephen took the last bag from the fridge and closed the door.

Ashur jumped off the couch and came over to Bethany Anne, who put her hand on his head. Ivan stared at the huge German Shepherd. "Ivan, meet Ashur. He invited himself to a fight in Costa Rica a couple of weeks back and almost died. He's had my blood, and spent some time being fixed in TOM's ship." She pulled Ashur's head back. "Hey, pay attention. He isn't food. He's my friend, and Ecaterina's brother." Ashur's tail wagged. "Figures you would remember who spoils you with the treats you like so much." She let go of the dog and Ashur went over to sniff Ivan, who put his hand slowly on his head.

"He's beautiful."

"God, don't encourage him. He already has all the Wechselbalg on the ship claiming him as their mascot, and I swear he understands every word you say."

Ivan continued petting Ashur. "Is he going to start cursing soon?"

"Probably."

Bethany Anne heard Claudia come slowly up the stairs, as if she had to talk herself up each step. She nodded in her direction, pointed to the body parts still around, and mouthed the word "Claudia" at Ivan. He went to intercept her before she saw too much.

Stephen got off the phone. "They will be here within the hour. They have a completely secure van to take Claudia to a safe house, and she and Ivan can stay there until we come back."

Bethany Anne smiled. "Pretty sure we're going to get through this, aren't you?"

Stephen looked at her. "My Queen, just stay back. Ashur and I will take care of everything." He grinned when the Shepherd barked in agreement.

The trip to David's castle didn't go anything like Stephen had expected.

He had taken a shower and cleaned up, and shocked the hell out of Bethany Anne when he came back out of his room.

He was dressed in military fatigues with the patches removed. He wore them comfortably, so this wasn't the first time he had been involved in operations, she thought. Damn, this man had secrets. He had always been such a lighthearted "lover, not a fighter" type. She never considered he might have a past that would surprise her.

He went downstairs three times, and each time, he came back with wooden crates which proved to contain a large assortment of weapons. She chose an extra knife and retrieved spare mags for her pistols. They would be attacking, she hoped, at sunset. That would mean more humans—easier to simply shoot them and be done with it.

Ashur stood, put his front paws on the table, and seemed to look over the choices. She snorted. "See anything you like?"

He turned his head and cocked it at her as if to say, "I don't have opposable thumbs, dumbass." He turned back and sniffed around the boxes.

She mumbled, "I guess I just got told off."

Stephen looked at Bethany Anne's outfit. "Oh." His eyes widened with alarm and he practically disappeared, running back downstairs vampire-fast.

What the hell?

She heard him return, not nearly as quickly as he left, carrying one more wooden crate. This one wasn't as big as the others, and the wood was different. It wasn't a crate to carry stuff, but a special holding box. Stephen had her attention as he set it down, pushing a machine gun out of the way. He unlocked it and stepped back, waving Bethany Anne forward.

Smiling, she stepped forward, the excitement of opening the box akin to receiving a beautiful gift. When she opened the top, she stared, speechless. She picked up a striking *saya*, the handle of the sword melding seamlessly with the sheath.

Inside the *saya* was the most exquisite *katana* Bethany Anne had ever seen. "It's beautiful, Stephen."

"It is yours, my Queen. It is time you leave your functional sword behind and take up your mantle. It is said this sword can differentiate between someone who deserves death and one who doesn't. I think it has more to do with the person who bears it, but it is unbelievably sharp."

Bethany Anne went carefully through a few attack movements, feeling the perfection of the balance and taking in the beauty of the blade. She tied the new *saya* in place and it felt right, as if something had been returned to her. "Thank you, Stephen. It is a treasure." She approached him and reached for his face, kissing his forehead. "Are you ready?" He nodded. "Then let's get our stuff. We need to be at the airport in five minutes."

"How are we going to get there so fast?"

Ashur woofed as if to say, "Seriously?"

"Trust me." This time, it wasn't a question but a command.

Frank had dipped his hand back into his military contacts and procured a fast transport for the three of them, no questions asked, at the military airfield she had used to get to Florida. She translocated the three of them with two bags, one full of clinking metal and the other an insulated cooler for blood. The front security gate guard was surprised to see two people and a very large dog walk up to his post, each person carrying a bag. Once he got approval, they walked through the open gate, and a car arrived to pick them up to take them to the hangar. Stephen jumped up front so Ashur could ride in the back with Bethany Anne.

The plane was in the air ten minutes later, taking them straight to a small airfield in Germany. There, a Mercedes SUV waited for them. Ecaterina had outdone herself, Bethany Anne thought. The two of them got in the back seat after putting their gear in the cargo area where Ashur was riding. He could lie down easily, his head resting on the cooler of blood. She got her update from Nathan on what to expect, then handed the phone to Stephen in case he had specific questions.

They could both hear the conversation fine without putting Nathan on speaker and sharing any information with their driver.

They stopped in a small village to gas up, then continued. Bethany Anne made one adjustment after seeing the topography of the valley David's castle was in. There was a tourist building two miles away but at a slightly higher elevation. The driver dropped them off at the restaurant/hotel. They paid top dollar for two adjoining rooms that faced David's abode. Management charged Stephen a three-week deposit to allow Ashur into the room. Bethany Anne looked down at the dog, whose face, she would swear, was saying, "What? I'll be good."

They went to their rooms, entering the first and opening the adjoining door to the second. As Ashur went around checking things out, Stephen put the bag with the weapons on the first bed. Bethany Anne opened the window. The hotel was only three stories, and they were on the top floor. She went to the first bag and found the sniper scope. Returning to the window, she started dialing in to see David's castle better. Stephen came up behind her. "How do you want to get over there? I imagine he has the grounds pretty well guarded by people and automated emplacements."

Bethany Anne pulled the scope back. "Automated emplacements? Stephen, you speak so deliciously right before an operation." She put the scope back to her eye. "We're going to drop in on them."

Stephen glanced at Ashur, who looked like he didn't have a clue what she was talking about either. He was trying to figure out why he had expected the dog to have any answers.

"I only see one guard up top. We need to get rid of him quickly."

"How? Are you a good enough shot to hit him from here? Plus, that will make an awful racket, and I don't know about you, but I can't run fast enough to expect us to get inside before they find the dead lookout."

"Oh, God no. Maybe Ecaterina or Killian could make that shot, but I can't. I'll shoot him with a pistol if I have to, but I hope to simply cut his throat." She put the scope away.

Stephen was completely at a loss as to what his Queen expected to do, so he simply accepted it would happen as she said it would.

Bethany Anne started stashing armaments on her body and in her holsters, so he did the same. Once she was done, she tossed the cooler of blood bags to him. "We're probably going to need that, but save some for Michael if you can. He isn't going anywhere, so if we fail, don't kill yourself. Drink the blood, and we'll try again some other time, got it?" Stephen nodded. This wasn't a request from her. He had been commanded to take care of himself first.

She looked down at Ashur. "Don't you make a lot of noise either. No barking or anything else unless you see something we need to know about." The dog returned her stare.

Tying her saya in place, she positioned Ashur to face the window. "Stay." She waved at Stephen. "Come up beside me. No screaming like a little girl, got it?" He was starting to understand what was about to happen.

"Will this be like John's story of attacking the large yacht?" Bethany Anne nodded. "Well then, yippee-ki-yay..."

Bethany Anne finished with him, grinning as they disappeared. "Motherfucker."

She had almost gotten the distance right but had undershot the castle by about three hundred feet. Still, she was high enough in the air to see the roof where the guard was walking, taking a drag on a cigarette. She translocated them again after falling fifty feet. Hopefully, no one had noticed them appearing and disappearing in the middle of the sky.

Bethany Anne let go of both Stephen and Ashur as soon as they came out of the second translocation and they dropped the last five feet. She landed on the balls of her feet and took off toward the guard. He hadn't finished the last pull on his cigarette when his head was lopped cleanly off, his body crumpling to the ground. She had to move quickly to dodge the arterial spray. "Gah!"

She walked back over to Stephen and Ashur, who were both on alert. With a look of surprise, she whispered, "This thing is dangerously sharp. I only wanted to cut his throat, but it took his head."

Stephen smiled. "Guess he was evil then, huh?"

She nodded her agreement.

They went in search of a way down. From the conversation with Anton, they assumed Michael would be in a dungeon. Nathan didn't have any information about the castle layout, so they were on their own.

Stephen looked at her. "Stay together or split up?"

She considered their options.

Her only priority was breaking Michael out of this mess. If they disrupted David's people, it was extra points, and should they kill David, she would do the happy dance.

"I'll look for Michael by going down as fast as possible. I want you two to stick with me. Should we get trapped, your responsibilities are to take the fight somewhere else and allow me to continue. Keep the fight going, then meet me back on the roof."

"How will I know when to meet you?"

"Oh, I'm sure I'll think of something. I'll yell it a few times down the halls if I need to. You two just pay attention, okay?"

Both nodded at her. That dog was freaky intelligent, she thought.

They went quickly down the stairs and only passed one person, a maid, on the way. Bethany Anne popped her on the head, successfully not killing her, and they laid her on a bed as if she were taking a nap.

It was getting late in the day. No one had seen them yet, but they hadn't found a way down to the dungeon either. Bethany Anne stopped and asked, "You have any suggestions?"

Ashur chose that moment to take the lead, sniffing along the floorboards. They sped up to catch him, then they went quickly from room to room. They found two security types and these they killed quickly, each one breaking a neck. They stashed them in a small room that looked and smelled dusty. Ashur went at it for ten minutes before he pawed at a wall in a hallway. Stephen grabbed both torch holders and tried to move them, then shrugged, mouthing, "It works in the movies."

The dog sniffed the wall, his head easily able to reach hand-height. Finally, he stopped and pawed at a brick. Bethany Anne felt around and eventually just pushed hard, and was rewarded with a click. Stephen shoved, and a section of the stone wall opened. The three of them entered and closed the stone door carefully. "Fuck my life," Bethany Anne whispered. "I didn't think to bring a flashlight."

There was another click and lights came on, revealing a circular stone staircase. Stephen took his hand away from the light switch. "We vampires are able to get with the times, you know." He smiled at Bethany Anne, who rolled her eyes. The three of them hurried down the steps, trying to listen ahead.

They passed a room that contained very old-fashioned torture equipment but nothing that looked like it could be used to hold somebody non-corporeal. Nothing smelled like it had been used recently.

Another level held cells and old-style metal restraints. The deepest level was a single large room with a copper device that reminded Bethany Anne of a diving bell in the center.

"This has got to be it. You two make sure I don't have company." Stephen and Ashur went back to the stairs.

She walked around the device.

TOM, do you have any suggestions?

According to the phone call, the idea is that if he becomes corporeal, it kills him. I would imagine it has a huge amount of pressure or a huge amount of vacuum. One would crush him, the other would explode him. If we could equalize the pressure, he could form his body again, and we can grab him and go.

Bethany Anne looked around and found the controls. She studied them for a minute.

Okay, any ideas?
Do I look like I run strange devices?
Do you really want me to answer that question?

The Pod-doc is not strange.

Okay, maybe I was asking too much. So, if I try to open the door on something with pressure, the door blows off, and God only knows what happens. Too much vacuum and there isn't a chance in hell I can pull the door open, not even with my strength.

Well, we could call to him and try to grab him Etherically.

Come again?

Tom was silent. This couldn't be good. She didn't like their other chances, and right now, she wanted out of this castle in the worst way. The whole place reeked of evil from ages past.

We could try to enter the Etheric right here and call to him, then move to where you "feel" him. Grab him and then move back out. You slip back into normal space, and we have him out of there.

And if I fail to judge the distance correctly?

Uh...boom?

Hold onto that thought.

"Michael, can you hear me?" Stephen and Ashur both turned their heads to look at her. She waved her hands, and they turned their heads back up the stairs.

She hissed a whisper, "*Gott Verdammt*, Michael! Answer me, you fucking pain in the ass."

Bethany Anne? It was weak, but she heard him.

"Yes. It's me, Michael. I'm outside this fucking contraption. I've got to get you out. Is there anything you can do to help me?"

No. I am barely holding on here as it is. My energy is low. Have you killed David?

"No, I haven't met him yet. I'll get around to killing him soon. Well, I hope so, anyway."

She got no response from Michael. It wasn't like she wanted his approval to kill David anyway.

You need to escape. David has killed Stephen, and he will kill you. Live to fight another day.

"Bullshit. Stephen is with me."

Truly?

"Yes, truly. I am not a lying bastard who says one thing and then disappears for a year. Oh, wait, that's you. Don't think I'm happy with you at the moment, but we can talk once I have you out of this fucking thing. Shit." Bethany Anne was getting impatient, which was not a rare occurrence for her.

"Fuck this. Michael, get ready. We have some blood out here. When you sense me not moving you anymore, you're safe to come back into your body. Drink the bag, because if you try to give me a hickey, you won't need to worry about David. I'll kill you myself."

She could hear chuckling in her mind. At least Michael's sense of humor wasn't gone.

"Bethany Anne?" Stephen called, concern in his voice.

She took out some blood and set it down beside the cooler. "Whatever you do, Michael cannot drink from me, understand?" He nodded. She pulled her sword off and set it aside.

"Michael, time to meet your maker." Let him chew on that comment for a minute.

She stepped into the Etheric, trying not to move any distance. It was a weird feeling as she lost the ability to see anything. Everything was by feel and sensory perception for her in this dimension right now. She could feel a sentience near her, undulating in and out of existence. It felt like he was maybe ten feet away? *Got you,* she thought as she tried to mentally walk toward him. There was nothing for her to grab. When she transported others, she always held onto them physically.

Dammit. She wasn't going to get this close and fail. She moved a little to the side to feel him from a different angle and then took another mental step. Michael felt like he was some sort of vapor, not wholly there. She needed vacuum.

TOM, can we pull a person into the Etheric and then push them out again?

Well, nothing precludes that idea. So far, we have moved

people into the Etheric and pulled them out. I'm not sure if that is factually correct or just how we understood it.

No fucking time like the present to learn something new.

TOM stayed quiet. It wasn't like he would change her mind, and she seemed to have an innate understanding of how the Etheric worked. He had not yet explained how many decades it might take a Kurtherian to master as much as she knew right now.

Bethany Anne inched toward the vapor, thinking how far she had moved inside the Etheric. She reached out, mentally grabbing the nebulous stuff and willing it to come into the Etheric with her. It didn't take long before the vapor became more solid in her mind. She decided to act as if she was transporting herself from a normal location and took a step back into the room. She had pushed Michael ahead of her, not wanting to find out what might happen if they were touching when she was back in the room. A very solid Michael fell toward the floor. She reached out enough to grab his shirt, and it ripped. She was successful in slowing him down a little before he hit the stone floor.

Ouch. That had to hurt.

He was unconscious. She grabbed a bag and was busy ripping it open when Stephen whispered, "Bethany Anne, we have company!" He pointed up.

She downed the bag herself and waved Stephen and Ashur toward her. "Grab Michael." Stephen picked up his Patriarch, and Ashur came over quickly. She tossed the canvas bag over her shoulder, grabbed a handful of Ashur and then Stephen's hand, and transported them back to their rooms in the hotel.

Twenty seconds later, David came down the stairs, sniffing in puzzlement. "Why does it smell like dog in here?" He went over to the device and checked the settings. Nothing had been touched. He walked around it, trying to figure out what was wrong.

"Master!"

David moved quickly up the stairs. He screamed in rage when he learned of his dead guards and rushed back down again.

He walked over to the device and slammed his fist against it. "How?" He turned and spotted a drop of blood on the floor. He looked back at the device, searching for any proof Michael was still inside. The device was working correctly, but he couldn't see anything.

David started yelling in a dialect lost to the ages.

The four of them appeared in the hotel room, and Ashur started sniffing the perimeter as Stephen laid an anemic-looking Michael on the bed. Bethany Anne pulled blood bags out quickly and tossed them to Stephen, who ripped them open and worked to get some down Michael's throat.

It took them fifteen minutes to get enough into him that he was able to start drinking the blood himself. His voice was calm, but his eyes blazed with anger. "Where is David?"

Bethany Anne snorted. "Really? Your first words are asking where that useless excuse is? Not, 'thank you, Bethany Anne, thank you, Stephen, for saving my apparently inconsiderate ass?'" She felt like slapping the man.

He managed a feeble grin. "My apologies. I guess I should have said, 'I appreciate the rescue, Bethany Anne and Stephen, and where is David so that I may kill him?'"

Mollified, she replied, "Well, at least you have one priority correct. He's back at his castle. I imagine he has figured out you aren't there and is having an epic conniption fit right about now. I hope he's worried about where you are and looking around every corner in fear. But you couldn't wrestle a squirrel, much less another vampire."

Michael looked down at his body, realizing the truth in her

words. "Yes, this is true. But I will be better soon enough, and then I will take care of him."

"Really? In a couple of hours, you'll be ready to go? What a bullshit answer. You'll be lucky to be at quarter-strength. You were almost dead; I could feel it. If you're better in two days, I'll consider it amazing."

Michael decided to accept the truth of her statements, although his anger demanded he kill David immediately. "How did we get out?"

Stephen handed Michael another bag. "Bethany Anne teleported us." She gave him an ugly look, and he shrugged. "What do you want me to do? He hasn't learned everything, so he won't have a clue if I give him the real explanation."

Bethany Anne growled, "Fine. Do we need to get out of the area?"

Michael looked around and through the window. "Where are we?"

"We're about two or three miles from his castle in a hotel."

Michael pursed his lips. "He might be able to feel me if he comes close, so I wouldn't say it's the safest place. Do we have a vehicle?"

Bethany Anne pondered that question. She reached into the bag again to pull out a pouch, but this time, she drank the blood herself and tried to gauge her level.

TOM, how am I doing on energy?

Amazingly enough, you have probably only used twenty percent since we left this room.

So I'm pulling energy through Ashur, right? Is it painful to him?

Does he look like he's bothered? I'm guessing he would let you know if it bothered him.

I wonder just how much energy I can pull. When we were in the Etheric, it seemed to be all around us, like I was swimming in the ocean.

A more apt metaphor would be breathing in air. You were

there in the dimension. **You were in the Etheric, so yes, you definitely felt it. It was beautiful.**

TOM, is that where your people are?

Tom was silent for a moment. **Some, yes. Those who had the ability, but far too many can't make the change.**

Stephen watched Bethany Anne for a moment. She seemed to be considering something. Michael leaned toward him while watching her. "What is she doing?"

The vampire looked at his father, the man who had left him to go to America centuries before. He almost felt compassion for his cluelessness. "I imagine she is deciding how to move us somewhere."

"How? Are we doing this transporting thing again? How far can she go? More than three miles?" Stephen nodded. "Ten?" Stephen nodded again. "Twenty?" Stephen decided to stop answering Michael's questions.

Bethany Anne focused again. "Okay, Stephen. How safe are Ivan and Claudia?"

"They're fine. They can move again tonight, but they are safe where they are right now. Why?"

"Because I want to make sure they'll be okay alone for a few days. Can I use your phone?" Stephen went to the gun bag and reached inside for a smaller cushioned pouch. Unzipping it, he pulled his phone out and turned it on, then handed it to her. As she waited for it to boot up, Michael stared at his son, realizing through his haze that he looked better than he remembered and that he was comfortable with technology. This wasn't the man he recalled or the man in the stories he had heard when he had been awake. What had happened while he was in that infernal device?

"Stephen, what is the date?" After Stephen told him, he continued, "Really? David will pay for that…" His voice trailed off as Bethany Anne put the phone to her ear.

"Nathan? Are you at the house? Can you go up to my bedroom and check to make sure no one is in my closet? Wait, don't you fucking look in my closet either. Just knock. Shit, okay. Look, make sure the floor in my closet is clear, but if you say one fucking thing about my shoe count, I will personally pull your dick up around your neck and strangle you with it, understand?"

Bethany Anne rolled her eyes when she heard Nathan try to hold in his snickering. "Furface, if I hear one mention, and that includes from Ecaterina, your ass is grass, *capiche*? Who else is there? Frank? Where are Dad and Patricia? Camped out next door for now? That's interesting. Watching movies? Netflix? God, I hope it isn't Netflix, and chill." She thought about who she was bringing with her and smiled. If she could pull this off, Nathan would wet his pants.

"Tell you what, Stephen and I need to drop in, but I have a huge German Shepherd with me. Yeah, Ashur. Really? Those guys just got on the boat. No telling what they think is large. Yes, we know where Michael is, and we have a plan to get him back to the United States." The Patriarch's eyebrows rose at that. He was clueless about why she wanted her closet emptied out. "It's dark here right now, so David is up. Mmhmmm. Right, Michael in the morning…stop, stop. No, no more arguing, that would be a bad idea." She didn't want Nathan to speak about Michael where he could overhear. She smiled evilly, her plan coming together. "Call Frank up there, would you? I'll want him there in a minute, and I'm sure he will want to meet…Stephen." She winked at her companion, who now had a good idea of where they would shortly be.

Ashur entered the room and Stephen pulled the bags together, taking the empty plastic blood bags from around Michael and tossing them in the gun bag. His father looked at him strangely, so Stephen answered the unasked question. "We don't need to leave anything behind that will make the maids curious."

Bethany Anne continued her conversation. "Yes? Frank is there. Good, make sure the lights are on, but you guys get out of my closet. Good, see you in a second." She pointed to a spot on the floor. Ashur walked over to it and sat. "You doing well enough to walk, old man?" She smiled, and Michael decided to simply go with the flow. He didn't have the strength to fight with her. She was a force of nature.

He rolled over slowly, got his legs off the bed, and readied himself to stand. She pointed at Stephen. "You." She pointed to a spot on the floor. "Here. Grab me, okay?"

She walked over to Michael, who struggled to a standing position. Bethany Anne stopped in front of him and looked into his eyes. "You know, I've wanted to slap your face ever since I woke up and your ass wasn't around. For now, you get a reprieve, but I haven't commuted your sentence. Understand?" He suppressed a grin. She didn't seem to be in a joking mood right then, or at least not one that was directed at him.

"What do you want me to do?"

She smiled. "Nothing, but if you pinch my ass, I will kick yours, understand?"

He didn't until she bent down and grabbed him around the waist, lifting him up in a fireman's hold. Now his head was staring right at her ass when she carried him back around the bed. From upside-down, it was pretty fetching.

Stephen reached out with one hand and grabbed the arm she used to hold Michael. She used her other hand to hang onto Ashur. "Let's go, boys."

They disappeared.

CHAPTER FIFTEEN

The closet was pretty close to how she remembered it. She lowered Michael to the floor. Even as pissed off as she was, she wouldn't leave him in such an embarrassing position when he met Nathan and Frank.

He looked around. "Where is this?"

Bethany Anne could hear Stephen introduce himself to the others. She knew that with Nathan's hearing, he would now know Michael was with them. Damn shame she couldn't see his face.

Ashur walked around, sniffing her shoes again. Then he went out of the closet and growled almost immediately. She yelled from the closet, "*Gott Verdammt*, Ashur. Stop your fucking alpha battles. Don't make me bitch-slap you again." He immediately calmed down.

"I swear, it's like going home at Christmas when you're seeing cousins." She held Michael's arm, giving him some support as they walked out of the closet. At least most of his color had returned. "We're in Key Biscayne, Florida. Miami is a few minutes from here."

She had to pause as he stopped walking. "Truly? You just

moved us from Germany to Florida? How?" Stephen took Michael's arm, sensing how tired she was.

Bethany Anne let him take his father. She sat down on a chair, pulled the cooler around, and took a pouch of blood out. "It's called using the Etheric to translocate. You might be able to do it now, and you will certainly be able to after I fix you."

Stephen helped him lie on her bed. Nathan's face was a mask, not revealing anything. She smiled at him, and he finally rolled his eyes and walked over to her. "What happened?"

"David had him in a device that would kill him immediately if he was in a normal body. Don't ask more about that, but suffice it to say, Michael was almost dead. We got him out, and now we're here. I'm sure David and Anton know they don't have him anymore. We'll have to get him healthy again. For the next couple of days, he's going to be healing. He and I have some talking to do, which reminds me—" She looked at him. "Michael, I'm throwing the strictures out the fucking window. That bullshit has fucked up so many lives, it's ridiculous. I've run into a couple of situations where I understand why you did it, but we have to come up with another solution."

He looked at the three men around him and the white dog lying on the floor. She truly *was* a force of nature. He wasn't sure what had happened while he was gone, but it was obvious that the biggest mistake of his life had been allowing David and Anton a free hand, and that his biggest success was sitting right in front of him. She was everything he had hoped and so much more, and he had nothing of himself invested in her success. He spoke after careful consideration, reflecting on his thoughts while in the chamber. "Maybe it was appropriate for another time."

Bethany Anne nodded her head, closing that conversation. She believed that was the most Michael could bend right now. Nathan simply stared, first at Michael, then back at her. The strictures, the rules the UnknownWorld had lived under for hundreds of years, had just been torn apart, and an agreement had been made between the two most powerful beings he knew to forge a new destiny. He sat heavily on the couch, at a loss for words. Frank noticed his reaction and itched to get his notebook. He hadn't known what to expect when Nathan had asked him upstairs, and he wasn't prepared.

Anton's Residence, Buenos Aires, Argentina

At his desk, Anton reached for the ringing phone, one he'd had for three years but never used. It stayed charged, and was one of three he used to communicate should David call him.

He smiled as he answered the phone. "Hello, David. Tell me dear old father is dead."

Anton's face lost its color. "What? How the hell did he get out?" Anton screamed into the phone. "You told me *you had him*. He was *dying at any moment*." Anton stood and paced his office. "Well, fucking find him, you jackass."

He listened for a minute. "Don't worry about that bitch, and stop trying to change the subject. I know where she is, and I have a plan to take her out. You find dear old dad and take care of him — What?"

Anton stopped pacing and sat behind his desk. "That isn't a bad idea. If he goes back home, we will take care of him there. Yeah, I'll put the word into a couple of ears, and they'll watch for him. Dammit, David. I handled my side of this. You know Michael won't forgive me for killing Bill. No, I guess he won't be too pleased with you, either. I'll have to push forward on the serum. No, I'm out of the original. I've got our changed version. No, we had to kill the three most recent subjects. The last one was impressive, though. A real monster. Yeah, I imagine you do need more protection now. Michael won't let this go. You have a target on your back, and you're not willing to leave that stupid castle. It'll be the noose around your neck. Fine, I'll take care of myself, and you take care of yourself. Thanks a lot for being such a worthless fuck. Why you didn't just encase him in cement, I will never understand. Yeah, goodbye to you too." Anton stood and slung the phone as hard as he could. It shattered against the wall, the sound like a gunshot.

There was a knock on his door. "Boss?"

Anton looked at the pieces scattered everywhere and called to the closed door, "Francisco, find someone to sweep up for me. I need to go to the research lab. Call up the car."

"Yes, boss." Footsteps walked quickly away.

The Queen Bitch's Ship *Ad Aeternitatem*

Bobcat, Marcus, and William stood around the frame William had pulled together, with help from the engineering crew. This version of the ship had most of Bobcat's design but very little of Marcus' yet.

They discussed what should work, and with the scientist's insights, what certainly wouldn't work.

William sighed. "This isn't going to fly, is it?"

Marcus shrugged. "We have an untested engine, a nominally untested airframe design, and not a clue exactly how we are supposed to steer yet. The one individual who might be able to help us is in Europe, right?" He looked at Bobcat for verification and got a nod of agreement from him. "Okay, so we have some details, but can't fully bake everything in at this time. Is there any harm in trying it out? What happens if we lose it?"

William snorted. "It sinks?"

Bobcat rubbed his chin. "I don't think Bethany Anne wants us littering the ocean floor with our efforts. We had better put scuttling charges on it. If we lose one of these things, no one should be able to figure out how we have it working by what's left of the parts."

Both men nodded their agreement.

Marcus could understand the secrecy, but as a researcher, he still had trouble with the concept that knowledge which would benefit all mankind was being hoarded. Once he'd had a discussion with Bethany Anne, his desire to release any of the technology early had been squashed, along with his desire to leave and pursue research anywhere else. The woman was fascinating. That she was beautiful never entered Marcus's analysis. Then he had met Gabrielle and walked around in a daze for ten minutes before he recognized the mirth in Bobcat's eyes. He had the good grace to at least blush at his scientific infatuation with the women.

CHAPTER SIXTEEN

Today was not a good day to fly. At least, not if you were the first effort by Bobcat's team.

Captain Wagner put out to sea after retrieving the last of his crew from their shore leave. Once he located an area safely outside the viewing range of other boats, he permitted the team to put the testing vehicle on a pontoon platform they lowered off the side.

Bobcat had the ship move off a quarter of a mile. At first, the craft didn't respond to any commands. It took another hour for the team to communicate with Bethany Anne, who replied with the answers. She apologized for not being there, but she was needed in Miami for a little while longer. She hoped to be there that evening.

They were surprised to find out she was in Miami.

The team decided to move ahead with ideas, incorporating the input they got from Bethany Anne. After three more hours, they tried again.

Everyone who was available went up to the main deck to watch the "amazing liftoff." After they counted down from ten to one, the team hit the button to test the ability to launch on its new gravity-based engine. The cheering was loud for the first few seconds as the triangular-shaped rocket, all of twelve feet long, rose slowly off the pontoon platform. It attained about five feet before Bobcat sent the command to reverse gently and land. Unfortunately, something wasn't wired or coded correctly, and the craft accelerated in the down direction at its maximum velocity. The pontoon boat disintegrated, pieces flying fifty feet into the air as the heavy vehicle went straight through it. Bobcat quickly sent the command to detonate the scuttling charges, and the team saw a large number of bubbles boiling to the surface thirty seconds later. Marcus wondered how far it had gone down in the scant time before Bobcat had hit the command.

One person said they should label that version the X6. Apparently, he was a fan of *Top Gear*, and since the team was Bobcat, Marcus, and William, it seemed fitting to call them Team BMW and name their first failure after the car Jeremy Clarkson had dubbed the "stupidest model BMW ever shipped."

Captain Wagner asked them if there was anything they needed to do about salvaging the rocket. Bobcat told him no, they had the electronic recordings sent before the scuttling charge activated, and there wouldn't be anything of value after they went off. Besides, the water was too deep there to salvage anything.

The captain did have a team retrieve the parts of the pontoon boat. There was no reason to litter, and if anyone wanted to know what had caused the large explosion, at least he would have some physical evidence to concoct a story around.

Down in the workshop, Marcus reviewed the electronic data they had been able to collect. Bobcat came into the room with a bucket of ice and beer. The scientist looked up from his laptop and gave him a curious glance.

The pilot smiled. "Look, if the numbers don't make much

sense, maybe our minds aren't lubricated enough to understand them." Marcus smiled and reached for the first beer of what would become a serious effort to lubricate the hell out of his mind.

William joined them an hour later. He had helped the team retrieve the pontoon boat's remnants and taken some serious shit about the test. One of the engineering guys grabbed a couple of pieces they had retrieved and made a casket to put the pieces in, along with a headstone. He brought a three-foot casket and headstone back from the engineering section. The headstone read, R.I.P. Pontoon 001. We Hardly Knew You. May Pontoon 002 last a little while longer.

William had to suffer the congenial ribbing. Captain Wagner thought it was a hilarious effort, and had the deckhands clear a small area to put up the headstone and coffin. The original jokester asked William how large they should make the graveyard, and he flipped him off as he walked away.

They were well past their third round of lubrication when Marcus came across some numbers that didn't make sense. He swung his laptop around, pushed it across the table to William, and asked him to review it. William was sober. He didn't want Bethany Anne coming in and smelling any alcohol on his breath. It took him about ten minutes to figure out what the problem was. He put his head down on the table and proceeded to beat it slowly against the hard surface.

Marcus and Bobcat stopped in mid-swallow, recognizing that their sober teammate might have figured something out.

William tried to explain what he thought was wrong, but his teammates had lubricated a little too much. They agreed to sleep it off and get back together in the morning. He made sure Marcus was able to get back to his berth. The scientist didn't seem to be able to hold his alcohol any better than he could, while Bobcat could probably have passed a sobriety test so long as they didn't breathalyze him.

. . .

Las Vegas, NV, USA

The microwave dinged, and Tom got up from the table. He brought back the chili con queso he had warmed up and pushed the corn chips in his companion's direction, offering him a few. Jeffrey grabbed a handful, dipped his chip in the cheese, and munched the whole thing in one bite. No double-dipping for him.

He talked around his chewing. "We're getting closer to decision time for the most important aspect of this whole AI project."

Tom grabbed his Wagner's Draft Root Beer and raised it in a toast. "I know. Exciting, right?"

"Pretty momentous. This decision could be great, or it could get us ridiculed for decades. Hell, possibly centuries."

Tom looked at his bottle. "Maybe this is too light? Need something heavier for this discussion."

Jeffrey concurred, so he went to the refrigerator and brought back two Cokes. "Need caffeine for this discussion." They clinked the bottles together, Tom reading the *Hecho en Mexico* written on the side aloud. "Why does this stuff taste so much better than what they bottle in plastic?"

"Real sugar?"

"Maybe, but fuck, it's good."

Jeffrey sighed, put the Coke on the table, and stared at his partner. "Okay, we've put this decision off long enough. Male or female?"

Tom barked out his answer. "Female!"

Jeffrey closed his eyes in weary acceptance. He'd known they would have a disagreement, just not this fast. "Seriously? You want another female AI voice? Aren't SIRI, Cortana, and whatever the hell Google names their voice good enough for you?"

Tom thought for a second. "You know, I don't know what they call their voice command. It's just Google Now, right?"

Jeffrey snorted. "Maybe they call it Julia. I don't know. Stop dodging the question. Do we want to follow everyone else, or strike out on our own?"

"Like they did in *War Games?*" Tom lowered his voice to sound like an electronic computer. "Would you like to play a game?"

Jeffrey stopped to consider his point. "Yes, I see what you mean. Plus, there's Dave from *2001*." He thought about that for a moment. "Seems to me the idea is that a male voice comes across as more menacing."

"Yes, but then you have the female coming across as too mothering. 'Here, let me lock all the doors so you can't leave the house. Then you can't possibly get hurt.'" Tom thought for another second. "Great, she could decide we don't need to leave the planet, and here I wanted to get voice samples from James Earl Jones."

Jeffrey looked at the man, shock on his face. "Darth Vader? You want to give *Darth Vader's* voice to our AI? Hell, why not use what's his face? Hannibal Lecter?"

"Anthony Hopkins."

"Yeah."

Tom looked at him. "What, you want to give him Mickey Mouse as a voice? If you made me squeak all the time, I would definitely choose Team Evil."

Jeffrey calmed down. "This is our world-shattering discussion and hang up? What if ADAM decides to research the actor or actress and model its behavior on the actor or the part?"

"Good point. No psycho killers, agreed?" Tom asked.

"Agreed. What about a scientist, like Einstein?" Jeffrey reached for another chip.

Tom scratched his chin. "I don't know. What if the scientist is just a theoretician? Do those guys ever get any real work done?"

Jeffrey smiled. "Lawyer?"

His colleague's face scrunched in disgust. "Fuck you and the horse you rode in on." He smiled evilly at his boss. "Politician?"

It was Jeffrey's turn to be disgusted. "I hate you. I really, really hate you."

He reached down with his chip, but the cheese was gone.

CHAPTER SEVENTEEN

The two men tabled the question and went back to Building One. Jeffrey brought up the next point of concern. "Okay, we start with a core download to give the system enough information to start figuring out causality and questions to ask. What should we inject second?"

"What have you thought of so far, and what have you rejected?"

"The classics, but which classics? We could go for religious, the Bible, but then the whole Old Testament eye-for-an-eye thing. The Qur'an? No, thank you. Plus, I don't want to take the chance of giving the thing a god complex."

"So, we believe whatever we feed it will start it down the path we want it to go?"

Both men sat there a moment, then Tom looked up. "Why don't we punt?"

Jeffrey returned the man's look. "Call Nathan?" Tom grinned as he reached for his phone.

Nathan answered after two rings. "Yes, Jeffrey? Is ADAM awake already?"

Jeffrey snorted. "No. Actually, we're trying to decide on an input path. Are you on speaker?" He explained what they had considered doing and what their concerns were.

"So you two have done what, moved it up the chain?" Jeffrey could hear the grin in Nathan's voice.

"Pretty much. What are your thoughts?"

Nathan snorted. "Like this is my baby. I'm going to do what great men have done before me."

Tom butted in. "Punt it up the chain?"

"Exactly, and the person I need is in the house both literally and figuratively. I don't think you've met her, but she's the one who runs this whole thing."

"Bethany Anne?" Both men were curious. They knew of her and had been instructed about her concerns, but neither had spoken to her, only with Nathan.

"Yes. One minute." The phone was muted on Nathan's side. It wasn't too long before it was un-muted and Nathan was back. "Jeffrey, Tom, let me introduce you to Bethany Anne. Please give her the same overview you gave me. Maybe the four of us can wrangle this question."

Her voice was pleasant over the speaker. "Hello, Jeffrey. Hello, Tom. I appreciate the opportunity to speak. What's going on?"

Tom liked that the head honcho didn't sound pretentious, but rather down to earth. He explained how ADAM worked, and how what they fed the software could potentially affect the learning path to sentience.

Bethany Anne spoke slowly, like she was forming her thoughts while speaking, "Soooo, let me understand. We feed the software *Mein Kampf,* and we get a digital Hitler?"

Tom explained, "Not exactly, but we'll have to work on the sense of ethics with you eventually. We just don't want to skew the direction unnecessarily."

She replied, "So, we want to give it a broad education. I know this might sound off the wall and trust me, I have a reason, but what about using science fiction? Some of the classics dealt with ethical issues and large societies and the chance to meet alien cultures. The best and worst of humanity are in those stories."

The two men looked at each other, trying to figure out what the software would do with the stories.

"Guys?"

Jeffrey jumped back in. "Sorry, both of us were trying to figure out what the software might do in that situation. You're suggesting we give it stories and let it read about the potentials and results of humanity? What about simply feeding it history?"

This time Bethany Anne snorted. "Because I don't want it to make a judgment on reality. I want to have a discussion about stories. I would have a hard time arguing, say, the stupidity of World War II and the atrocities over the last eighty or so years. I would rather have what-if discussions. Much easier to converse when the facts aren't available."

The talk lasted another hour, but in the end, they decided to follow her lead. They also decided to leave off the last couple of hundred years of history in the core data load.

Ecaterina was sweating, trying to keep up with the Were team. She had taken Bethany Anne up on the chance to train and gone to Pete. Everyone in his group knew she was with Nathan, which guaranteed nothing but courtesy from the new recruits.

Pete, however, wasn't willing to cut her any slack. She felt as though she had gotten out of shape because of muscles that were in revolt and rebellion. Her body was one large sack of pain, completely incapable of following even the simple muscle commands.

Like "Stand up."

She lay on the mat, breathing through her pain, her eyes closed as she tried to get her stomach muscles to stop cramping. Vaguely, she could feel someone step onto the mat with her. If that prick told her she should stop being a whiny human one more time, she would eventually get her muscles under control enough to flip him off. Maybe a "Fuck you" would be enough? That is, if she could stop the effort of breathing enough to waste the time to speak. Back to the flipping-him-off idea, it was.

She opened her eyes to see Bethany Anne's face inches away. "Sh… Sh… Sh… Shit!" She continued panting while Ashur went over to the other Weres, who stopped what they were doing and greeted him like a rock star.

"How's my little out-of-shape Romanian ducky doing today, hmmm?" Bethany Anne straightened up and reached down. Grabbing Ecaterina's outstretched hand, she pulled the woman up off of the floor but had to steady her so she could stay upright.

"Dying. I'm dying here." She continued the effort to get her breathing back under control. "That guy is a sadist. An animal." Bethany Anne looked up to where Ecaterina tried unsuccessfully to point.

"Who, Pete?" Bethany Anne watched as the Romanian girl changed from a sort-of-pointing to a sort-of-thumbs-up gesture. Bethany Anne waved him over. He obliged and smiled as Ecaterina finally arched her back and seemed to get herself under control.

"Yes, my Queen?" Pete greeted her.

Bethany Anne rolled her eyes. Him, too? Ecaterina was still a little sore over the Pepsi incident, but not sore enough to sneak any into Bethany Anne's personal fridge again. For now, they stayed in the galley.

"How is Wonderbutt here doing?" Bethany Anne smiled as Ecaterina tried to get her finger up to flip her off. Finally, she used her left hand to pull up her right middle finger.

Pete watched her while answering the vampire's question. "Pretty fantastic, I would say. I trained her like you asked, making sure she was pushed like a Wechselbalg. For a human, she ranks pretty high. Probably has more stamina than Scott, actually."

Ecaterina's mouth dropped open. She was being trained to the TQB Guards' standard? She didn't know if she should be proud of herself or locate the nearest gun to shoot them both. She would probably shoot her foot off since she couldn't lift the damn thing at the moment.

"What about the other three?"

"Not even close to John or Darryl. John, for obvious reasons, and Darryl because he came back from the sandpit and never stopped pushing himself. Eric has good days and bad, but overall, he's still pretty solid. She'll need another month to catch him."

"Hmmm. Going to have to make sure Gabrielle works him more." Pete grimaced; he hadn't meant to point out that Eric had bad days. It was something that happened only occasionally, but even trying to throw a bone to help him out would get Bethany Anne's attention fixated on the subject. He shrugged. What didn't kill you made you stronger.

Bethany Anne called Ashur over and helped Ecaterina limp back to her temporary room on the *Ad Aeternitatem*. The Weres had been moved in order to get accustomed to the boat they would protect, and all of them had been "sworn in and sworn at." Pete had taken them all aside, individually and collectively. He would allow nothing less than the best they had in them. They were the first cadre, which would be the greatest cadre of Wechselbalg Guardians. They would set the standard every Guardian would need to meet for decades to come.

In Pete's eyes, every one of the new team, from Tim and Joel to Rickie, Joseph, and Matthew, had been measured and found wanting. They would by God measure up, or they would die trying. His expectations for each of them, unique to their own accomplishments to date, were stretch goals. Even Tim found himself working to reach a goal above his own expectations.

To live was to believe. They would be the hardest, fastest, meanest Guardians ever, including those who came after. They would never accept defeat.

Over the next century, the core beliefs Pete instilled and these men accepted became the cornerstone of the Guardians. Even when killed to the last fighter, the enemy would know to expect another group to come to take the position and retrieve their brothers' bodies. Often, if a position was held by the Guardians, the enemy would try their damnedest to go around. Occasionally, they simply decided it wasn't worth it and went elsewhere.

CHAPTER EIGHTEEN

While Ecaterina cleaned up, Bethany Anne worked with Team BMW and heard the first-hand account of what had happened and what they had figured out.

With further insights, which she was able to provide with TOM's input, the team confirmed the information Marcus and William had surmised was the problem. She stayed an extra hour, detailing new technologies for the scientist, who was able to grasp the concepts if not the details. He could not figure out how she was able to review such technical documents and figure out the solutions so quickly.

It wasn't until she admitted she was communicating with a technical representative of the aliens' technology to help them that he understood and then sat down, completely overwhelmed.

"You are speaking to an alien?" He shook his head, trying to come to terms with the reality.

She stared at him, not understanding his seeming inability to accept that she was talking to an alien. "You've seen the spaceship. I've taken you through it. Well, certain parts. You still have a problem believing I'm communicating with an alien?"

He looked up at her. "No! No, I don't doubt you're doing it."

He waved his hands at the blueprints and calculation sheets the men had been working on. "I can tell a lot of this is over your head." He looked back at Bethany Anne, his neck coloring. "No offense intended."

She smiled. "No offense taken, Marcus. I'm not a rocket scientist. I merely know someone who is."

I'm a pilot.

You're an alien whose whole naming structure begins with the answer to a mathematical problem. I think I can throw in "rocket scientist" as the least of your accolades.

Well, since you put it that way, I suppose I am.

Having made TOM feel better about himself, she continued, "If I could—and we really should have figured out a way to do this already—I would give others access to communicate with him. But I warn you," Marcus held her gaze, "he can be a handful and a bit of a smartass."

William snorted. "Sounds like he fits right in."

"Yeah, he fit in just fine. I'm sure he will fit in again."

The men had no clue what she meant by that.

After her conversation with Bobcat's team, she and Ashur took Ecaterina to Bethany Anne's home in Key Biscayne. Exiting the closet, the Romanian was surprised to see a man sleeping in the vampire's bed, even if he did look a little under the weather. She hissed at her, "You've got a man in your bed!"

"Yeah? That's Michael. He got messed up pretty badly in Germany. He's sleeping, getting himself rested up and healed. Right now, he's a sort-of invited guest."

"Yeah, but he is kind of cute in an older man kind of way." Ecaterina stared at him, making no effort to leave the room. Ashur went to the foot of the bed and lay down. Bethany Anne walked back over to stand next to her.

"Yeah, as in much older. You realize he is probably as old as your great-great-great-great…" She stopped for a second, counting on her fingers, "How many years is one generation? I'm not sure how many greats to say, frankly. Fuck it, he's at least a thousand years old."

Michael's voice interrupted them. "And he is trying to sleep, not listen in while two women describe him as an old man." Ecaterina put a hand to her mouth, her eyes flying open.

Bethany Anne smiled. She had monitored his breathing and heartbeat, so she had known he was awake before they left the closet. "Well, don't be a bump on a log then, codger-boy. The blood will be here tonight, and we'll get you back in action soon. So rest up and let your betters talk about you while we pretend you can't hear us, okay?"

Michael opened one eye and stabbed her with a hard gaze. "Wait till I am better. I'll put you over my knee—"

Bethany Anne interrupted him. "And probably lose your concentration while staring at my ass, you lecherous old coot." Ecaterina's eyes grew impossibly larger, her head jerking around to stare at Bethany Anne, not believing what she was hearing.

"It is a chance I will have to take, isn't it?"

Bethany Anne only harrumphed and pulled the other woman to the door. "He really does need his sleep and blood. I probably shouldn't be around to make his blood pressure rise like this anyway."

Michael's eye closed and his lips broke into the slightest grin. It was the first time he had scored any points against the fiery woman.

Stare at her ass, indeed.

After shutting the door behind her, Bethany Anne started toward the stairs. Ecaterina asked her, "Why did you need me here?"

"One, you're becoming useless without getting your Nathan injection." The Romanian slapped her arm but then rubbed her hand, realizing she wouldn't hurt the woman that way. Bethany Anne pointed at her. "See? You're already so wound up that any little thing sets you off."

She smiled at Ecaterina, who finally simply went with the flow and whispered, "Damn right! We will have to get a room at a hotel or risk damaging your sensitive ears." They went down the stairs.

"God, I only wish it was just you two. I'm more worried about—" They arrived at the bottom of the steps as the front door opened. Lance and Patricia entered, both smiling. "Speak of the devils. Patricia, let me introduce you to Ecaterina." The two ladies exchanged greetings, but Bethany Anne saw the older woman eyeball Lance when she realized the beautiful woman was the Ecaterina Lance would occasionally mention. It was probably a good thing Patricia had the good manners not to kick him in the shin right there in front of his daughter.

Fortunately, Nathan was close behind them, and the two gave a very public display of affection. Bethany Anne stepped between them and almost physically pushed them apart. "Hey! I've got to get back to talk with Pete. You two make nice for those of us with sensitive eyeballs."

"Damn right," Lance added.

The vampire spoke over her shoulder. "Not you. I'm pretty sure your DNA doesn't have any sensitivity in it."

"Ha! That DNA is in you too." Patricia elbowed the General.

"And it has been refined by alien technology to remove all horrible aspects. That was probably why it took six months to fix me."

TOM sniggered in her mind.

"Ecaterina, I need you to work with Patricia and get her up to date on what you know. She is a master at handling things and has decades—"

Patricia interrupted, "Hey, now!"

"Of experience. Good Lord, am I going to leave here without another interruption?" She let the faintest red glow enter her eyes as she stared at them. Her father wasn't bothered, but it got the right reaction from the other three. Lance was smart enough to keep his mouth shut. "So, get together with her, and I'll get you back for your workout tomorrow morning after you spend the night here, for obvious reasons." She shook a finger in Ecaterina's face. "Don't give me any lip about your workouts. If you didn't make it through them, boy-toy here wouldn't have signed off on your joining the covert group. Before you get your panties in a twist, he *is* the covert group lead, so you had to pass before he gave approval. I'm happy to say you did."

She stepped away from the two affectionate individuals and kissed her dad on his cheek. "Looking good, old man, looking good. Talk tomorrow about the businesses?" Lance nodded. Michael hadn't wanted anything back in his control. He rather enjoyed how Bethany Anne had taken over. But Lance was using as much time as Michael would provide to come to grips with the vast holdings. Frank was constantly under the vampire's feet until Bethany Anne told him to go work at a Starbucks or she was going to find and burn his notebooks.

He left in a hurry, carrying considerably more notebooks than usual. Stephen went with him to experience more of the United States. She figured Frank would find a bank and rent a safety deposit box. He really was passionate about acquiring information, and the vampire was happy to talk to him. The old man was in heaven.

Apparently, Ivan and Claudia were doing okay. Claudia was healing after the deaths of so many in her life, and Ivan made sure everything with the house, and Claudia, were taken care of.

Bethany Anne went back upstairs to fetch Ashur. She knocked once and entered. The dog stood, and she shut the door and walked to her closet. This time, Michael was actually asleep.

She shut the door, and the two of them stepped back to the *Ad Aeternitatem* and the special room reserved for her comings and goings. Once there, she told Ashur to stay put, but left the door open in case something happened and he needed to leave. She didn't want him involved when she was sparring with Pete's team. Satisfied he'd obey, she headed toward the gym. One of Todd's Marines caught up to her before she'd gone thirty feet and stayed a respectful five feet behind her. Those guys were getting as bad as John's clique. She waved behind her to let him know she was aware of him and not trying to be inconsiderate.

When she entered the Weres' training area, she moved to the side, allowing the Marine to step in with her. Joel was squared off against Rickie, whose sarcastic wit worked overtime as the two of them tore into each other. When Pete finally called it, Joel had broken his opponent's wrist. He grimaced in pain but didn't let even a squeak come out of his mouth. The Marine stared as the broken wrist started to heal itself and Rickie tested it.

He leaned toward Bethany Anne, forgetting for a moment that Todd had told him to be seen but not heard. "They are some tough sonsabitches, aren't they?"

She whispered back, "They are, but they are also a little sensitive about their moms being called bitches so I wouldn't use that term freely. Mmmkay?"

The man straightened and nodded his head once sharply.

The fight over, she walked into the group and got Pete's attention. She looked at all six guys. They had come a long way in just a few days, although they had been balls-to-the-wall days only Wechselbalg could do. Pete had them sleeping for four and training hard for twenty. He had done something amazing there, and she was glad he had asked for the chance. "Okay, you pussies feeling pretty good about yourselves?" She saw Tim straighten his back, incensed by her rudeness. Matthew let it roll right off him, and Joseph's eyes narrowed, trying to determine the play she was making.

Pete didn't let it faze him. She had called her personal guards much worse and more often. "Why? What do you have in mind?"

"A little Were-on-vampire action." Tim tried, but couldn't control his snort. She gave him a small smile. He would pay for that reaction.

Pete asked, "How do you want to play it?"

She looked around. The mat was twelve feet wide and twenty feet long. "I'll leave and give you two minutes to come up with a game plan. After the two-minute mark, I want you to 'protect' the…" She picked up a towel, ripped it down the middle, and tied the two pieces back together. "Flag." She tossed it into the middle of the mat. "That will have to be protected, and yes, you have to leave it there until I come into the room. Then, you can do whatever you want with it. The only other rule is that you have to stay off the mat until I enter. Agreed?"

When she got nods all around, she walked out, pulling the Marine with her. He looked over his shoulder. "What, can't I watch?"

Bethany Anne shook her head. "No. The first time is always embarrassing. They need to keep this one in the group. Unless you want to take Pete on for the right to watch?" She shut the door. He turned a little white and shook his head. "Got a timer?" He nodded and pulled up his watch to set the alarm, and she waited.

She considered moving into the room through the Etheric but decided that might give them something to whine about. It was important to make sure they got the message—again—about how dangerous Nosferatu could be. When the Marine called time, she dropped into vamp mode and pushed the door open. Thankfully, no one had been stupid enough to wait behind the door or they might have become paste. She was surprised that one of the guys was in his wolf form, just off the mat.

That was smart. They were going to try to play keep away from the vampire. What a cute little Were game. She had just stepped inside when the werewolf moved toward the towel.

She figured Pete would have at least two of them ready to ambush her, expecting her to move directly toward the mat to save the flag. Instead, she turned to her right and sped up, running into, onto, and then over Tim, who had been there to try to grab her. She cold-cocked him in the temple with her elbow for good measure. Make fun of her sexually without permission? No fucking way, even if it was a normal reaction. Unfortunately, he would miss the rest of this fight, since he would be out on the floor. Sucked to be him. She increased her pace a little, keeping her speed within the range of a very fast Nosferatu but not anywhere near her top speed. Spotting a ten-pound dumbbell, she reached over to grab it, twisting around to offset the sudden weight. The werewolf was halfway to the flag. That was fine. It wasn't like it was a problem if they moved it.

She saw Rickie step out from behind a large box with a six-foot-long bar used for free weights in his hands. As he emerged, she tossed the barbell toward his head. His eyes grew huge when he realized how much weight was coming at him, and he tried to duck. Her hands were now free, so she slid between his legs, grabbed them, and pulled him down behind her. She flinched at the sudden banging of the metal bar but didn't wait to see how he made out. Unfortunately, she had lost the barbell. She could have caught up to it, but not without using her best speed. Instead, she let it hit the far wall. Captain Wagner would hear that crash up on the bridge for damn sure.

Two down, one in werewolf form, and one she was sure of on the other side of the door. Bethany Anne darted straight toward the mat, then realized those crafty bastards would probably try to get the flag out of the room. She had to hand it to them. If that was the plan, it was a smart one.

A second later, another werewolf tore out of a cubby, running toward the door and gaining speed.

Gott Verdammt! She changed her angle to move back toward the door. Sure enough, the first werewolf grabbed the flag and made a beeline to where the second was already running toward the door. Passing, the first wolf handed the flag to the second. It was beautifully executed, if a little late.

She saw Joel on the other side of the door, heading in her

direction. That probably meant one of the wolves was Matthew and one Joseph. Pete wouldn't be a runner. She glanced around, trying to figure out where he might be.

With a bad feeling, she decided to look back at the door. She spotted Pete, all in black and behind it to the right. Oh, fuckity fuck. If she allowed Joel to slow her down, there was a chance they could get the flag out. If it didn't become a win—because she would chase their asses down—it would be a moral victory. She wouldn't allow a moral victory. She just didn't feel very moral at the moment.

Coming up on Joel, she reached out for the arm he used to try to stiff-arm her. Pivoting, she used his momentum to bring him back around and flung him ass-over-appetite into the second werewolf. Both hit the wall with a resounding and painful crash. Joel was out as well, and it looked like the wolf was pretty messed up.

Four down, one wolf and Pete to go. The first took off toward the mess of arms and furry legs to get the flag, and Bethany Anne headed to the door.

Pete stepped out when it was obvious the plan was a bust. She wouldn't tell him how close they had gotten for a while. She didn't want to hurt him, but she wouldn't go easy on his training, either. The problem was that in his human form, he was superior to humans but inferior to vampires. Since they didn't have many weapons for this exercise, he was actually without many options.

In her vamp state, she had plenty of time to think.

TOM

Yes?

She acted as if she would head toward the flag. Pete's eyes narrowed, and he changed his direction to intercept her.

Why do the Wechselbalg only change between man and beast? We have stories that there is a middle form. A man-beast, if you will.

It could be that the group which infected them didn't have

the scientific abilities, or it could be they didn't have a way to learn how to do that.

So, you don't think it is impossible?

No, I don't think it is impossible, but I can't tell for sure unless we research the idea.

She took a last step, making sure Pete was committed to running as hard as he could before she broke left, heading straight for the door. His eyes widened in alarm.

So if we test one, we might find a cure?

You mean a cure for their condition or a cure to help them stop in man-beast form?

Well, I guess both. Maybe some don't want this situation, but I was really discussing the option to give them a better fighting chance. Going up against vampires in their human forms doesn't work very well.

Bethany Anne made it to the door and slammed it shut, jumping to the side and pushing off the wall while turning around in the air. Pete ran to get back to the door and she grabbed an arm, flinging him faster in the direction he was going. He made a resounding smack when he hit the wall, and she heard him sliding down. She didn't think he was unconscious, but she doubted he was thinking clearly at that moment.

The first wolf had grabbed the flag and taken a few steps toward the door when he realized Pete wouldn't get up to open it for him, and he lacked opposable thumbs.

He bit down hard on the flag, not willing to give in to the inevitable, and braced for impact. She admired his tenacity. There was no backing down in any of this team. She wished she knew if there were any sensitive spots on a wolf's jaw that would cause them to involuntarily open it. This would certainly hurt the wolf a lot more than it would hurt her.

Reaching him, she leaned down and slowed some, not wanting to fling him very far. She turned and swung the wolf a few feet higher in the air, wanting to see how many times she could cause him to flip before he landed. He tried to arch his back, seeking some way to get his feet under him before he crashed into the floor. Somewhere around flip number five, the flag left his jaws and went flying. She used both arms to catch the wolf, getting scratched up when the nails sliced through her wrist. In the same motion, she rolled him like a bowling ball across the mat in the opposite direction from the flag. She sauntered over to the flag and picked it up, then went to Pete, who looked at her dazedly from the floor, a nasty gash healing on his forehead.

She looked a little closer at the gash. "You should probably get that looked at. Talk to me after your AAR, okay?" He nodded. She opened the door and stepped out, closing it behind her.

Thirty minutes later, Pete came by the hold where TOM's craft was berthed. She was talking to Todd when he arrived. The Marine looked him up and down and cocked his head. "You don't look good. Everything okay?"

Pete pointed at Bethany Anne. "We played Capture the Flag and got our asses handed to us. Tim is still trying to get his wits back. What did you do to him?"

Bethany Anne smiled. "Thou shalt not snort."

"Yes, he understood that was a bad response when it happened. I'm not sure he'll remember anything at the moment."

"Well, he was in the way. Maybe I hit him with an extra elbow?" Todd winced. He had heard how Bethany Anne had used a forearm to knock a werewolf out once from Nathan. The Were nodded. He had thought it might be an object lesson. Well, Tim seemed like a fast learner, so Pete expected the one time would be enough.

She pointed her thumb at the craft. "Here, come with me." She punched in the access codes. Todd was never sure if she would show up and go in the front door, or if he would be standing guard and she would suddenly exit after transporting in.

The two of them went inside and the door shut. Pete looked around. "Seems tiny."

"Yes, TOM's people are shorter than us. I want to show you the Pod-doc area." She took him into the white room with the medical Pod in the middle of the floor and waved at the machine. "This, as you know, is what started vampires. It's what was used to change Michael, and a thousand years later, it was used to change me. It fixed Gabrielle's sensitivity to the sun, and was used to modify Ashur."

Pete shifted his gaze from the Pod to Bethany Anne. "It can handle non-humans?"

She nodded. "According to TOM, it's all about genetics. It can read DNA and figure out what the code is supposed to do. During our little game, I thought about how you guys are at a disadvantage against vampires. For weapons, you have to be in human form. For ultimate speed and to have claws and teeth, you have to be in your werewolf form. I asked TOM if there was a way you guys can have a middle form."

"Historical stories suggest there were Wechselbalg who could do that, but it was lost centuries ago," Pete told her.

"That's my theory. I think the basics are there, but either the knowledge is not, or the genetic changes that allow you guys to change have mutated. Something is different."

He shrugged. "Beyond me, and I don't know of anything offhand. You want me to jump in?"

She smiled. "Am I that transparent?"

He grinned back. "Pretty much, yes. When you get an itch for something that doesn't make sense, you use a large tool to beat it until something comes up. When that tool doesn't work, you get a bigger one. You want to know why we can't change, and it matters for our safety. Mind you, I know we will be more powerful and dangerous, and that works perfectly for my Guardians. But your first thought was that we're at a disadvantage against vampires, so I take it you're concerned with our safety first and our abilities next."

"That's…fair, I guess."

"So, want me to jump in? How long will this take?"

TOM?

Just to run an analysis? Probably a few hours. He *is* human, so we have most of the details already. The Pod only has to figure out a few mutations, not an entire sequence like on Ashur.

"Have you back in time for dinner. At the latest, breakfast?"

Pete shrugged. "Who's going to take care of my team?"

"Who would you suggest?"

"Well, Tim, if he wasn't working on getting over a concussion. Probably Matthew next."

"Okay, I'll do it that way. If Tim is still out of it, I'll have Matthew handle it until we get you back."

Pete nodded. Bethany Anne explained he had to strip. It wasn't a big deal to him since werewolves stripped all the time to change. She pulled out the little bench, and he folded his clothes and dropped them there. As he climbed into the doc, she assured him, "I'll be here when the tests are done. Get in, put your arms by your side, and close your eyes. You'll fall asleep and wake up seconds later. Piece of cake."

Her "piece of cake" comment had the opposite effect on him than he presumed she was going for.

Once the Pod-doc was working, she left and told Todd no one was to go near the craft for the next few hours. He nodded, and she went to help Pete's team. Tim was tracking just fine by the time she got there. She told them Pete was working on a project with her, and he wouldn't be available until that evening.

They talked for a little while, going through the game and how she had worked it from her side. She admitted they'd had a really good plan, but if they had gotten the flag out the door, she would have tracked them down. Matthew had been wolf number two. He explained he would have run out of the room and then jumped off the back of the boat. Wechselbalg could tread water for a very long time.

Startled, she stared at the guy for a few seconds and then smiled. "That was damn devious. You guys are fucking nuts, and I mean that as a compliment." The guys high-fived each other. They felt good about Pete's plan and their effort, and really good about surprising Bethany Anne so thoroughly.

She left them when they started to figure out how they might best her next time.

CHAPTER NINETEEN

Bethany Anne was back inside the medical room on TOM's ship, sitting next to Pete's clothes. She was trying to come to grips with what TOM was telling her.

You mean someone from your group changed them too?

Well, not my group. I think it was one of the Seven. The missing piece is in him. He can change to a man-beast form, but it'll be hard to control.

How did they get here? Are they still here? What a fucking mess. You Kurtherians are worse than a soap opera. That's what you guys are, a Gott Verdammt *space opera. It's like twelve siblings going around the galaxies stirring up shit.*

TOM stayed quiet.

She exhaled loudly.

What's the chance of him ever changing if we don't modify him?

Not high. The nanocytes in his body are a different type. Maybe a slightly older version than yours? They aren't as sophisticated.

Well, for not being so sophisticated, they sure seem to work efficiently with the Etheric power load.

Yes, well, that's true. I'm not positive how that works, and it would take putting the computer back into the ship to possibly figure it out.

No. Fucking. Way. I am not going through that shit again.

I wasn't suggesting it, merely explaining what it would take to understand the energy transfer and how it is accomplished. It would mean no more blood drinking.

TOM, you can be an ass, you know that? You really want to know how this works? Well, have you considered that Ashur might be a clue?

How do you mean?

How much energy do you think I pull through him when we go traipsing across the world? It has to be a huge spike. What makes him able to pull it when I can't? The Wechselbalg all pull a huge amount of power, but they turn into a canine. At least, I think wolves are canines. There are bears, too. Well, okay, animals. Have you considered the animal side of this yet?

In a word? No.

Fine, work on that angle before you start trying to bribe me with not drinking blood. For now, I've got Ashur the Wonder Battery—not that I would use that phrase around him.

He does seem remarkably smart.

Are you sure you don't know what happened to him?

I told you he would be smarter. Dogs are already early-childhood smart. He might have gone late childhood?

How late? Are we talking out of diapers, out of cribs or, God forbid, teenagers? Because a hundred and whatever pounds of snarly teenager with teeth is not my idea of fun.

Well, he hasn't required much in the way of blood.

Yeah, but he eats bags of dog food, not to mention he cleans every plate someone leaves unattended in the mess. He should weigh five hundred pounds by now.

She stood up.

This isn't getting us anywhere. I have the answer, but it just leads to more questions. I don't know what to do with Pete—change him, or keep him as is.

What would Pete want?

Balls to the wall, I bet. He's putting everything into the Guardians. If he could learn something to make them even more badass, I'm sure he would do it. However, this isn't Pete's decision, it's mine. Why am I doing it? If I knew he could control it, I would do it in a heartbeat.

What about any of the others?

Oh, God, no! I only trust Pete in this situation. I don't need a Tim with this ability if we don't know how it is suppressed or how they control themselves. Tim is bad enough without Hulk urges.

Hulk urges?

Big green guy, grows into a mountain of muscle. Wears purple pants for who knows what reason. What was the original setting, can you tell?

Yes, it was supposed to turn on when under a substantial amount of duress.

Kind of like a Berserker. Well, if Pete was ever in that situation, I can imagine it would be a good time to have a chance to change things. How long will it take?

Just a few minutes to change the settings. I don't know how long for it to change throughout his body. I would guess a couple of days at the minimum.

Will he still have his mind when this happens?

Where would it go?

No, I mean will he have his ability to think when in this state? Will he be able to tell friend from foe?

I can't tell from what we have seen so far, but I would be very surprised if he couldn't.

Why is that?

Because the Seven weren't known for wasting their people by having them kill each other unnecessarily.

Oh, trust an enemy to be smart about it, huh?

Yes.

She tried to figure out all the angles and finally went with the one she trusted the most—her gut.

Okay. Let's make it happen.

She hoped she wouldn't regret it later.

An hour later, she was back there and cracked the case for Pete. He blinked his eyes, getting his bearings.

"How did it go? Did you learn anything?" He sat up, shaking his head.

She pulled on his arm, and he hopped off the bed. "Yes. Get dressed, hooligan." He grabbed his clothes and complied.

"Not only do we have a good idea who was responsible for creating the Wechselbalg—"

Pete interrupted her. "No fucking way!"

"Way. Now shut up and stop interrupting me, or you will be the first and last of your kind." He shut up. "The guilty party is another of the Kurtherian clans."

Pete almost let another comment slip but caught himself in time.

"Unfortunately, not the good guys. Wechselbalg do have a latent ability to allow them to change to a man-beast form." She had his full attention, and she could tell he was anxious to ask questions. "But it comes with a price. So, knowing the original intent comes from a race of inimical aliens—"

She noticed his desire to interrupt again. "Fine, what is it?"

"Inimical?"

"Hostile."

"Why didn't you just say 'hostile?'"

"I'm trying to teach the wolf a new word, now shut up again." Pete smiled at her. "So, back to the basics: bad aliens make changes to humans for their own purposes. You guys have a switch to change into raging man-beasts full of destructive power. Should we try it out?"

"I have a choice?"

"Of course, you have a choice."

"Then let me back in and let's do this. No time like the present."

"Ah, no need."

Pete stopped buttoning his shirt. "You already flipped the switch, didn't you?"

"Well, I had a discussion with TOM, and we agreed it would probably be what you wanted."

"You discussed my future with an alien—an alien related to the ones who created Wechselbalg—and came up with 'change him already?'"

Bethan Anne smiled, popped the Pod-doc, and pointed to it. "Want me to change it back?"

Pete put his hands up, waving her off. "No, no. I'm very good exactly like I am."

"Really? Because with as much shit as you're giving me, I'm pretty sure you are about to either get another dose of the doctor, or you'll be treading water for a really, really long time."

Pete grimaced. "Matthew spilled the plan, didn't he?"

"Not so much spilled it as we had an after-action review. You had an amazing plan."

He tried to fish for information. "Would it have worked?"

"Against a Nosferatu? Possibly. No, probably. They are more desire-driven than intelligence-driven. On me? No, but I wasn't trying to be me, so yeah, you guys might have pulled off a win. That was some seriously creative shit your team came up with. I'm impressed."

Pete looked at the Pod-doc, the top still open. "Um, are we good here?" He waved at the Pod-doc.

"I don't know. Do you think we are? I wouldn't want you second-guessing my second-guessing again. As in, ever." She stared frankly at the young man.

"No, no, I'm really good." Pete looked down, trying to school his face and stop it from betraying his mirth.

She closed the Pod-doc. "Good, now finish getting dressed. The short answer is the change can happen anytime, but it is generally duress-driven."

"Like, stress-driven?"

"No, I think it's a more action-oriented or highly emotional state change, if you want to get a little more clinical." She adjusted the controls on the Pod-doc to reset. This time, TOM didn't have to direct her.

"And if I want a more simplistic answer?" He finished tying his shoes.

"Don't get really, really mad. People might not like you very much when you get mad."

"Ah, got it." They left the room together.

Todd confirmed everyone was out as Pete went to join his team. Bethany Anne translocated over to the *Polarus* after she had grabbed Ashur.

CHAPTER TWENTY

Before Bethany Anne was able to sleep for the night, John cornered her and gave her a piece of his mind. In this case, it was a short and abrupt diatribe about her "tearing off across Europe" without him…uh, without the team. She decided to ignore the clarification. She knew where he was coming from, but couldn't promise she wouldn't ever do it again.

They sat down at the conference table and had a frank talk about what she could and couldn't do. Right now, she was able to pop easily between Miami and the boats, but she wasn't sure how many she could take or how far she could go. She had moved two humans and Ashur a couple of miles easily enough and then moved them all to Miami. The problem was getting everyone to touch.

John considered what she'd said. "What happens if they aren't touching you?"

TOM?

Well, technically, you could do it, although the power needs go up, directly correlated to how far away from you they are. Those who actively touch you require the minimum amount of energy.

What happens if I run out of juice?

When? I don't think you could partially pull a person into the Etheric, but our race rarely took chances, so I don't have anything to support my assumptions. If you run out of juice on the way to the other side? Good question. Either you lose people, or everyone simply stops in between. If you should lose your connection to them, I imagine they would be stranded. I can't believe too many humans left in that dimension would last very long, either physically or mentally. It would be bad.

She answered him finally. "I'm not comfortable trying that yet. The farther away, the more energy I need, and while Ashur hasn't let me down yet—" She was interrupted by a woof from her bedroom. She rolled her eyes and continued, "I don't know how much energy it is truly safe to pull through him. TOM says the amount of energy could go up exponentially with distance. So, how many people can we deal with? I have to hold onto Ashur."

John was quiet for a moment. It was obvious she couldn't take the whole team with her every time. "How did you take Stephen and Michael to Miami?"

Bethany Anne stood and went to the refrigerator, bending over to make sure she could see into the back. Satisfied no Satan-spawned beverages were hiding, she pulled a Coke out. "You want anything?"

He didn't, so she closed the door and came back to the table. "I slung Michael over my shoulder and held Ashur with one hand, and Stephen grabbed my arm, I think. Well, that's what I remember. We were a little busy."

John latched onto that statement. "So, it's fine if people grab you?"

Bethany Anne gave him the fisheye and he blushed, putting up his hands. "Not what I meant."

She continued eyeing him while his face got redder. She

finally let him off the hook and smiled. "I know. I'm just kicking you while you're down. I wanted to see if you could lighten up a little. I know my trip to Romania upset you, but I wasn't about to try going that distance and put you guys in danger." She held up a hand. "Don't. Just don't. I will never do it, no matter how much you complain, okay?" He finally nodded. "Yes, I suppose I could put out one arm and maybe the five of you could grab hold, but it isn't something I'm happy trying out yet, okay?"

That was the best John could hope for, so he took the small victory when he could. They finished talking about inconsequential things. Bethany Anne asked whether he had had a chance to hook up with anyone on either of the boats, and he pulled up his empty wrist to stare at it. "Oh. Look at the time, got to run. Great talking to you and everything, boss, but someone is calling my name." Nothing happened, so John raised his voice, "I said, *someone* is calling my name."

Eric's voice came from the other room. "John, come quickly. Someone is calling your name." She smiled as he waved and fled the room. She got up from the table as she heard John smack Eric and tell him, "You ass." Eric's laughter followed her into her room as she shut the door.

The next morning, Ecaterina was surprised when Bethany Anne came out of the closet, John and Eric with her.

John nodded at the startled Romanian as Eric exclaimed, "That was badass, boss! You beat the Disney World rides hands down—oof!" He bent over a little, holding his stomach. Ecaterina assumed Bethany Anne hit him.

Bethany Anne smiled at her. "Feeling better?"

She was up for it today. "Yes, filled to capacity, and slept very well." Making sure there would be no misinterpretation, she added, "Dinner was nice too." The vampire smirked. The Ecaterina of old was back.

The Romanian woman asked for her phone, telling her she needed to add a couple of phone numbers. Bethany Anne handed it to her.

The vampire headed to the door. "Everyone ready downstairs?" She noticed the vampire wasn't lying on her bed. "Where's Michael?"

Ecaterina turned to walk out of the suite with her, the two men following them. "He grabbed an SUV and went for breakfast. He also said he needed different clothes. He's a changed man, from what Nathan told me." They started down the stairs.

Bethany Anne was confused. "Changed how? How much can you change a guy who's lived a thousand years? I can't change my own—" The front door opened and Lance came in. "Dad. How are you this lovely morning?" He certainly looked younger. He had gotten a high-and-tight across the top since his hair was coming back in dark again.

Lance smiled. "Hi, baby. I see you have the terrible twosome with you this morning." Lance preferred his daughter to have protection and loved how it annoyed her at the same time. As a parent, you got your kicks where you could.

Bethany Anne's smile brightened a notch. "Yup, and you will be happy to know they're staying here for a while." His smile dropped. "What? Why?"

The General closed the door, so Bethany Anne grabbed his arm in hers and moved them all to the living room. "Because I'm popping between here and the ships so much, Gabrielle, Dan, and John prefer to have the protection at both locations. Plus, *you* aren't protected here."

Lance followed, but felt his freedom slipping quickly away. "I've got Nathan here. He's a hell of a guard, right?" He looked over his shoulder to see if John would jump in to help him. The look on the Guard's face told him he was screwed. He turned, resigned to having shadows again. Dammit!

John and Eric both smirked after the General turned away. John was more worried about Bethany Anne when she was there. She made a good point that they would have duties on the home front if she was back on the boats.

She looked around. "Where's Stephen?" Frank sat on a couch, typing on his laptop.

Ecaterina answered, "He went with Michael."

Bethany Anne went into the kitchen to grab some water, "Really? I wonder how that's going?" She came back into the living room and sat down on the loveseat. "Where's Patricia?"

Lance sat next to her. "On the phone with some old contacts. We might have a way to get the base early."

She leaned forward. "Really? That would be freaking fantastic. God, that would make things easier right now."

He nodded. "Yes. It seems a multinational corporation has been making quiet but very interesting inroads with both senators and congressmen, especially one from the great state of Florida. Since the company is willing to help some of the military who have family in the area and are paying tax revenues, there is a lot of political desire to make this happen. The company is willing to pay a twenty-million-dollar bonus if the closing of the base and movement of military personnel happens quickly. They have also agreed to help significantly and asked for a ninety-nine-year lease, so that was the last hurdle. Should the government go to war, they have the right to reinstate parts of the base."

Bethany Anne's eyes grew frosty. "Dad, that could be a liability. You *know* we are going to war."

Lance smiled. "Well, the legal language requires the war to be with a known terrestrial country. It can't be with anything less than Russia, China, or a coalition having a minimum of one million soldiers. That will, in fact, preclude them from grabbing the base if we go to war with say, Iraq, again. Plus, since we lease the base, they would lose the income and have to mobilize everyone back. Once we have the base and everyone is happy, I'll go back and renegotiate, but it gets us the base quickly."

She thought about the downsides and had to agree this was probably the best solution right now. Satisfied, she leaned back again. "Well, that's good news, but make sure we have a bolt hole. I don't want some trumped-up agency knocking on the front door and telling us to leave everything and get out. I want there to be doors we can use to get out the back with our stuff."

Frank looked up from his typing and grinned. "Not very trusting, are you?"

"Hell, no! I've worked for the government, remember? I put away some of those creeps. I trust them to either be altruistic, which has its own set of problems, work for themselves, or work for the money. I've never found them to be very pragmatic unless there was a political reason for it. So, no. Speaking of that, how is our Congressman Pepper?"

"Helpful, at least so far. We haven't asked too much, and he is careful about making demands of us, with all the dirt Frank has on him. He's talked to Anton but told him off, so we think we have him bought and paid for. Anton invited him to an event he's having in two weeks, but Pepper told him he was stuck in meetings and couldn't make it."

Bethany Anne's eyes narrowed. "Hold on, did you say Anton is having an event? Why is this the first I'm hearing about this?"

Nathan chose that moment to arrive. His hair was an unruly mess, but he looked pretty relaxed. He went over to Ecaterina and gave her a kiss. "What did I miss?"

Bethany Anne answered for her. "You missed telling me Anton is having a party." Nathan sat down next to his lady love.

"Yes, Bethany Anne, Anton is having a party. I told them not to tell you until I had more to go on. With Michael here, I have more information and the beginning of a plan. The problem—" The front door opened again. Bethany Anne could hear Michael and Stephen talking as the door shut, discussing fashion. This was becoming a damned reality tv show.

She put up a hand to stop Nathan from continuing and turned to Lance. "Is Patricia coming in anytime soon?"

Her father shook his head. "Unlikely. She had a list of over twenty names. She should be busy for at least a couple of hours."

Michael and Stephen walked into the room, both dressed fashionably for the Miami weather. Stephen looked good as always, but Michael was a significant step above. He had lost his age, and a very scrumptious thirty-year-old smiled as he walked in. This man would get jumped if he walked into a bachelorette party anytime soon.

"Hello, you guys. Take a seat. I'm just getting up to speed on what you have all been making happen without telling me."

Stephen grabbed two chairs from the kitchen and gave one to Michael, who was remarkably calm and seemed to be enjoying life. Bethany Anne noticed that even Nathan didn't shy away from the man as he reached over to shake his hand. Something was going on behind her back. That they were all happy meant something. She just didn't know what yet.

The two vampires sat next to each other. Bethany Anne was having a hard time figuring out what was going on, so she looked around the room.

Stephen and Michael talking and looking relaxed together. Weird, check.

Nathan shaking Michael's hand and not flinching. Cold day in hell, check.

Ecaterina and Nathan happy with each other. Well, at least one thing was nice and didn't give her ominous feelings… Wait a minute.

She speared Nathan with a finger. "You prick! You're sure you know how to nail Anton and don't want me to be part of it."

Stephen's large grin let her know she was heading in the right direction. Michael's face gave nothing away, and Nathan just winced.

He started to protest. "Not exactly. It's simply that we have a good idea of what Anton is going to do, and we think we should discuss options."

"I'm listening." She sat back, her arms crossed in front of her.

"Anton has this party, which I was about to tell you. The thought is to use Pepper's invitation, and you be his plus one. Once you get in, Pepper will leave again. You can deal with Anton. We'll have Killian and Ecaterina at two separate locations with views into his house."

Bethany Anne's voice was a little short. "You know where he lives?" She was already considering getting a plane ticket and flying down there right now. Make that three tickets, and one for a dog. Damn, she would have to have Paul Jameson come get her. Fuck, she couldn't make this happen fast no matter what.

Nathan turned to Frank, who spoke while he turned his laptop around. "We have the location of the party. I don't think it's his main house, so right now, no. The man is very security-conscious, so I highly doubt he is there except for the party."

There went her need to call Paul right away. That was when she noticed Ecaterina smiling, still holding Bethany Anne's phone, which she hadn't returned.

She smiled back. Sneaky bitch. Her team knew her too well.

Michael chose to interrupt her efforts to go kill Anton right then. "Bethany Anne, have you ever wondered why I didn't kill Anton a long time ago?"

She turned back to him. "Hell, yes. That prick needed to be gone a long time ago, and certainly after World War II."

The vampire leaned forward in his chair. "Granted. I didn't know about his actions in World War II or I might have tracked him down—or I might not have." Frank turned his laptop back around and started typing while Michael talked. This was history talking.

Like, literal history. The man should be in a museum answering questions. She smirked to herself. Maybe she could get him to do something like Chippendales. Oh, shit. Her face locked in place. She was trying desperately to not laugh out loud at her own thought. Michael strutting his stuff at Chippendales for the ladies. God, that was too much! Time halted as she willed herself to stop thinking about the subject. *Anton, Anton. Need to focus on killing Anton.*

Michael caught the facial expression and raised an eyebrow but continued. He assumed she was pissed, but it was better to not ask. "The problem is that when you kill him, you will have a major uprising among the Forsaken in all of South America. He is the lesser of two evils."

Her face carefully controlled, she asked, "So, kill him, and potentially hundreds or thousands die due to vampire politics as others try to take control?"

Michael nodded. "Yes. That is the sum of it."

Chippendales forgotten, Bethany Anne thought out loud. "We went through a period of this in San José." Michael looked at her. "Costa Rica, not California." No one seemed to have updated him on anything that had gone on before they rescued him. Then again, he had been asleep for a large part of the time, too.

She stood and started pacing the living room. "What happens now if a powerful vampire kills the highest-level vampire in an area to take control?"

Michael didn't like the direction this conversation was starting to go in but answered anyway. "Unless someone challenges him or her, the new vampire controls what goes on. But if you have a non-Forsaken take over a Forsaken area, you will still need to clean up everyone who believes vampires should rule humans."

She decided not to correct him. Vampires *were* humans, just genetically modified. Which, when you went down that path, meant they had genetic mutations over humans, and that left you with vampires were mutants. Back to square one.

"Michael, why did you allow this bullshit to continue?" She wasn't accusing him, but rather was genuinely curious.

Everyone looked at him. He wasn't giving off the patriarchal air he was accustomed to wearing, and no one seemed to be judging him. He sat back in his chair. "Two reasons. When it started, I lost them. It wasn't easy to track people back in those centuries." Frank nodded since it made sense to him. "The second was that I thought it was a phase—like teenage boys? Something they would grow out of eventually. The men they were before they were vampires weren't the men they became. It was like when they changed into vampires, something within their minds changed as well. I felt a duty to the men I had changed to give them another chance. Over time, my inactivity allowed them to grow until fixing the—"

Bethany Anne finished his sentence. "Fixing the problem was a bigger challenge than leaving it alone." He nodded his agreement. She could understand both the emotional and practical issues, but it didn't make her happy. She still had a little girl's desire to slap the shit out of him.

She went back to her seat and sat down. "Which brings us back to Anton. I'm sorry, but that psychotic bastard is going to die. Not only for having been the head of the group which killed Martin, but for all the people in those camps, and I'm sure the hundreds if not thousands since. He is messing with the formula in some form or fashion, so he has to go."

Nathan took up the conversation. "So there it is in a nutshell. We have the place, we have the time, and we have the beginning of the plan. You couldn't have done anything with the information before now, and after talking to Michael, I understand the political situation better. I don't have a solution for the massive number of San José-style operations we will have to do to clean up South America."

Bethany Anne put her elbows on her knees and her chin on her hands, thinking. "Michael, what do vampires understand better than anything else?"

He was quick to answer. "Power."

"Who is the most powerful vampire in all of history as far as they know?"

Michael was a lot slower answering this question and showed significantly less enthusiasm. "Me."

She turned to him with a smile. "So, once Anton is dead—and I will be there making sure that bastard is dead—*you* are going to clean up South America. Consider it your penance for making this mistake so many centuries ago." Her voice got a little harder and more commanding. "In fact, consider it penance for the thousands of people he has killed over the decades, and the hundreds of thousands he probably was at least partially responsible for. Your honor has been compromised, and I will beat you with it until you make this right. David and Anton signed their own death warrants." Michael's face grew decidedly less friendly when she mentioned David. "And we will execute them, both because they deserve it, and because I can't have a problem on my back if I'm dealing with other…things." She didn't want to mention the aliens at that moment and lose the momentum on the present subject.

Adding the honey where before she used a stick, she softened her voice. "Will you do this, Michael? Will you take control of South America when Anton is out of the way?"

He pursed his lips. "What about Europe?"

Stephen jumped in with, "I've got that. I might need a new house after the latest dustup, but I've already committed to fixing Europe."

Bethany Anne cocked her head. "How about two houses? Of the floating variety?"

Stephen looked at her. "Your ships?"

She nodded, "Yes. I'm about to move to a fixed base in

Colorado, or at least I hope so. The ships need to move since they've been in and around South America too long. I will 'sell' them to you so if someone tracks me, it looks like a legitimate change of ownership. The Guardians need to get some seasoning. I'll be here in North and South America, so the TQBs can help if Michael needs it, and the CG will help you. We need to get a few more fronts going. Keep my translocation areas clear for me and a"—she looked at John—"*small* team can come over on short notice, and a much larger team with planning. Plus, Nathan needs to work in Europe too."

The Were seemed surprised by that.

She turned to him. "I don't want you in America while dealing with the Chinese, or what we think are Chinese, network attacks. Plus, if ADAM comes online…"

This time Michael interrupted. "Adam?" She put up a hand to shush him. He was both surprised at her rudeness and amused he didn't cause her to shiver in her boots. He had spent a long time in that device under David's castle, and it had caused him to rethink a lot of his previous attitudes. Being a little less quick to take offense had been one of his choices.

She continued, "If ADAM comes online, I don't want him in the United States. I'm not sure how we will move him around yet, but I would rather he be somewhere outside of a major world power, I think."

She stopped herself. "Oh! That gives me an idea. Hold on, folks." She walked back to Ecaterina and put her hand out, retrieving her phone. She typed into the messaging app for a second and then put it away in her pocket.

"Okay, consider what I just said." She turned to Michael. "ADAM is a potential artificial intelligence my team—well, what used to be *your* team in Las Vegas—is working on."

"How much have you accomplished since I was taken?" he asked.

She looked at the people in this room alone, thinking about

how many dozens of others she had spread out across the world. "A fair amount. But let's focus on killing Anton at the moment, and I'll bring you up to speed on the rest, okay?"

He nodded his agreement. Bethany Anne was beginning to like Michael 2.0. She hadn't known Michael 1.0 for very long, but he had been a ranting scrotum lord. Well, thinking back, she hadn't been the easiest person to deal with either, but hey, she was the one who would freeze before Michael did. At least, that was the excuse she gave herself.

Wait until she explained the Wechselbalg. Then she'd see just how changed the man had become.

CHAPTER TWENTY-ONE

Congressman Pepper hadn't been too hard to convince. He was invited onto a private jet with Ecaterina as his hostess, then Chris flew them both to the *Polarus* in the Sikorsky. They hid Shelly over on the *Ad Aeternitatem* and kept the ship far enough away that he couldn't see it when he was on deck.

The crews of both ships had been ready to move. While some downtime was appreciated, the crews were all adrenaline junkies in one form or another.

Bethany Anne had translocated Michael, Stephen, and Nathan through the Etheric. John and Eric would stay in Miami. John didn't like it, but he had to admit that with Michael, Stephen, and Gabrielle, she should be adequately protected. She wanted to ask him, "What about *my* mad skills? Don't they count for anything?" but simply grabbed his ears and pulled his tall-ass head down so she could kiss his forehead. The whole time, the beast of a man was yelling, "Ow, ow, *ooww*." Eric smiled and ducked his head down. He was no fool. She kissed his forehead too, then took the group in two trips.

Michael, fully awake for this trip, was amazed. He had some

memories of the trip from Romania, but he had been too dazed to remember much. Ashur left, probably to hit someone up for handouts in the galley.

The vampire looked around the closet. "Shoes. You really, really like—" A finger was suddenly two inches from his face, followed closely by Bethany Anne's squinting eyes.

She spoke in a decidedly curt tone. "Don't. Say. One. Fucking. Word. You deal with your stress your way, I'll deal with mine my way. My psychiatrists are named Christian Louboutin and Jimmy Choo, and I have an occasional meeting with Blahnik and a couple others. Lay off, and if you so much as mention Imelda Marcos, I will send you to your maker early. Got me, buster?"

He agreed serenely, but on the inside, he smiled. He had another hot button to push. She was deliciously full of fun. This was the first time in ten centuries a woman could stand up to him, and he understood better what Stephen saw in her. Now, if he could only understand this Chippendale name he had caught a glimpse of earlier before she stopped thinking about it hard enough for him to mentally eavesdrop, he would be golden. He might ask Stephen about it, or maybe Gabrielle. She seemed fun-loving.

He followed her out of the closet and closed the door behind him.

The ship's crew kept Pepper happy until Bethany Anne was ready to meet him. She despised him immediately as being slimy and pretentious in the extreme, but he was an easy ticket to the party, so she put up with the man.

She had taken Ecaterina and Killian over to the *Ad Aeternitatem*. Those two plus a couple of others took off in Shelly and went to Buenos Aires early—she assumed to establish good hides before the party, although she really didn't know. She trusted Dan to have her team ready when it was time.

On the day of the event, Pepper and Bethany Anne would be ferried to a landing spot only a hundred yards from the party location. The team couldn't have any vampires onboard since Anton might be able to spot them by their scents. That was the same reason she couldn't have any of Pete's team, either.

She had worried about a lack of decent armament, and Michael had noticed her down mood the previous evening. Finally, she confessed to him that she hated going in without her pistols or her sword. Although she would have a knife under her hair, it didn't provide much comfort. She had refused to go in a dress so she could hide a small pistol, but it would only be enough to shoot a human. Basically, not much good for anything since she didn't want to kill humans.

Michael took her aside and provided the nicest gift—other than an extended life—he could have given her. He taught her to create cutting surfaces with her hands. She could almost kiss him for that alone. With TOM's help, what had taken him a significant amount of time to perfect, she was able to make useable within the first two hours.

It seemed the older vampire had figured out a way to pull energy from the Etheric and channel it into his hands and forearms. Studying the blades Michael formed in this world, she then went into the Etheric, telling him not to move a centimeter. She was able to figure out what was going on from that side as she felt the energy flow. When she reappeared in the room, she concentrated, mentally thinking about a small hole of energy releasing power, running along her forearm and up the side of her hand and then to her pinky finger. It didn't look like much, but she could feel the energy.

She walked over to a metal serving tray the crew used to bring her food. She wasn't particularly fond of the design and had complained a couple of times that it was gaudy. Bethany Anne picked it up with her left hand and swiped at it. She produced about a quarter-inch cut before her hand hit it and the cutting stopped.

Michael came over. "You have to think harder, like you're pushing more energy into it when cutting."

She pulled the tray up. "It takes more energy once you're cutting?"

He nodded.

Focused, she tried again and made it all the way through. She noticed the drag on the energy as she pulled more from the Etheric. Eagerly, she looked around the room, trying to find another object to test. Nothing she would want to replace caught her attention, so she turned the tray on its side and swiped it again. This time the cut was quick, the second piece dropping to the floor. She studied the cuts, amazed at the cleanliness.

She whispered, "This is seriously badass."

Michael smiled.

Now they were landing. If they found her little pistol, it was fine with her. Pepper had talked about himself the whole damn trip. She had been tempted to put him to sleep, and if she had known how to do that correctly, she would have tried. Since she didn't, she suffered and suffered, and fucking suffered some more. She had no one to blame but herself for accepting this little part of the assignment. No wonder Frank had smiled at her the whole time he laid out the plan.

The land around Buenos Aires is relatively flat with no mountains close enough to block the sun, so the party was scheduled in the evening. Sunset was around eight and the party was scheduled for nine, but the invite suggested those arriving via helicopter should get there early. They chose to arrive at eight thirty.

Chris landed them nice and clean. He had taken lessons from Bobcat, whom Bethany Anne surmised was doing something in

Shelly tonight. If everything worked out, she would come in, meet Anton, he would die, and then she'd translocate through the Etheric back to the boat. Wham, bam, kill a man and leave.

A nice group of people had gathered, and she let Pepper take the lead. He knew some of those present, and having an American congressman with her was a nice front. Most considered her window dressing for the man. She wanted to kick a couple of ladies in beautiful dresses and sparkling jewelry who looked down on her pantsuit. That most of the men ignored those women and were captivated by Bethany Anne only irritated the sparkly women more.

If the ladies had realized Bethany Anne wore no makeup, their heads might have exploded.

Pepper capitalized on the opportunity to meet and greet, not realizing his sudden popularity had little to do with him or his name.

Walking around and talking lasted about an hour before the buzz in the crowd changed noticeably. Bethany Anne inhaled and tasted the scents.

Vampires had arrived.

Anton walked through the underground tunnel to the party. He had bought the house decades before and used it for most of his lavish affairs. Two hulking Nosferatu walked behind him.

He was inordinately proud of these two creations. Out of the fifty-two subjects, they alone had survived. Unfortunately, the previous two subjects had been able to break out of the straps, and had killed three of the research support staff and put one of his scientists in a coma. He had been close enough to provide a little of his blood to the man, so he would heal and be able to go back to work for him soon enough.

These two hulks were not as easily commanded as the subjects who had been injected with the Japanese serum. He had to be there to tell them what to do, and the massive musculature was abnormal for most humans so he couldn't use them in crowds without causing a minor panic.

But for tonight, they would be very useful. His contacts had told him the *Polarus* had left, heading south. Furthermore, he had discovered Pepper had decided to join him after all. Imagine his surprise when he found out Pepper was aboard the *Polarus*.

Stupid bitch. Who did she think she was messing with?

He had enough information to know she could walk in the sun, so she was either Michael's or Stephen's. Since Stephen seemed to work for her, she was one of the older vampire's. Anton was aware his father was free and somewhere out there, but David was supposed to clean up that mess. He made it, he needed to fix it.

Or at least die trying.

Anton had his top three children with him. They would move through the crowd and fetch those he needed to speak with. It was a shame Clarita had died. She used to do it so nicely. A smile, a word in the ear, and they would practically run to speak to him.

Another annoyance Bethany Anne needed to answer for. He had toyed, no matter what he had told David, with how to turn her mind toward what the world needed with the Forsaken as leaders, but decided she would be too much of a handful. He had been lucky with Clarita. She was a fairly subservient woman and hadn't been too much trouble afterward. He understood Stephen had endured decades, if not centuries, of pestering from *his* daughter.

Oh well, he would take care of Michael's mistake. His father could thank him later.

He came into his office from the back stairs, hidden from view. When he entered the room, he opened the drapes and looked out over the courtyard. The grounds covered an acre of carefully cultivated bushes and trees, with tasteful decorative lighting throughout. It had two large fountains, lighted from within the water, and one stony brook between them. It was very tranquil, and occasionally, he would have the groundskeepers light it up and he would go there to contemplate the future: the efforts he had undertaken to help create a centralized world government, and what to do next. He stood in front of his desk, the dark wood gleaming in the lights from the walls. He touched it with his finger. It was too oily.

Reaching into the second drawer, he pulled out a towel. He had learned long ago that killing the maids only created more problems. He would find out if this one was good in other ways and not let her oil his desk again.

If she wasn't good at anything else…well, he needed to drink from time to time.

He told the two hulking guys to stand, each in a corner. He had tested their abilities to understand his commands back at the research facility, including kill, attack, and subdue. He had done it in a different order, of course. They subdued, then attacked, then killed. It was beautiful to watch. He'd gotten a little ahead of himself in his excitement, and got too close to the action. Unfortunately, he had to change clothes when a bloody arm hit him in the chest, one recently ripped off the test subject. The man, a research scientist who'd had a bout of conscience after witnessing the fruits of their labors, had asked to speak to him. Anton had nodded and kept asking the scientist to "let his heart out and tell him what he felt" until the scientist finished, happy to finally let his conscience speak.

He became the test subject, his obvious keen intellect and curiosity not enough to drive him forward any longer.

Finished wiping down his desk, Anton sat down.

It hadn't taken long for George to bring in the first person, a local constable who hadn't been introduced to Anton yet. George nodded when the vampire asked if the prime guest had arrived.

Anton listened to the man for a couple of minutes, which allowed a connection, the control to slowly insinuate between the two of them. Once he felt the connection grow, he turned the conversation slowly from what the constable thought about his district to what Anton needed the man to be on the lookout for and what he wanted him to ignore. By the end of the ten-minute conversation, the constable shook his hand, believing fully that Anton was his biggest supporter, and agreed to take care of a couple of inconsequential items for his benefactor.

When George opened the door to let the man out, Anton continued, "Why don't we get the main attraction up here? I don't want to be on pins and needles all night. These two brutes can then go back down to the tunnels—and make sure they keep the blood off my floor when they take her away." The lackey had almost walked out the door before Anton spoke again. "George!" The vampire stopped and looked back. "Get someone up here to take these chairs out. They're antiques." He nodded, and seconds later, a couple of men in tuxes came in to take the loose furniture out.

Satisfied he had done enough to minimize the destruction, he sat back down.

Five minutes later, his assistant entered, followed by a very beautiful woman, her black hair radiant in his wall light. She wasn't wearing a dress. and didn't smell like a vampire. He looked at George. "Are you sure this is the right lady?"

She spoke up. "If you mean, am I Bethany Anne, the answer is yes. What, does the fact that I smell human throw you off?"

Anton waved George back. "Where is Pepper? I'll want to talk to him later."

Bethany Anne explained, "He's gone back to the ship. I wanted to have a personal conversation with you."

Anton flipped his hand. "No matter; we will grab him there. What? I see a small flinch. Did you think I didn't know about your ships? Those two beautiful boats will be changing owners, much like they did when you took them over, yes? Got rid of the original owner somewhere out at sea and purchased them on the cheap?"

He was enjoying himself. He had seen a slight movement, a tightening around her eyes, and knew he was getting to the woman. She wasn't human, he was now sure of that, but he wasn't sure how she hid her scent.

That was when his men attacked her ships.

CHAPTER TWENTY-TWO

The Queen Bitch's Ship *Polarus*

It was a good time. Not a very trying time, but a good time.

Both the *Polarus* and *Ad Aeternitatem* had moved out beyond the twelve-nautical-mile limit of Argentinian waters, so they weren't near the city when the two speedboats raced toward them.

Captain Thomas called his gunnery officer and told her it was "weapons free" but to fire a warning shot.

Jean complied, asking Darryl and his crew to place a few ranged shots as the boats sped toward the ship. Nothing seemed to faze the craft, so Darryl put a couple into their glass. The boat turned sharply to the right but then returned to speed, heading in their direction once again.

Darryl was near Jean and was able to overhear her. "Good, I was hoping they wouldn't puss out."

She ordered over her command headset, "Team one, please uncover and be ready to fire on my mark."

One of the aboveboard emplacements shed its metallic cover. It was ripped away, in fact. Previously, it had appeared to be an equipment locker. Now, two gun barrels rolled down and tracked the boat.

"Fire."

The barrels kicked back with a whoomph. The *Polarus* barely rocked. Darryl watched the cigarette boat explode into pieces, one body wheeling at least forty-five feet into the air before he lost it in the night sky.

Jean spoke again. "Captain, orders?" She listened. "Understood." She switched channels. "Team, stand ready. We are heading toward the *Ad Aeternitatem*. They don't have our armament."

Gabrielle returned from her position at the side of the ship, where she had been prepared to repel boarders. She spoke while approaching. "Anyone seen Michael or Stephen?"

On the *Ad Aeternitatem*, Captain Wagner was calm and collected. He spoke to Todd and Pete. "Men, we are about to have boarders, probably Nosferatu. I will move all crew I can into protected areas and lock them down, but I can't allow boarders on my ship, and we can't let anything happen to Bethany Anne's spaceship. The *Polarus* is on its way, but it will be at least five minutes before they can help. Suggestions?"

Pete was calm. Todd was also, but he understood what was coming at them so he asked, "Any chance we can get Bethany Anne to join us?" Pete nodded. It was a good suggestion.

"Unfortunately, no. I was able to hear enough to know she's in the middle of something herself and can't break away." There was a bright flash and an explosion to port, and all three looked in that direction, "That was probably the end of the boat attacking the *Polarus*. Maybe she will arrive a touch sooner." He turned back to them.

"I don't want any casualties, and I don't want any of these

bastards running around on my ship. Is this understood?" They acknowledged and left the bridge.

Pete looked at Todd as they walked. "Will your guys trust my team?"

The Marine looked at the young Were. "Why? What are you thinking?"

They reached the main floor. "Six of us, four of you. I've got a situation that makes me possibly need to work alone. I say we make up two, maybe three teams. Let my team soak up as much damage as possible while your team shoots the fuck out of them. My guys know fighting, but we haven't worked on weapons so far, and I don't think we want them doing that on a boat in the middle of this much water."

Todd thought he was rather dry with his wit. "Three sets of three?"

"Works for us. I'll send Tim with two of yours, Matthew and Joel with someone, and Joseph and Rickie with you." Todd agreed, and they went to finish suiting up.

All ten men met on top of the ship, waiting for the speedboat to come within range before shooting. They didn't hope to hit much, but better shooting off the ship than on.

His Guardians had their weapons, some blunt, some sharp. Those who had sharp weapons were told to be careful around the Marines. Pete started to get undressed when Todd looked back. "What the hell? Is this some sort of werewolf rite of passage?" He honestly looked perplexed, so Pete didn't take offense. He had informed his guys of what he would try to do.

"Trust me, and don't get between me and those assholes."

Todd asked, turning his head back to the rapidly approaching boat, "Does this have to do with you being on the alien ship the other day?"

"Yes."

The Marine nodded. "Stay out of the way of Pete, everyone.

I'm not sure what he and Bethany Anne have cooked up, but I want a front-row seat. Ready to go?"

He got a bunch of "oorahs" from his guys.

Pete left his pants on. He would feel stupid if he was fighting with his tackle hanging out, so he would risk a pair of pants getting ripped off. He was pumped up, his blood racing through his body. Fighting was all he wanted to do. Ever since John Grimes had slugged him on the airport field, he had wanted to be worthy. Had wanted to have John's respect, and he had earned it. He had earned Nathan's respect, and even Gabrielle's when he took over the pack. His father had called him and told him how amazed he was, how proud a father he was after he and Tim had had their alpha fight.

Now he was fighting for his own future, as well as the future of the world, using a gift that had probably been intended to hurt people on his own planet. He needed to understand this final change and how to control it. He could feel his blood, feel the tension leave his body, along with the heightened senses that were muted before.

"Oh, fuck me sideways." Pete looked at Joseph to his left, who was usually the quiet one. Someone had turned the lights up, he thought.

"What?" Pete's voice was a little surly, and the Marines took a step back. Todd turned around to watch the Were's fur start to cover his body and his fingers grow claws.

"Pete, I think Bethany Anne gave you an upgrade, buddy." Todd pointed to his hands.

He looked down, clenching his hand, the two-inch claws making it a little difficult to squeeze. His legs were growing out of his pants.

The Were shrugged, his shoulders larger than before. He smiled, his mouth full of razor-sharp teeth, making it hard to talk. He was able to communicate his feelings as he watched the boat come closer. He walked toward the rail and clasped it with hands that were bigger and stronger than his normal hands. Calmly, he looked over his left shoulder, then his right. All of the men grabbed their weapons, and he turned back to the boat coming at them, yelling in a deep baritone, "Brrriiinnng ittt, bbii-itchessss!"

Todd ordered, "Rifleman, fire."

The battle for the *Ad Aeternitatem* had begun.

The Nosferatu jumped from the boat, heading toward the first blood they could smell. The Were team split to the left and right, and the Marines jumped behind them. Pete ignored the small fry and focused on his target, the vampire.

Manet had been a vampire for over thirty years. A fourth-generation vampire, he was considerably stronger than his generation should be and often made third-generation vampires walk around him. He was power walking; he was Death, and he was there to take this ship. He had been winged by one of the bullets, and it had pissed him off.

He hissed at the enemy seeking to stop them from getting on the ship. He smelled the Were but didn't know what to make of the mutant in the middle bellowing at him to "brrriiinnng ittt," whatever the hell that meant. If he wanted a fight, Manet was more than willing to kill him first.

Eager now, he bounded onto the boat, grabbed a line, and pulled himself upright beside the soon-to-be-dead furry guy.

He made it as far as the railing when both of his hands were clasped and he was swung up and over the rail to the deck. This fool would make it too easy.

That was when he belatedly realized the beast hadn't let go and the momentum didn't allow him time to get his feet under him. His body smashed into the deck, his bones cracking.

Manet pulled his arms apart, but they were pushed back

together quickly. This werewolf wasn't weak. The vampire felt the first twinge of concern that this wouldn't be easy, which was when two bullets slammed into his chest. His left arm was free, and he tried to reach around to clutch something for leverage when a large clawed hand grabbed his neck. Instinctively, he reached to pull the arm away, but the hand clenched, crushing his larynx. He ceased thinking when the claws pulled back and tore his throat out.

The vampire died on the deck of the *Ad Aeternitatem*, the first powerful vampire killed by a changeling in single combat in over four centuries. Seconds later, the last gun fired and the final Nosferatu died. Tim and Matthew went around cutting heads off.

Pete surveyed the ship, anger and hunger running through his mind. Everything was clear for him, as if it were daylight. He felt a hand on his shoulder, and he spun around. It was Todd. "Come back to us, Pete. We need you too much. We're done."

The Were smiled. They had won. They had fought, and the Guardians were 1-0-0. He took the feeling of anger and the desire to continue dealing death and felt it through his body, then he commanded it to leave. He would be the first, but he would not be the last. His people, his world, and his Queen needed him to beat this. Pete shattered the rage and unshackled the bonds in his mind, and he could feel the energy leaving as he changed back to himself.

Pete Silvers, the little rich boy who had been slugged that day on the tarmac in New York, was destroyed. Peter Silvers, the first and arguably the best alpha of the Guardians, stood proudly among the men who had protected this ship and these people from the death that had come for them. He looked around and held out his hand to Todd, and they cemented a friendship that would be talked about for centuries. Together, they architected the first Guardians cadre of Marines.

The Wechselbalg Guardians would forever be paired with humans.

The teams threw the bodies overboard and laughed over who would claim the fast boat. It didn't take long for the *Ad Aeternitatem's* crew to come up top and help them grab the expensive boat before it floated away. Later, Rickie lamented how those bully Marines had shot up his beautiful boat. It took two seconds before three men jumped him, and he laughed as he changed it to, "Our boat, our boat." They made it to within three feet of tossing him overboard before dropping him on the deck.

CHAPTER TWENTY-THREE

Anton continued explaining his method for capturing her ships. "A few Nosferatu and a vampire for each boat, and now they belong to me. Well, actually, two vampires for your *Polarus*. I know you have the lady Gabrielle on board that one. I'm not an ass, so I'll let her decide if your ship is worth saving or if she would like to live a few hundred years more. I'm sure she will see the right decision open up before her."

Bethany Anne's eyes went to the hulking brutes in the corners. "Friends?"

Anton smirked. "Of course. Newly-made, as it were. We've finally got a decent recipe." He looked to his right, talking as casually as if explaining the benefits of purchasing a new car. "Stronger than the original version, and able to take a significant amount of damage before it quits working. Still tinkering with the intelligence, of course, but I would have to rate them a solid seven out of ten. Overall, something I can finally be proud to bring out in public." He looked back at her. "Well, by 'public,' I don't mean daylight yet, but you know, small steps and all that."

"I see. So you only now figured this little recipe out? Because I have to tell you, none of your other toys have been much of a challenge."

It was Anton's turn to be annoyed. She had reminded him of the many times she had messed up his plans. "Yes, well, I wasn't aware of you until recently, so I hadn't exactly planned on you crashing my party. Well, like you're doing right now." He smiled. "You weren't invited, and yet here you are. I can only assume it was to create mayhem and maybe get a little revenge, hmmm? Clarita not enough for you? I honestly didn't participate in any direct action, nor did I order the death of your friend in DC, so you can't lay that at my feet."

Bethany Anne marveled at how the conversation was going. It was as if the man thought he would get a pass for the thousands he had killed in the past. "Martin was one of my best friends, a man who helped a lost woman find direction in her life. An ear to bend when there was no one else to talk to, but then you probably don't know much about that, do you?"

"Oh, *au contraire*. I was just listening to one of the research scientists bleed his heart out after he had misgivings over the results of their efforts. I truly did listen and encouraged him to get it all off his chest." She wasn't positive, but she was pretty sure he hadn't told a lie.

"Well then, you might be able to appreciate how it helps a person."

"Yes, I do."

Bethany Anne was perplexed. This wasn't the way she had expected the conversation to go, but now she was wrapped up in the story. "What happened to the scientist?"

Anton did that waving thing with his hand again, as if the end of the story were unimportant. "He was used to test the obedience of my two friends here. I told you he bled his heart out, right? I'm almost positive I said that." He gave her a sincere smile at how he had worked the death of the scientist into his story.

Bethany Anne wondered why she even cared; he was not only

powerful but obviously mentally unstable. She turned and saw George by the door. "You might want to move a few feet to your left."

He gave her a funny look and then glanced at Anton, who shook his head no. "She seeks to disturb you. What did you find on her?"

George pulled a small pistol from his pocket. "Just this."

Anton looked back at Bethany Anne.

"Don't say I didn't warn you," she told George and turned back to Anton. "What?"

"Really?" He pointed to the little gun "That isn't even enough to piss me off."

She nodded. "I totally agree, but I should have help arriving in three…" She turned toward the door and George jumped to the side, prepared for action.

"Two." Anton stood, ready to command the two Nosferatu to attack whatever came through the door.

He began to speak. "I don't hear—"

"One."

"Anything."

Supersonic rounds from two sniper rifles chambered for .338 Lapua arrived from half a mile away, so close together you wouldn't be able to tell which hit him first. Anton's head exploded, brain matter spraying the wall and door in front of him. George was covered in gore, surprise evident on his face.

Bethany Anne spoke as the mostly decapitated body slumped over the desk. "My friend always asks, 'What is the bait?' Well, Anton, I'm the bait."

George spoke into the silence. "Oh, God." He wasn't looking in her direction.

She hadn't made a move to attack him, but realizing he wasn't looking at her, she turned quickly to see the dumb stares of the two Nosferatu replaced by cunning looks.

Her eyes grew wide. "Oh, holy fuck."

CHAPTER TWENTY-FOUR

Stephen felt the surprise and shock and immediately understood it had come from Bethany Anne, then he felt pain.

Michael looked at him, "What's wrong?"

"Something is wrong with Bethany Anne. I can feel it."

"How? Where?"

Stephen stood. "How do we get to where she is? She needs help."

Michael joined him. "Do you know what direction she's in?"

The other vampire paused, concentration etched on his face. He pointed through the door toward the coast. "That way."

Michael nodded. "Come with me." They broke into vamp speed, racing down the corridor and up to the main deck. When Stephen arrived, Michael turned to Myst and grabbed him, then streaked toward the coast. The younger vampire was surprised to find himself inches above the waves, feeling more than seeing the area around him. He could also hear Michael's thoughts and feel his concern for Bethany Anne. *Maybe feelings a father wouldn't have for a daughter, hmmm, Michael?*

They approached the bay quickly. "To the left, Michael." His thoughts both sounded in his mind and echoed from close by.

He didn't think this was how his father normally communicated.

He felt another large burst of pain, and the older vampire made an effort to speed up. Michael had connected with him to get a direct read on his ability to sense her.

Bethany Anne was tossed over the second-story railing. She tried to twist around in the air and was successful in getting both feet underneath her. Unfortunately, she didn't have enough time to take a good stance, and ended up falling backward and skidding across the floor to come to a painful stop against a piano leg.

"You cock-sucking shitbag," she screamed. She was getting her ass kicked, but if she ran, they would turn on the other humans, and that wasn't a good thing. George had bolted as soon as he realized the Nosferatu were free. Well, no plan survives contact with the enemy, especially when the stupid enemy had a deadman's switch on two hulking pains-in-the-ass.

It was time to get some of her own back. Beast number one jumped at her from the second floor—aiming, she figured, for her head.

Bethany Anne rolled out the way and pushed to her feet. "Look, you catatonic flea-fucker—" She had to dodge as its partner came unexpectedly through a wall above her. In a second, she had the whole room to herself, the partiers having decided this wasn't a cool room to be in.

She stood motionless, facing the two large Nosferatu. "Okay, you want to party?" Her voice deepened, and malevolence was the song. "Let's fucking party." Her eyes glowed red and her fangs descended, and the two assailants charged as she ran toward them.

The clash was over in less than a second. One lay on its side, its leg cut off, while the other screamed in rage. What was left of its arm sprayed blood. Bethany Anne picked herself up off the floor where she had landed, the wall being polite enough to stop her after she was thrown by the second beast.

She reached down to peel off the hand, attached to a forearm, that still gripped her leg. Calmly, she straightened and popped her neck, walking toward the beast with the missing arm. It screamed in frustration and pain and charged at her, and she pivoted to the side with the missing arm. Making a complete circle, she continued toward the second beast.

The first one continued running, smashed into the wall, and the severed head fell to the side. The second was able to pull himself around in time to reach out with both hands. She grabbed them and put a foot against its chest, and it screamed as she dragged each arm slowly out of its socket. Finally, she yanked hard enough to pull them both off. "Dude, shut the fuck up!" She sliced its head off. Covered in blood, gore, and body parts, she looked around the room. When she heard two sets of footsteps approaching quickly, she headed back toward the main entryway

She sighed. It sounded like George had gone and enlisted support.

CHAPTER TWENTY-FIVE

Michael was worried. Getting into the house became an effort of dodging the screaming, fleeing people. Finally, he left the mass behind, and he and Stephen became corporeal. They could easily pinpoint Bethany Anne from the cussing and screams of frustration and pain.

They ran around the corner and both slowed and stopped, looking at the sheer destruction and blood everywhere. She wouldn't win any best-dressed contests, they decided as she looked back at them.

"You guys are late. Usually I complain about guys coming early, but you are definitely late." Stephen snorted at the joke. Michael didn't get it.

The older vampire looked around. "I see you redecorated the place. Anton?" She pointed above his head.

"He's up there, or at least his body is. I don't think Ecaterina and Killian left enough brain matter to regenerate. I have to admit, he wasn't the only thought on my mind. Fucknuts had these two beasts, who went apeshit when the prodigal wank-lover unsuccessfully tried to stop two copper-jacketed lovers with his skull."

Michael turned to Stephen with a confused look on his face. "Anton's upstairs with his head blown off. I'll go make sure he is still dead." Stephen headed upstairs at vamp speed.

The other man turned back to Bethany Anne. "Are you okay?" He looked her over, trying to see if any of the blood was hers.

She looked at herself. "Well, I could use a bath... Hold it. Here comes more fun."

Her gaze slid over his shoulder to the entrance of the room. Four sets of footsteps raced toward them but slid to a stop when they smelled the vampire on Michael.

George, the one in the lead, held a shotgun in his hands. "Look, buddy, I don't care who you are, but you're in the middle of a disagreement. This bitch..." He jerked his head in Bethany Anne's direction.

She looked around. Was there another female in the room?

"This bitch just killed Anton, so we're going to finish her off and get South America settled before this becomes well known."

Bethany Anne was curious as to how Michael would handle this, but steps could be heard above them. The four looked up to see Stephen at the rail. George started the same spiel, but Stephen put up his hand. "I heard you the first time, jackhole." The man looked like he wanted to protest being called a name, but Stephen simply talked over him. "My name is Stephen." That got everyone's attention. "I'm sure you know she is Bethany Anne?" George gave him a quick nod. "Good, that helps. Since she is my Queen, I'm sure you understand I will not allow you to continue with your plan?"

The hapless man's face looked like he had just eaten a sour lemon.

Bethany Anne put her hand on her hip and stared up at Stephen. He wouldn't allow? What was this man-breast-beating bullshit?

"Be that as it may..." Michael pulled everyone's attention back to him. She spared a glance at Stephen one more time. He would have his ear twisted, for damn sure. Michael's eyes turned black, his voice surrounding them all and coming from everywhere and nowhere. "My name is Michael." He disappeared.

Bethany Anne had to admit, that was one fucking scary-ass introduction. She tried to see him, but she couldn't.

His voice still filled the room. "There is no question about who is in charge in South America." All four vampires looked around, behind them, and in front of them, and one even stared at her as if she had a clue. Bethany Anne simply smiled at him.

She reached into the Etheric, and could vaguely feel Michael. He was in the hallway behind the vampires. Well, they were trapped, because they wouldn't get away from her. She walked slowly into the middle of the room and stared them down. Now, they spent half their time looking at her and half looking around.

A massive feeling of fear hit all of them, and even she was affected.

TOM, what the hell?

One second...

The fear turned off.

Got it. He was affecting the mental areas that drive fear. Pretty fantastic. That is a level of control I hadn't thought about.

Look, you can finish the Michael Adoration Society meeting later. Don't let him affect me again like that.

A voice they all heard screamed, "**I am Michael, and *you will kneel.*"**

She stabbed a hand at Stephen, who held himself upright by force of will.

The other four, however, couldn't drop to their knees fast enough.

He reappeared in front of them and spoke, his voice a deadly whisper. "South America is mine. I am changing the strictures here. There will be one power, one voice, and one rule. Mine."

Bethany Anne waved at Stephen to come down, and he was beside her in a second. "Yes, my Queen?"

She smiled at him. "Michael is busy doing something he should have taken care of a long time ago, and I need a bath. Are you staying?"

Stephen looked at his father, and his face broke into a mischievous smile. He offered his elbow, and she proceeded to lock her arm in his, then they disappeared.

One of the four vampires stared past Michael, who turned. He noticed the two of them were gone and realized what she had probably done to get his attention. He turned back to the four to continue telling them what they would do to help clean up this mess—or, of course, they could choose a slow death.

He would find her and speak to her again. Oh yes, he would. She wasn't going to get rid of him this easily. He had time on his side.

Gabrielle heard the shower in Bethany Anne's suite, so she went inside and stopped short. Her father sat on the couch, leafing through a fashion magazine. He looked up.

She pointed at the shower. "Michael?"

Stephen smiled. "No, Bethany Anne."

Her eyes narrowed. "Where is Michael, and how are you in this suite while she is taking a shower, father mine?"

"Michael is—or was when we left him five minutes ago—where Anton held his party. I'm here because she didn't tell me to leave, and there were no security agents up front."

She pointed at him, then at the suite door. "Consider the security here. Now get out. She normally comes walking out of there naked, and I don't need your old geezer heart exploding with lust."

He closed the magazine. "That was what I was counting on. I hear the stories and never get to—" The pillow hit him squarely in the face.

"Go!" He stood and walked out. He actually hadn't known she would walk out naked, but he liked giving Gabrielle a hard time.

He found Darryl and Scott jogging toward her suite. "She's taking a shower, and Gabrielle is in the suite." Darryl nodded and moved on. Scott smiled at him as if there was a shared joke and walked past.

CHAPTER TWENTY-SIX

Germany

David stood outside his moonlit castle, looking down on it from a quarter of a mile away. It had been his fortress for hundreds of years, the one place he could depend on to protect him.

It had failed.

It had taken him three days to realize he was not in a good position at this location. Michael knew where he was, and he wouldn't be able to trick him and capture him again.

Briefly, he had considered booby-trapping the whole castle, but couldn't. Maybe he would be able to survive this, and if he did, he didn't want to come back to see this beloved place, so full of memories, destroyed.

He heard the car coming down the lane a full minute before it arrived. His legs caught in the headlights, he looked at his home and then turned and walked to the open and waiting back door and slid inside. The driver closed the door, then the car made a U-turn and traveled down the road.

. . .

Las Vegas, NV, USA

Jeffrey was sleeping on a cot. His head had hit the pillow thirty minutes before. He had tried to go to sleep earlier but had a short argument with his wife. She was not happy he was there for the second night in a row. If he hadn't brought his kids there, and they hadn't told her about everything including the kitchen and the cots, she might not have believed him.

A buzz woke him. He looked around groggily as his phone buzzed and blinked. He grabbed it to see Tom's ugly mug. He hit the answer button and closed his eyes, the phone against his ear. "What the hell, Tom? You're two buildings away. Couldn't you just walk over?"

"Jeffrey, it's asking for more input."

"Then feed it and let me go back to sleep." Jeffrey rolled over.

"Jeffrey! Wake the fuck up."

He tried to wipe the sleep out of his eyes. "Fuck, Tom, no need to yell. Who wants food, and why are we feeding them?"

"Jeffrey, you awake yet?"

He sat up with a grunt. "I am now, so answer my question."

"ADAM is awake, and he's requesting data."

"ADAM is awake, and he—" Jeffrey's eyes opened wide. "He wants more— Oh, shit. Be right there."

Jeffrey scrambled to get his clothes on, buttoning his shirt as he jogged over to Building One and practically ran into the security door. He stopped and punched in the code, taking two tries to get it right.

He walked into the main room, which was dark and had green and blue lights flickering all over. Tom was at the desk, which had two monitors on it. One had a command prompt window, green text blinking on a black background.

He stared at the message, which reminded him of a grocery list.

"Please provide the following >>"

There were forty-three lines of requests. He sat down next to Tom.

ADAM had just woken up.

FINIS